Love Hacks
The Next Generation Book 2

ANNETTE MORI

ALSO BY ANNETTE MORI

<u>Single Books</u>
Compound Interest
Georgetown Glen
Artist Free Zone
Disconnected
The Others
Sculpting Her Heart
One Shot at Love
The Panty Thief
Pleasure Workers TWC2
A Window to Love
The Book Witch
The Book Addict
The Dream Catcher
Unconventional Lovers
Captivated
The Termination
The Review
The Thanksgiving Baby Caper
The Ultimate Betrayal
Locked Inside
Out of This World
Asset Management
The Incredibly True Adventure of Two Elves in Love
(Affinity 2014 Christmas Collection)
Love Forever, Live Forever
The True Story of Valentine's Day
Vampire Pussy...Cat
Nicky's Christmas Miracle X3

(It's in Her Kiss, Affinity's Charity Anthology)
Donner Junior Saves the Day

Series
San Diego Series
Undercover Love
Politics of Love
Love Bonds

The Next Generation Series
The Next Generation Book 1
Love Hacks Book 2

Co-authored
The Organization with Erin O'Reilly

Co-authored with Ali Spooner
Heart Strings Attached- TWC3
Free to Love
Trouble in Paradise -TWC4

Love Hacks
The Next Generation Book 2

ANNETTE MORI

Affinity
Rainbow Publications

2024

Love Hacks
© 2024 by Annette Mori

Affinity E-Book Press NZ LTD
Canterbury, New Zealand

1st Edition

ISBN: **978-1-99-104065-7** (paperback)
ISBN: 978-1-99-104066-4 (EPUB)
ISBN: 978-1-99-104067-1 (PDF)
ISBN: 978-1-99-104068-8 (KINDLE)

Editor: Angela Koenig
Proof Editor: Sue Lee
Cover Design: Irish Dragon Designs
Production Design: Affinity Publication Services

ACKNOWLEDGMENTS

A huge thank you to Ali Spooner, who was the only beta reader I sent this book to (hopefully that will not end up being a mistake). I would also like to express my gratitude to Affinity Rainbow Publications—JM Dragon and Nancy Kaufman—who continue to provide feedback to tighten up manuscripts that need help and publish my unconventional work. I am eternally grateful for the opportunities they give me to let my stories see the light of day. Thanks to Angie for her magic as the final editor to further tighten the story. She is a delight to work with. Inevitably, those pesky errors slip through, and I am thankful that the final proof editor caught those before the book went to print. Thanks to Nancy Kaufman for the final cover. A huge thanks to all the other readers and fellow writers who have sent personal emails, written reviews, and posted nice things on Facebook (you know who you are). The Affinity authors are an incredibly supportive group and often share posts or send words of encouragement. Finally, my wife, Jody, continues her support even when it interferes with our time.

DEDICATION

To nerds and geeks who keep us safe in the world. And to my beautiful wife, as always.

TABLE OF CONTENTS

The Organization
Family Tree

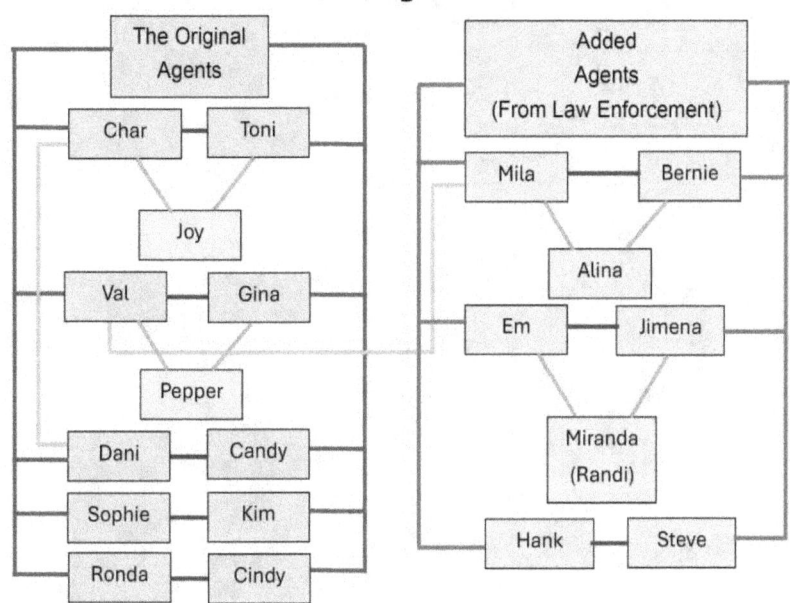

Key:

Children: ═══════
Marriage: ▬▬▬▬
Siblings: ═══════

CHAPTER ONE

Joy Stiles rotated her neck. Spending so much time on her supercharged laptop was not healthy. She knew that but couldn't seem to break away. She'd been in a non-stop battle with the mysterious hacker who had gained her grudging respect. It was time to call her mother because now this person was popping into her attempts to hack the NSA.

Absently tying back her long red hair, Joy reached for her phone and made a video call. "Hey, Mama T, I think I might need your expertise to hack the NSA."

Toni's smiling face appeared on the screen. "Mmm, hon, the NSA is a tough nut to crack. So why do you want to whack that hornet's nest?"

Her other mother slid into the chair next to Toni. "Is this a private genius-to-genius conversation, or can I get in on the fun? I never get to see you anymore," Char lamented.

"You might get bored, but you're always welcome to join us. Actually, I'm glad you jumped on the call. You probably

1

need an update, anyway. So, in answer to your question, Mama T, I was poking around on the dark web and picked up some disturbing chatter," Joy answered.

"You sure that isn't some nutty conspiracy theory crap?" Toni asked.

"That's why I wanted to hack the NSA. Now I'm more convinced than ever that I found at least some kernel of truth." Joy leaned back in her chair before turning when Randi poked her head into her room.

"Hey, Joy. Alina, Maria, and I are going out to get some pizza and have a few beers. Do you want to join us? Oh, whoops, hi, Aunt Char and Aunt Toni. Um, root beer," she amended.

Char and Toni laughed. "I'm pretty sure the entire world knows you're not having root beer, Randi, including your moms. We aren't that old to forget what college was like. Besides, I'd be disappointed if Joy hadn't created fake IDs for you," Toni said with a smile.

Char playfully nudged Toni's shoulder. "Goddess, Toni, do you want the kids to turn into delinquents? I swear, knowing something and blatantly expressing your approval are two very different things."

Toni held up her hands. "What? It's a crime not to use the talents we've been given by the Goddess. And fortunately, Joy has many talents."

Joy answered Randi, "I'll meet you guys later. Pete's Pizza?"

"Yeah, but you better not bail on us again. Shit, if you could have sex with your new laptop, you would," Randi scolded. "How's that neck of yours doing?"

Joy waved her hand. "Go. I want to talk with my moms. And don't ever say something so gross like that again. I'll be there."

"Alina told me to tell you she saw your crush there the other day," Randi teased.

Randi bounced out of Joy's room, and Joy returned to her conversation. "Sorry about that."

"Crush?" Char asked.

"Don't get your hopes up. She doesn't even know I exist despite spending the last year in the same graduate program."

"Honey, you're a beautiful, talented, brilliant, kind young woman. I'm sure she knows you exist. You got your mother's beauty. There isn't a man or woman alive who could resist those gorgeous green eyes. Maybe I should have taught you more than how to hack into any secure space. Catching someone's eye is easier than avoiding detection when we enter those fortified sites."

"Now you make that offer," Joy grumbled, but she was more interested in solving her current dilemma, which had nothing to do with her nonexistent love life. "Can we get back to the reason I called?"

"Of course, honey," Toni said.

"There's this other hacker who keeps popping into my computer, leaving irritating messages whenever I poke around in the dark web, especially when I entered this site with the concerning intel. Then, when I tried to crack the security code in the NSA, she stuck her nose into my business again," Joy explained.

"Her? Interesting. How do you know it's a woman?" Char asked.

"She sent me this animation of a beautiful dragon with long eyelashes." Joy groaned. "See, who does that?" She

3

continued her explanation. "I'm describing a dragon as beautiful. No wonder I can't get a date. Mama T is a cool nerd, and I'm just your run-of-the-mill geek, hiding behind my computer and letting my skin get pasty."

"You'll thank the universe for that when you turn fifty, and you've no wrinkles on your skin," Toni joked.

"Not funny, Mama T."

†

Toni wondered if, in her excitement to show her daughter the joys of all things tech, she missed the boat by not teaching her other life lessons. She'd felt so bad when Joy confessed to how miserable she was two years ago before Alina, Maria, and Randi moved in during Joy's final year in her undergraduate program. Pepper, Joy's other close friend, had finally filled Char and Toni in on the fact that Joy hadn't spent her time enjoying the life of a typical college student. The reality was that Joy had spent nearly every weekend at Pepper's place. Char had tried to talk to Toni about letting up on the "lab time," wanting Joy to have a more normal childhood. Toni had passed that off, insisting Joy would grow out of her shyness once she gathered more confidence. And what better way to gain self-assuredness than by mastering technology? By the time Joy hit college, she could hack almost any site, and Toni couldn't have been prouder.

Deciding to stroll into the lane she was more comfortable with, Toni ignored her daughter's confession about being unable to get a date and moved on to why Joy called in the first place.

"Okay, honey, I'm going to take control of your screen. Let's see if we can get a peek at the NSA. It's been years since I poked around. The key is to only stay for brief periods. Ten minutes or less," Toni advised.

Toni's fingers flew over her keyboard as she typed in commands and created a string of code. Her first two efforts failed miserably, but Toni was nothing if not persistent.

"Yeah, I tried that," Joy said.

"Hang on. This might be a little unconventional, but it could work. Fucking paranoid government," Toni grumbled.

Char laughed. "For good reason, with you two geniuses constantly outplaying them. I'm glad you're on our team."

"Ha! I got it!" Toni exclaimed.

"Frickin' brilliant, Mama T. I'm taking a screenshot of the code. Shit—"

A shimmering, definitely female dragon appeared on the screen, waving a scaly claw that looked almost manicured, with bright red nails. Toni would have laughed if it hadn't been so frustrating to be thwarted by the very hacker Joy had lamented about.

The dragon's message was simple. "Naughty, naughty." The hacker promptly kicked Toni and Joy out of the NSA, and Toni lost control of Joy's screen.

"I'm not really into threesomes, newbie," the dragon's sultry voice declared.

"Oh no, you did not just do that. You fire-breathing glorified lizard." The hacker incensed Toni.

"See, this is what I've been dealing with. I got this, Mama T," Joy growled. "A dragon isn't really a lizard, though," she added. "Maybe more of an evolved dinosaur with special abilities."

An Amazon warrior appeared on the screen wielding a dangerous-looking sword. "Not looking for a third, so fly away, little dragon, before I skewer you and roast you over your own fire. I'm mighty hungry right now, and you look delicious."

The dragon laughed. "I knew you were a woman, but that doesn't make it any less inappropriate for you to poke your nose where it doesn't belong. Even if your nose is lovely."

Toni laughed. "I think your hacker is flirting with you. It's time for your old mother to bow out of this challenge. I'll send you more code similar to what we tried before. You might need to tweak it a bit. There has to be a way to go in undetected. Whoever this is, she's good, but after thoroughly dissecting the code accompanying her dragon, I'm confident we'll find her weak spot, giving you time to sneak in. Have fun!" Toni teased. She ended her call with Joy.

Char kissed Toni's cheek. "Good call, hon. I know you've been worried about Joy, but there is a lid for every pot. Joy doesn't need to change a thing about herself. She just needs to find the right pot or lid."

Toni leaned back in her chair and smiled. "Yeah, we started out as foes, and look how that turned out. Although, I think I had a little more game than our daughter."

Char chuckled. "More hubris, too. But we were never actually foes. You just thought we were."

"True. And maybe the fire-breathing lizard isn't an enemy either. But she's definitely a good match for Joy. So, at the risk of sticking my nose where it doesn't belong, I feel compelled to track the lizard and discover her identity."

"Hmmm, do you really think that's the best idea? And stop calling her 'the lizard,' especially if she ends up being someone Joy starts to date," Char chastised.

"She started it," Toni defended.

"Oh, for shit's sake. You're in your fifties. Time to act like it."

"Why? It's all part of my charm. I'm never growing old. I simply refuse to do it," Toni insisted.

CHAPTER TWO

Before blinking off her screen, the dragon gestured with her red-tipped claw, pointing to her amber eyes before turning her dragon fingers to Joy's screen. "I'm watching you, newbie."

With nothing more to do than wait for her mother's code to play with, Joy decided to keep her promise to Randi. Grabbing her sling pack, she headed for the door and sighed. Was her mother right? Surely the hacker wasn't actually flirting with her? Maybe she started it with her comment about the dragon looking delicious? She hadn't meant it like it came out. That was more Alina's style.

Their pizza hangout was within walking distance of their home. Joy hurried along the sidewalk, not making eye contact with anyone who crossed her path. Even a simple greeting caused Joy to blush if she was acknowledging a beautiful woman. She spotted her friends right away, and they waved her over.

"Holy shit! You actually made it," Randi said.

Maria poured beer into an empty glass for Joy. "I am glad you joined us."

"So, did you break into the NSA or not?" Alina asked.

Joy frowned. "We did, but then the hacker kicked us out. Mama T was pissed, but then she kind of laughed it off and teased me about the hacker flirting with me. She's going to send me code that will hopefully allow me to sneak in for a few moments."

"Why don't you just take that job they offered you?" Alina asked.

"Because Sadie works there," Joy mumbled, almost too low for her friends to hear.

"Sadie, the woman you've been drooling over for the past year?" Randi asked.

Alina jabbed Randi with her elbow. "Shhh." She jerked her head toward the door.

Joy's eyes traveled to the door, and she slunk lower in her seat. "Crap."

Sadie had just confidently walked into Pete's Pizza, and her eyes seemed to momentarily travel to their group. She smiled and nodded.

"Wave back at her," Alina prodded. "Even better, we should ask her to join us. She looks like she's alone."

"I can't," Joy hissed.

"Sure you can," Randi answered. "I'm getting us another pitcher." Randi stood and grinned.

Joy couldn't hear what Randi was saying to Sadie, but she had a big smile on her face. If it was possible to disappear, Joy would have gladly chosen that option. Randi paid for the pitcher the bartender had just filled for her. Sadie grabbed an empty glass and followed Randi to their table.

"You're sure it's okay to join you guys?" Sadie asked while shifting her focus to Joy.

"Yeah, yeah, of course." Randi set the pitcher on the table and motioned for Sadie to sit in the empty chair that magically appeared beside Joy when Alina jumped up and grabbed the spare chair from another table.

"Hey, Joy. I hear you haven't decided which job to take," Sadie said.

"Um, no, not yet," Joy mumbled.

"I know the NSA would love to have you join the team." Sadie laughed. "They've been bugging me to talk to you, so I'm glad your roommate asked me to join your group. I was supposed to meet Carson here, but she's late, as always."

Maria filled the empty glass sitting in front of Sadie. "Hi, I'm Maria, Alina's girlfriend and another roommate. I think you've met Alina before, right?"

Sadie laughed. "Yeah. Alina's kind of hard not to remember. Nice to meet you." Sadie offered her hand, and Maria shook it.

"Is Carson your girlfriend?" Maria asked.

Oh, my Goddess, this isn't really happening. Joy stood quickly, nearly knocking over her full glass of beer. "Um, I have to use the bathroom."

Sadie smiled. "Okay, but when you come back, I'm going to do a hard sell on the NSA. I know you have a lot of other offers, but I promised I would make a pitch."

As Joy rushed to the bathroom, she heard Sadie say, "Goodness, no, Carson is my best friend. We would kill each other if we tried to give that another go. Both of us are far too competitive. Been there, done that, and figured out we were better as friends."

Joy pushed open the door to the bathroom and sighed in relief that no one was there to see her meltdown. She was going to murder her roommates. Something clean, like an altered dart. Blood and guts weren't really her thing. With her hands braced against the sink, she tried to slow her breathing. She could do this. It was only pizza and beer. Maybe her friends would control the conversation as usual, and she wouldn't have to talk. She could sip her beer, have a few slices of pizza, and make a graceful exit. *Oh, who the hell am I kidding?* There was no such thing as grace, charm, or confidence in the world of Joy. *I'm going to have to answer her questions if someone really tasked her with trying to recruit me. Then, Sadie will know precisely how much of a loser I am.*

The door to the bathroom opened, and Maria cautiously entered. "Did I do the wrong thing by asking Sadie if Carson was her girlfriend? I just thought that might be good for you to know."

Joy turned on the cold water and splashed it on her face. "She's going to guess that I have a crush on her, and then I'll be totally humiliated when she makes it clear she has zero interest."

"Or something wonderful might happen. I do not think Sadie has zero interest. She was very warm when greeting you."

"Because the NSA wants her to convince me to join their organization," Joy mumbled as she grabbed a paper towel to wipe her face.

"Come, Joy. Pretend she is another roommate, not the woman you want to have sex with," Maria said.

"Maria! Alina is rubbing off on you and not in a good way."

Maria smiled. "Yes, Alina rubs on me often. It is a good thing, trust me."

†

Sadie didn't know why Joy Stiles always looked away whenever she caught her eyes. Sadie had tried that one time to get Joy to join them, but she had politely refused. She'd caught Joy staring at her on more than one occasion, but Joy had never even attempted to join their study group or bothered to interact with any of their classmates. She supposed someone as brilliant as Joy didn't need to link up with a study group. Joy had always been at the top of their class, although Sadie felt proud that she'd given the woman a run for her money on several occasions.

Maria frowned when Joy abruptly left and excused herself, following Joy into the bathroom. Clearly, Joy was uncomfortable. Sadie didn't know if her bringing up the job offer with the NSA was the right thing to do or not. She'd wanted to get to know Joy all year, but after Joy politely declined her invitation, she thought better of asking a second time. Joy clearly gave off "stay away" vibes, and Sadie was no stalker. Well, at least she didn't consider herself a stalker, merely curious about the beautiful woman. She'd done her fair share of research about Joy but had come up empty. Joy was not on social media, and her attempts at gathering information about Joy, even in the less than reputable places to find information, had gone unanswered. Sadie preferred to label her efforts as mere curiosity. Surely, she hadn't crossed a line.

"Is Joy okay?" Sadie asked. "Did I do something to upset her?" Sadie shook her head. "I came across too strong again. I have a habit of doing that."

"Okay, you can't say anything to Joy." Alina grinned as she looked at Randi, who nodded. "We might have to take drastic measures if you ever let her know we told you."

Sadie laughed. "Drastic measures, huh?"

Randi kept nodding. "Yup. Not an idle threat. Alina can be impulsive at times," Randi said seriously.

"So, it's like this. Joy's had a massive crush on you all year. I've tried to coach her, but she's a total geek, like one hundred percent, and really shy," Alina said.

"Three-quarters of our class were nerds. Joy is absolutely stunning. Plus, she was the smartest person in our class. And that's saying a lot since we all graduated Summa Cum Laude in our undergraduate programs. We just thought she didn't want to associate with us. You're pranking me, right?" Sadie asked.

"Nope." Alina made the sign of the cross over her heart. "Not a joke or a prank. So, if you are at all interested, you're going to have to make a move because she never will. Although, I can't guarantee a positive reaction. She may internally combust." Alina chuckled.

"You're serious?" Sadie looked between the two roommates.

"As the heart attack that she'll probably have. Yup!" Alina answered.

"Okaaay." The word came out in an elongated fashion. "Say I am interested. What should I ask her to do that would put her at ease?" Sadie's mouth was suddenly dry, so she took a big gulp of beer. She'd noticed Joy on the very first day of class but thought Joy was way out of her league. She could get lost in those keen green eyes and shiny red hair. If she didn't know better, she would have thought Joy was in the wrong room, but clearly, the National Defense University did not have a modeling school.

"Now, that is an excellent question," Randi said.

Before they could continue the conversation, Maria and Joy approached the table, and Joy slinked into her seat, failing to maintain eye contact. Sadie didn't know how she would get Joy to agree to go out with her if she couldn't even look her in the eye, but that didn't stop her from blurting, "I'm not going to give up, Joy, so have lunch with me this week. Wherever you want to go, it's on me." Sadie gently touched her arm, hoping Joy would look at her.

Joy blinked twice. "Lunch?"

Sadie laughed. "Yeah, that midday meal most people have. Unless, of course, you get so sidetracked by your computer, like me, you forget to stop and eat. Or we could have coffee if you would prefer."

Alina, Maria, and Randi all had huge smiles on their faces. "Breaking Joy away from her computer is a monumental feat, but everyone has to eat. I know for a fact she has nothing on her calendar all week," Alina answered.

Joy took a moment to glare at Alina before reluctantly answering, "Okay. A recruitment lunch, right?"

"Sure, if that's how you'd like to frame it. I can go with that for now. How about I pick you up at noon tomorrow?" Sadie asked.

"Um, maybe I should meet you there." Joy lifted her beer and drank half the glass.

Sadie touched Joy's arm again and said, "My mama taught me better than that. What kind of woman isn't willing to go the extra mile to pick up their date?" Sadie chuckled. "Besides, you only live a few blocks from me. You guys are in the nice brownstone with the rainbow flag, right? I just moved to the neighborhood."

"Date?" Joy sputtered.

"She'll be ready," Randi interjected. "We'll make sure she doesn't get lost in her tech tomorrow." Randi topped off Sadie and Joy's beers. "Drink up, ladies. Here's to new friends." Randi lifted her glass. Maria, Alina, and Sadie enthusiastically raised their mugs. Joy's eyes darted back and forth between her roommates and Sadie but finally touched her glass to theirs.

A waiter interrupted the toast and set down two large pizzas at the same time Carson entered the restaurant. Sadie noticed her best friend looking around and waved her over. Carson smirked and quipped, "Found a way into the cool kids' table, huh?"

Randi jumped from her seat and grabbed a chair for Carson. "We sort of kidnapped your friend."

"I seriously doubt Sadie feels like you've kidnapped her. She talks nonstop about Joy, who won't give her the time of day." She turned her gaze to Joy. "You are Joy, right? I mean, how many gorgeous redheads are there that frequent Pete's Pizza and hang out with a small gang of equally attractive lesbians?" Carson plopped into the chair Randi had brought over.

Right about now, although everything Carson said was accurate, Sadie wanted the earth to open up beneath her and swallow her whole. Joy did her blinking routine again, and the rest of the table sported enormous smiles.

Thankfully, Maria jumped in and asked, "What kind of pizza do you guys usually get? We have meat lovers special and vegetarian, but I think a third large pizza would be good to add to the ticket."

"Hawaiian? That work for you, Sadie?" Carson asked, clearly clueless about what she'd just blurted. But that was Carson. She didn't have a filter. Now it was time for Sadie to gather some space.

"I'll go to the bar and see if the waiter can put in that order." Sadie grabbed an empty pitcher and added, "And I'll get us another pitcher of beer."

She heard Carson introducing herself to the table of women as she made her way to the bar.

†

Joy experienced an overwhelming amount of warring emotions. Was it actually possible Sadie was interested in her? She tried hard to keep up with the boisterous conversation at the table, but her mind would not let her stop obsessing over what Carson had said. Even if she had anything to contribute to the conversation, who could get a word in with Alina, Randi, and Carson dominating the discussion?

Joy watched as Randi's rapt attention focused on Carson's every word. Carson had just begun her FBI academy training at Quantico. If Joy thought Sadie was outgoing and confident, next to Carson, Sadie appeared almost as shy and reserved as Joy. It was either that or Carson had managed to embarrass the perpetually poised

Sadie. Not one person responded to Carson's outburst about Sadie talking nonstop about Joy.

"The place is enormous. Like 547 acres. You'd think that by now, I wouldn't have to deal with a bunch of sexist asswipes, but the guys still want to try to show their superiority. It really chafes their little tighty-whities when I beat their times," Carson relayed to her interested roommates.

"How did you get into the academy? Were you heavily recruited? Damn, I wish I could fast forward a few years, or my moms would let me quit college and join the army," Randi complained.

"Moms?" Carson asked.

"Yeah, Joy, Alina, and I have two moms. They work for the same company. That's how we all know each other. The moms thought it would be good for us to room together. It's been great. We have a lot in common," Randi explained.

Joy almost didn't hear the question directed at her because she was so focused on staying under the radar so she wouldn't say something inane and cause further embarrassment. She felt a slight puff of air next to her ear as Sadie whispered, "What's it like to have two moms? I imagine that would be very cool. Coming out to them would be a breeze." And then she heard that sultry chuckle in her ear.

She listened to what Carson said, but somehow it didn't quite sink in. How did Sadie know Joy was a lesbian? Even though she hadn't actually tested that theory with anyone, Joy just knew because she'd never noticed boys or men.

She knew she should say something. An answer was required of her. So she blurted the first thought that came into her mind. "We're close. We have to be. My Mama T is a genius who literally saves our asses when we're in a tight spot. I wonder if I'll ever be as good as her."

Joy wanted to yank the words back into her mouth. What the hell was she thinking, letting that tidbit slip out? She hazarded a glance at Sadie, who looked perplexed. It was clear that Sadie had gathered her confidence again, not letting Carson's spontaneous revelation affect her ability to speak with Joy.

"As good as her at what? From my vantage point, you must be used to being the best at everything you touch. You certainly were in our class. I'm not saying you were a braggart or anything. In fact, it was the exact opposite. If our instructors hadn't called on you, no one would have ever known how smart you were."

Thank the Goddess Sadie ignored the "literally save our asses" part of what Joy had just verbally vomited. Fortunately, it was getting easy to engage in conversation with Sadie. She made it so Joy could actually answer with more than one or two-word responses.

"I was fortunate that Mama T enjoyed our time together in her lab. I swear I spent my entire childhood there. That's the only reason I did so well in class. There's a running joke that my mother found a way to splice two eggs together, but that didn't happen. And that running joke also applies to my friend, Pepper. She looks like her birth mother but has eyes like her other mother. My moms went the traditional sperm bank route. I'm the spitting image of my Mama C, but my passions are all Mama T because of how much time we spent together in the lab."

Joy was sure that was the most words she'd ever said to anyone, including her best friends. It was like an alien had taken over her body. Sadie was looking at her with a mix of astonishment and mirth. Joy couldn't maintain eye contact and looked away, feeling the flush rise in her chest and undoubtedly make it to her face.

"You're not at all like I thought you would be." Sadie nodded. "I'm so delighted about that. Now I'm really looking forward to lunch tomorrow. To be honest, I was a little scared you'd turn me down."

"I probably should have. I'm not at all accomplished with small talk. Or any kind of conversation, for that matter," Joy responded.

Sadie smiled. "You seem to be doing just fine right now."

"You kind of make that easy. Plus, it helped what your friend said. Not because it embarrassed you or anything," Joy quickly added. "More because I guess I could see you're human like the rest of us."

Sadie groaned. "Can your genius mother invent a time machine and take us back to before Carson opened her big mouth?"

Joy laughed. A genuine laugh, not something forced. "If anyone can do it, my mom can. She's that brilliant. She's helping me with a minor problem I have right now. I'm sure she'll have sent the code for me to play with by the time I get back home."

Sadie's eyebrow rose. "That sounds interesting. Care to share more?"

"And have your view of me shattered?" Joy teased. "Admitting to my mother that I needed her help was bad enough, and now you want me to reveal the gruesome details?"

"We could commiserate together. I'm having my own challenges trying to keep everything secure. You have no idea how many hackers put on their bucket lists to penetrate the NSA. It's like they want to do it just to have bragging rights. It reminds me of those frat boys who want to add another notch on their bedpost, not caring about the consequences." Sadie shook her head.

Joy was sure her face had lost all its color. She hadn't ever thought about causing problems for the people who worked at the NSA when she tried to hack their site. Would she be the reason someone like Sadie lost their job because she was obsessed with learning more about the rumors flying on the dark web?

"Hey, are you okay?" Sadie asked.

"Um, yeah, I don't usually drink a lot. Maybe the beer is going to my head or something. Can you excuse me for a moment?" Joy pushed back her chair and fled to the bathroom again, leaving her phone on the table.

†

What the hell just happened? Everything was going so well. Sadie had managed to get Joy to open up and talk. She'd even seen a side to Joy that Sadie was sure she only showed her closest friends. Joy had actually teased her. Maybe she shouldn't have talked about the NSA. Joy could be thinking that the only reason Sadie wanted to take her to lunch was to convince her to accept the job they offered. Or maybe Joy thought Sadie was only trying to use her for that big brain of hers. That couldn't be further from the truth. Sure, it would be nice to collaborate with the most brilliant woman she'd ever met. Sadie could learn a lot from Joy. She was sure of that. But that wasn't why she was interested in Joy. There was something about her that drew Sadie in. At times, she seemed confident and sure of her skills, but then things would turn on a dime, and Sadie could almost see the self-flagellation play out on her beautiful face. Joy's phone rang, and Sadie saw a picture of a stunning woman flash on the screen. At first, Sadie was jealous, even though she had zero right to those feelings. But upon further inspection, the woman looked like an older version of Joy.

Sadie saw Alina's eyes travel to the phone, and then Alina abruptly stood.

"I'll go," Alina offered.

Maria turned to Sadie and reassured her, "Do not worry. Alina can sometimes be like the bull in the china shop, but they have known each other since they were very small. Alina loves Joy. It is hard to know what goes on in Joy's head. She is very, how you say…introspective."

"Yeah, poor Sadie has been trying to figure Joy out for over a year," Carson said.

Sadie rolled her eyes. "I'll deal with you later, Ms. Verbal Vomit. It's bad enough I came on too strong, but you just had to reveal my interest. Did you ever think that maybe I should be the one to tell Joy I've been crushing on her for the last year?"

Randi shrugged and grinned. "Meh. It's in the open now. And neither of you had to send a note with checkboxes. Do you like me? Yes or no," she teased.

"I'm pretty sure both of us are adult enough to have the conversation without our gaggle of friends interfering."

Randi arched her eyebrow. "Oh, yeah, because you were doing a bang-up job of that for the past year."

Carson laughed. "Got you there, Sades."

Sadie leaned forward. "Okay, if you're so smart, why do you think Joy left again? Was it my frat boy bedpost comment? Does she think that I just want to have sex with her or something?"

Randi shrugged again. "Who knows? I haven't been around Joy as long as Alina. You could ask Alina, or how about conversing with Joy because you're both adult enough to do that, right?" Randi laughed.

"Fine, I'll do that at lunch tomorrow. In the meantime, how about y'all stay out of it? Clearly, your matchmaking skills aren't helping. I'm going to check on her," Sadie declared with a challenging glare.

†

"Oh, for fuck's sake, Joy. You're not going to cause Sadie to lose her job. The NSA employs thousands of people. No doubt there are also hundreds, maybe thousands of hackers out there trying to penetrate their security. It's highly doubtful you're the one hacker pitting your skills against Sadie. Do you know the odds of that?"

Joy opened her mouth to share the calculated odds, knowing that about 32,000 people worked at the NSA, but guesstimating the number of hackers skilled enough to even try hacking into the NSA was likely less than one hundred. But Alina put her hand up.

"Do not spew some number you've just calculated in that big brain of yours."

"Fine, point taken. Thanks for talking me off the ledge. I just humiliated myself again." Joy hung her head. "Didn't I? Don't fib because I'll know."

"Yeah, but I don't think it matters. Sadie looked equally horrified when her best bud spilled the beans on her fascination with you. Okay, don't freak out, but I better confess to doing something. You'll probably find out, anyway. I kind of did the same thing."

Joy narrowed her eyes. "What did you do, Alina?"

"Um, the first time you went to the bathroom, I figured if giving you pointers wasn't working, I'd try offering my words of wisdom to Sadie. I might have let slip that you had a big crush on her and told her you'd never ask her out, so she would have to be the one to take the plunge."

"Is that the only reason she asked me to lunch? How could you, Alina? A pity date?" Joy's breath started coming in rapid hiccups. She was on the verge of full-on panic mode when the door opened, and Sadie stepped in. Joy's eyes went blurry, and nothing seemed to maintain focus as she slid down the wall. She heard the voice and felt the comforting touch as her heart continued to race.

"Breathe, Joy. You're having a panic attack. Come on, take a deep breath with me. Focus on putting oxygen into your lungs. That's all you have to do right now. Nothing else."

Joy knew it was Sadie's voice, and she tried hard to listen to her, but it wasn't working. Knowing it was Sadie watching her meltdown made it worse. Far worse.

"Hey, you have absolutely nothing to be embarrassed about. I only know how to stop an attack because I used to get them at least once a month. Now please, breathe with me, or I'll hyperventilate right along with you, thinking I've caused this," Sadie consoled.

The words finally seeped in, and Joy slowly blinked as she forced herself to take deep breaths and slow her heart rate. She looked into Sadie's concerned face. Through the slight haze, Joy heard Alina's phone ring, and a frown formed on her face before Alina slipped out of the bathroom to take the call. Joy's focus swung back to Sadie, who had such a serene expression. She reminded Joy of an angel, or at least her vision of what an angel might look like.

"There you are." Sadie smiled. "Listen, I think our friends might have our best interests at heart, but they haven't been helping, have they? Look, I like you. I want to go out with you and not just to put a notch on my bedpost, if that's what you assumed. If I came on too strong, I'll do my best to tone things down."

"You...You get panic attacks?" Joy asked.

"I used to. Meditation and therapy do wonders for my ability to cope in stressful situations. Ready for pizza to soak up some of that alcohol?" Sadie winked.

"You're not coming on too strong," Joy barely whispered.

Sadie smiled. "Good to know."

CHAPTER THREE

Sadie wasn't lying to Joy when she told her she'd had panic attacks, too. What she shared, however, happened a long time ago. In high school, to be exact. When Sadie entered college, she'd reinvented herself through a steely willpower that no one thought possible. Only one individual knew anything about her at the university thousands of miles away from the tiny town where she'd grown up. When Sadie earned that scholarship, she became someone new. As if she'd shed her old skin, emerging shiny and pristine. Not unlike a snake, but she didn't like comparing herself to a snake. Her best friend Carson was the only person who knew the broad strokes of her past. Carson often reminded Sadie that she sometimes took the "new you" to an unflattering level of confidence and arrogance. She wanted the old Sadie to come out and play because she missed that Sadie—the version that showed glimpses of her previous self to Carson as they got to know one another.

Well, that's what Sadie had done tonight. She admitted her imperfections. Something she rarely did in front of others. But she hated seeing Joy struggle. At the same time, Sadie was restless tonight. It felt uncomfortable retreating to the person she used to be. She needed to settle herself the only way she knew how. Flipping open the lid of her laptop, she began her quest for dominance. She was the queen of the dark web, and Sadie would be damned if she'd let some novice hacker beat her at her own game.

"Shit, the nerve of this person. Very clever," Sadie mumbled.

She had to admit the code was nearly flawless. If she hadn't been paying attention, she would have missed it. But Sadie knew whoever this person was, they were relentless and wouldn't give up. She couldn't let that happen. At first, she'd assumed the group was just a collection of crackpot conspiracy theorists, but now she knew that wasn't true. Sadie suggested they shut down their conversation and develop a new back channel that was more secure until they figured out what to do. She had hoped that after Carson finished her training, she could help because this was a lot bigger than a handful of talented hackers discovering dangerous intel. If Sadie could uncover the other hackers' identities, she suspected this new person could as well. That made it unsafe for all of them. No one would believe them without hard proof. Sadie was working on that. At first, she didn't accept it either. Not until she started working at the NSA. Her curiosity was going to get her killed. If this woman was working for him, they were screwed. Sadie knew it was stupid to underestimate a woman, and she was not stupid.

"Time for Dragonfire to torch the pesky warrior." Although Sadie did approve of the avatar the unknown hacker chose the last time they had a confrontation. And now Sadie was second-guessing her assumptions about this hacker. What Sadie couldn't figure out was if she was working for him, why would she need to hack into the NSA?

Sadie decided to take a less aggressive tack. Finding her way into the hacker's computer, her dragon flew across the screen and said, "Why are you interested in joining our online game club? I thought my previous messages clearly communicated we are an invitation-only group."

The Amazon appeared with a very lifelike expression of amusement. "Oh, please give me some credit. Keeping me out of your little clique and the NSA. Why? Clearly, you are in over your head. You're just a bunch of nerds trying to play heroes and heroines. You're going to get yourselves killed. Are you even old enough to drive?" the Amazon taunted.

Sadie made her dragon roar as fire torched the Amazon, leaving tiny wisps of smoke curling above a very lifelike corpse. "We are not afraid of him. We're going to find The Crusaders before he does. You're just his pathetic lapdog."

The Amazon quickly reanimated and lifted her sword, cleanly slicing off the head of the dragon. A puff of smoke emerged from the severed dragon's head in the form of a dying cough.

"Rude. Your dragon's breath is nasty. Him? Crusaders? Don't presume to know who I am or what side I fight for. Then, when you're ready to play nice, you know how to hack me. Bye-bye for now," the Amazon taunted.

An impressive display of colors splashed across the screen before the clever hacker locked Sadie out. She watched in horror as the Amazon used a new set of codes and barreled into her secure site. No matter what she did, she could not prevent her from accessing every conversation and piece of information they'd collected, except for his name and the proof from the NSA that she'd locked away in a separate vault on the dark web. At least for now, that was safe.

Maybe it was time to shut down the site. She might need to do her own research to find The Crusaders. At this point, all she knew was what the NSA had discovered, which was still not a lot to go on. The only intel they had uncovered were witness statements that the saboteurs were almost exclusively women. Women who had elite army fighting skills. Sadie couldn't let him uncover this fierce group of mostly women. She knew for a fact he was trying and had gotten the NSA to do the dirty work on his behalf. Fortunately, these women clearly had their own connections to the government; she was sure of it.

†

After returning from Pete's Pizza, Joy was too wired to sleep. She barricaded herself in her room, sending an unmistakable message that she did not wish to scrutinize every minute of tonight's near disaster. Thankfully, her friends accepted her need to be alone.

Toni had provided the code. Joy really wanted to talk to her mother about her upcoming date, but she didn't have those kinds of conversations with Toni. So, she ended up calling her Mama T, proposing they hack the site together.

Joy activated her video phone. "Hey, Mama T. Are you up for another sneak attack? Besides, I want you to see everything on this site. Whoever these guys are, they've stumbled onto something that could get them killed. I'm a little worried about them, even the irritating dragon woman. No doubt she works for the NSA, too. I think they're trying to play the hero."

While Joy was taunting the dragon, her mother worked in the background unnoticed. It was the perfect plan to find this woman and hopefully protect her and her group. After they gleaned all the information they could from the site, her mother could scrub its existence. Leaving any crumb behind could attract the wrong attention.

Joy was a little surprised at the dragon's fresh approach. She seemed slightly less aggressive out of the gate, trying to persuade Joy they were merely an insignificant gaming group. Now she really needed to find out who they were because they had a name. This was the first real break The Organization had in two years to discover who was pulling the strings. Or at least one name of someone high enough to keep their efforts to a minimum impact. Unfortunately, Joy experienced a queasy feeling when the dragon mentioned The Crusaders. Her gut told her that The Organization was more at risk of discovery than at any point in its long history.

"Did you get enough information, Mama T?" Joy asked.

"Why didn't you tell me they were tracking our organization?" Toni asked.

"I thought I could find out more about what they may or may not know about us before coming to you. It's why I've been so obsessed with breaking into this group and hacking

29

the NSA. When the one with the handle Dragonfire mentioned the NSA in one of the posts, that got my attention. I assume our irritant is Dragonfire. Can you track her?"

"Yup. Within two hours, I'll know everything there is to know about the lizard, from her brand of toothpaste to the color of underwear she prefers. Do lizards even brush their teeth?" Toni laughed at her own joke.

"Dragon, Mom. Not lizard."

"You say dragardo, I say lizardo."

"Oh, Goddess. And I'm the child here." Joy leaned forward and stretched her sore back, realizing she'd been slumped over her laptop in the same exact position for far too long.

Char's face popped into the screen. "Hi, baby. I heard you have a date tomorrow. Good for you. This is the young woman who was in your class, right?"

"Just because I can't kill Alina doesn't mean I won't post pictures of her when she had braces—all over the internet," Joy grumbled.

"Joy," Char began with her soothing mom voice, "You are a beautiful, talented young woman. From what I hear, Sadie is intelligent enough to recognize what a catch you are. Don't try to be something you're not, because clearly, she wants to date you, not some trumped-up version of the perfect woman. Don't clam up, okay? That's my mom advice for you."

"Believe it or not, Mama C, I was able to have a conversation with her before I went into panic mode again, thinking that I was causing her problems at the NSA. Then, I was reminded of all the secrets we have to keep. Doesn't help, you know?"

Char sighed. "I'm so sorry, hon. We haven't made it easy for any of you, have we? But don't give up. Toni and I have good intuition when it comes to assessing people. If this Sadie person is worthy, I'm sure we can make an exception. Look how many we've allowed into the fold. There are always ways to accommodate love."

"Love," Joy squeaked. "I haven't even gone on a first date yet. I know very little about Sadie."

"I'll do a deep dive on her," Toni offered.

"No!" Joy exclaimed. "Please, can you just stay out of it? It's not that I don't appreciate your help and advice, but with this...I just want to have a normal experience. I loved growing up in the adoring arms of The Organization, but it was far from ordinary. Even the college experience wasn't exactly what I had in mind when I moved away." Joy shook her head when Char opened her mouth to speak. "Don't apologize. Neither of you. I would not change a thing." Joy chuckled. "Okay, maybe I would change my bitchy roommate, but other than that, not a thing. Being involved in The Organization's missions these last two years more than makes up for those three awkward years in college."

"Okay," Toni answered hesitantly. "Do you still want me to find out who this lizard is?"

Joy laughed. "You are insufferable. Dragon," she reminded. "And, yes, because I don't have all that fancy equipment to do it myself."

"If you came home more often, then we could work on it together," Toni hinted.

"I miss you too, Mama T. And Mama C," she added, not wanting to leave her other mother out. "Maybe next weekend. I need to decide what conventional cover job to accept. I'd love to talk with both of you about that. Alina thinks I should take the NSA job because I'd have more access to the information we need."

Toni shrugged. "We've always been able to hack the government sites. We're happy to discuss this with you but don't feel the need to take a job there if you aren't feeling it. Cover jobs help, but they aren't mandated. You could be a bratty rich girl, spending your wealthy mothers' money," Toni teased.

Joy yawned. "I think I'll head to bed now. If I don't, I'll be up all night trying your new code and hacking the NSA. I'm sure whatever there is to learn won't disappear in one day. You don't have to work on finding out who Dragonfire is tonight. That can wait, too. It's late."

"Ha, like that will happen. You do know your mother, don't you?" Char teased. "I'll keep her from calling you, though. Have fun tomorrow and relax into it. It's lunch, baby, not a lifelong commitment."

"Thanks. Love you both."

"Love you, too," Char and Toni said simultaneously, then her screen went blank.

Before Joy logged out of her laptop, she saw the dragon appear on her screen, relaxed against a rock where she appeared to wait patiently while a surprisingly accurate rendition of her Amazon slept as light snoring sounds emanated from her mouth and a trickle of drool escaped. Joy laughed despite the taunt. She decided not to respond because that would frustrate Dragonfire more than thinking up a clever response. Dragonfire would get kicked from her screen the minute she logged out. She didn't need to lose sleep playing the game. Joy would rather not have bags the size of a moving truck beneath her eyes for tomorrow's date.

She'd only hoped she could sleep versus ruminate all night. As it turned out, her emotional exhaustion had her dreaming about dragons and Amazons within the hour.

†

"Damn, this little lizard is good, but I'm better," Toni muttered. She'd been working on unraveling the rabbit holes the hacker sent her down for the last four hours. Finally, she followed the last thread, and she was almost there.

"Gotcha!" she exclaimed before looking up and finding a grumpy-looking Char.

Char shuffled into the lab, rubbing her eyes. "Seriously, Toni? I thought this was all behind us now. It's been months since you spent all night in the lab. You were the one who said we needed to hand over the reins."

"It's not all night." Toni glanced at her watch. "I'd say it's early. The evening's still young." Toni shot her wife an impish grin.

"It's two o'clock in the morning. I woke up to pee for the millionth time, and guess who was not in bed with me? I distinctly heard Joy tell you not to work on this tonight. You're never going to retire, are you?"

"But I finally got her." Toni returned to her screen and stared, not saying anything for several seconds as she looked at the name and physical address for the IP host she finally tracked. "Oh, fuck. It can't be. Do you know Sadie's last name?"

"No, Alina never mentioned it. Why?" Char asked.

"Because the lizard is a person named Sadie Harris. And she lives only a few blocks from Joy. That cannot be a coincidence." Toni's fingers flew over the keyboard faster than she could type in the commands to take her to her program that would make a copy of the entire contents of Sadie's computer.

Char sat in an office chair and rolled over. "You're going to do what you promised you wouldn't, aren't you?"

Toni glanced quickly at her wife, a pained expression on her face. "You're damn right I am. I want to know what the slimy little lizard is up to. I'll have her entire life history and whatever she's working on in less than an hour. If she thinks she's going to hurt Joy, she has another thing coming. You need to call Val right now."

"Whoa. Stop." Char put her hands on top of Toni's, stilling her typing. "You're jumping too quickly to conclusions. I will not send Val to scare this poor young woman before we verify her intentions. And, even then, unless she's planning to assassinate our daughter, which I highly doubt, I will not authorize elimination. However, I would be interested in learning more about this young woman and verifying she's the person Joy is having lunch with tomorrow. Joy might not be happy about your deep dive, but I agree it's prudent to determine if she poses any risks to Joy or The Organization."

"Her little dark web group has been far too inquisitive about an organization they call The Crusaders. They've been tracking our missions over the last year. So has the NSA, according to the lizard. There is also a vague reference to some mysterious man funding the search. It's unclear who the money is going to, though. One obvious thing is his pockets are deep. If the lizard is trying to cash in on what essentially amounts to a bounty and she has more information about Joy, it could be dangerous for her and us."

Char nodded. "I don't think Joy would blame you for unearthing everything you can about Sadie Harris. You want me to make a pot of coffee?"

"Please. Should we talk to Joy before her date?"

"Depends on what you learn. Joy's smart enough not to reveal anything about The Organization. And we've trained her to pick up on subtleties. So she'll know if this Sadie person is trying to glean information from her. I trust our daughter."

"I don't know. Lust sometimes blunts our self-preservation gene. Crazy things happen when we find someone attractive." Toni laughed.

"Like almost having sex with me in the bathroom? As I recall, you tried to put a bio tracker in me with your fancy business card. I'd say your paranoia gene worked just fine," Char retorted.

Toni smiled. "Come on, that was the best foreplay ever. Both of us trying to outmaneuver the other."

"Exactly. So what if Sadie is on the right side of this? Shouldn't we give them a little time to figure each other out?" Char asked.

"I don't know. It was different for us. We both knew more about the other, or at least had suspicions. Plus, you had The Organization's full support as we played our little games. Maybe we should activate someone to watch over Joy. I'd put bots in Joy, but she'd never forgive me if I did that. Is there anyone we can send that Joy won't immediately spot?"

Char stood and began pacing. "Maybe. We have eyes on a new recruit at the FBI Academy but haven't made contact yet. It's too soon for tomorrow. We might have to let it play out and take action after the fact if we're compromised."

"How about if we get Alina to put the bots in Sadie? That way, we can monitor her. If Alina has to follow them, Joy will assume Alina is just butting in as usual. I'll call Alina tomorrow morning with an update," Toni offered.

CHAPTER FOUR

Joy figured she had plenty of time to try her mother's new code before her date. She didn't know if Saturday was a good time to poke around in the NSA's database, but at least with the new code, she had a chance of not being discovered.

Not bothering to shower, she rolled out of bed, wrapped her long wavy locks in a hair tie, and searched for coffee with her laptop tucked safely under her arm. She could kiss Randi for insisting they purchase a coffeemaker that would brew the black gold on a timer. Temporarily setting her laptop on the granite counter, she pulled a large cup from the cabinet and filled it three quarters to the top, leaving plenty of room for her favorite creamer. The smell of freshly brewed coffee permeated the large living area.

It was a miracle none of her roommates were up yet. She'd left her other gadgets strewn across the coffee table and felt blessed that not one of her roommates was a neat freak. Not even Maria, who used to work in housekeeping at the Mexican resort. They weren't slobs, they enjoyed a certain amount of cleanliness, but they were not particularly concerned with tech spread all over the living room and tolerated her clutter just fine. She supposed it was because that same tech led them to their missions. Joy grabbed her coffee and laptop, spreading out into the living room as she nestled into the couch. She began her perusal of what the NSA was hiding in relation to their knowledge of The Organization.

Using her mother's new code, Joy slipped inside almost seamlessly. On a lark, she tried a search using the word Crusader. She'd set her watch for ten minutes, remembering the warning from her mother that she avoid remaining inside their network too long in one setting. Of course, that didn't keep Joy from embedding her own unique tracking mechanism. That was Joy's specialty now. She might not be the best hacker, but she could implant a string of commands inside any network once she hacked their firewall without notice, and that code was part of her elaborate notification system.

Just as Joy found a remote corner of the NSA network with an abbreviation of Crusader, her watch went off, startling her. She desperately wanted to chance it, but that might cause more trouble for The Organization. If Dragonfire was competent enough to stop Joy from nosing around, she might be able to track her, similar to what Mama T planned on doing today. Reluctantly, she backed out of their system using the same code that enabled her to sneak inside undiscovered.

"You still trying to get inside the NSA?" Alina asked.

Love Hacks

Joy jumped. "Shit, you scared the crap out of me. Yeah, Mama T gave me some code to use, and it worked. But right when I found a file in this obscure location on their network, I had to jump out. Too long inside puts us at risk, and no matter how much I wanted to tug on that thread, I couldn't chance it. No way is it a coincidence that the file is called *Crusdr*. I'm pretty sure that means the NSA is a little too interested in a group they're calling The Crusaders, same as that collection of hackers on the dark web."

Alina scratched her head and strolled to the coffeepot. "I think I need a gallon of this. Last night was fun, huh? Well…except for your meltdowns, but it turned out all right. You're not still mad at me, are you?"

"You called my moms," Joy said with a fair amount of aggravation. After she'd finished talking with Toni and Char the previous evening, she'd barged into Alina's room, catching her and Maria naked and in the middle of sex. After pulling the sheet up to their necks, Joy proceeded to ream Alina out for spilling the beans. She hadn't even waited to hear Alina's defense before marching out and slamming the door.

Alina held up her hands. "They called me. You left your phone on the table when you went to the bathroom. When you didn't answer, they contacted me. They were worried, so I had to set them straight. Well, not literally," Alina joked. "Isn't there a better saying, like as in when we're giving directions and we say never go straight, always go forward?" Alina poured coffee into a mug and added a healthy amount of sugar before grabbing the cream from the refrigerator.

"Enlighten. Redress. Ameliorate. There are probably hundreds of other ways to say it," Joy answered absently.

39

Alina clapped her hands. "There's our little brainiac. Anyway, they were thrilled to hear about the date. Speaking of dates, are you getting excited yet?" She lazily made her way to the couch and plopped next to Joy.

"She seemed sincere, right? I'm not projecting, am I?" Joy asked.

Alina shook her head. "No way. She's as much into you as you are with her. Carson pretty much confirmed what I already saw the few times I watched you guys interact."

"Bullshit, Alina. You never saw us interact because we barely acknowledged one another."

"*Au contraire.* See, I did learn some French in high school." Alina laughed. "It's all about the nonverbals, my friend. Never listen to the words; always pay attention to someone's tone of voice and their non-verbals. Y'all were so fucking obvious. I can't believe you never caught her looking at you. She did it a lot."

"Whatever."

Alina grinned. "By the way, if you want some sex pointers, you don't need to burst into our bedroom on the pretense that you were mad at me. We aren't into voyeur sex," she teased.

"I did no such thing. I *was* mad at you, and I'm re-evaluating whether to forgive you now." Joy playfully smacked Alina. "You're beyond reproach."

"Alina, your phone is ringing," Maria called from their shared bedroom.

"Pointers later. Gotta take this call. I hope it's the moms. I'm getting bored and desperately need a new mission."

40

CHAPTER FIVE

Toni continued to dig, finding out everything she could about Sadie Harris. She'd found a fuck-ton of information about the young woman. But what did it all mean? Sadie certainly had her reasons to hate the mining industry. At the same time, sometimes people who grew up in a one-industry town had a level of loyalty similar to victims who come to love their kidnappers. Personally, Toni had never understood Stockholm Syndrome, but Em and Jimena saw it enough for Toni to recognize it as something very real. Running the group homes for survivors of human trafficking, both women were skilled enough to work with the kids, but the psychological damage was real and took many forms.

Toni wanted to wait until a reasonable hour to call Alina and explain their predicament. She also needed to confirm that Sadie Harris was, in fact, the woman her daughter was crushing on. Toni grabbed her video phone and called Alina.

She made sure that Maria didn't call out that she was video phoning, lest she irritate her daughter.

"Yo, what's up, Aunt T. I can't give you more information about Joy and Sadie's date today. She's already mad enough at me," Alina whined.

"Too bad because I found out who the hacker is."

"What's that got to do with their date?" Alina asked as she plopped onto the bed next to Maria.

"Is Sadie's last name Harris?" Toni asked.

Alina scrunched her nose. "I'm not sure." She turned to Maria. "Do you know Sadie's last name?"

At the edge of the screen, Toni saw Maria shake her head. "No, sorry. I don't think Joy has ever said her last name."

"Well, I suppose I have enough information about her that I don't need you to confirm. Sadie Harris just took a job at the NSA, and she recently completed her Master of Arts in Strategic Security Studies at the National Defense University."

"Are you saying the hacker is Joy's crush?" Alina asked.

"Joy's class that just graduated from the National Defense University is not that large. I seriously doubt there are two Sadies in that class."

"Fuck me." Alina rubbed her hand over her close-cropped hair. "This is bad. Really bad. We've been pushing Joy to go out with the enemy."

"I think it's too early to determine whether Sadie is the enemy at this point. She has her reasons for hating the mining industry. It's possible she's cheering your missions, not trying to stop them."

"What do you mean she has her reasons for hating the people that run the mines?" Alina asked.

"Sadie grew up in a small town in Idaho where the only industry is their mine." Toni gulped the fresh cup of coffee Char set next to her. "Her parents both worked for the mine. Her father died in a mining accident, and the company somehow managed to avoid liability. Not only that, but they fired her mother shortly after his death, using some bogus reason. She died a year later from cancer."

"Damn, that sucks," Alina noted.

"Yeah. And there is a high incidence of that particular cancer in the small town where Sadie grew up. A reporter tried to write a story about the mine's toxic metals leaking into their nearby rivers and streams. The mining companies swore they would take precautions and clean things up, but with the push for less oversight, it isn't much of a stretch to link the high incidence of cancer with the mining company."

"So, how did Sadie make it to DC?" Alina asked.

"She lived with relatives in Maryland before securing a full-ride scholarship in Computer Science. She caught the eye of a recruiter for the National Defense University, who offered a generous deal for her to complete her Master's with them. That deal included a job at the NSA," Toni explained. "But something doesn't fit because Sadie is a wealthy woman. She did not need the substantial deal they offered, yet she took it. I'd like to know how Sadie accumulated her wealth."

"Okay, what do you need from me?" Alina asked.

"I know I'm putting you in a terrible position because Joy is already aggravated with you, but I need you to put tracking bots into Sadie."

Alina scrubbed her face. "Shit. Why can't Randi do it? Joy will never forgive me for this, especially if Sadie turns out to be a friend versus foe."

"Randi can't do it because Em and Jimena won't allow her to join The Organization until she completes her degree. She doesn't have the skills to do this without getting caught."

Alina snorted. "Yeah, I wouldn't be too sure of that."

With her phone sitting on the stand, Toni was free to put her fingers in her ears. "Do not say another word. Plausible deniability. I don't want to hear anything about what y'all are up to when we're not around. Please, Alina. It's for Joy's own good we're doing this. And to protect The Organization."

"Fine," Alina huffed. "But when this blows up in all our faces, I'm putting the blame squarely on your shoulders. Why don't you just talk with Joy and tell her everything you've told me?"

"Because I don't want to taint the date or Joy's opinion of Sadie. She might be perfect for Joy, and I don't wish to be the one to shatter that possibility. If what you told us last night is true, Sadie genuinely likes Joy."

"Yeah," Alina admitted. "I don't think she's faking her feelings. Sadie probably doesn't know that Joy is the person who keeps trying to hack into the NSA and the dark web group Sadie's associated with. Actually, Joy got in for about ten minutes this morning. She was going to try again, but not today. She found a suspicious folder. Apparently, the NSA is very interested in a group they are calling The Crusaders. I'll grab a quick shower and swing by to get your newest bots. We don't have any of those at the house. I should have enough time. I need to think about how to do this without Joy figuring out what I'm up to."

"If Sadie comes to the door, maybe you can get one in her before they even leave for the date. She's coming to pick Joy up, right?"

Alina nodded. "Yeah, that would be optimal. That way, I won't have to stalk her. Joy might notice that and ream me out for it."

"Thanks, Alina. I owe you," Toni said.

"Damn right you do," Alina answered. "I'm going to seriously consider how you can pay me back for this little job." Alina laughed. "Oohah, this is fun, having the great Aunt T owing me a favor."

"Don't get too carried away, Alina, or I'll forget my rule of never putting bots into an agent." Toni grinned. "I have numerous ways to make your life difficult. Never underestimate me."

"Psht. That's not your rule. That's Aunt Char's. But fine, whatever. I'm only doing this cause I love Joy and want the best for her."

"Good, because that is the most important reason for this mission, not because you want a future favor from me." Toni ended the call and looked at her wife. "Well, that went smoothly."

Char leaned back in her chair and crossed her legs, shaking her head. "Don't threaten the kids with that. You know you would never put bots in any of them. We already talked about this and decided that was a bridge too far, no matter the good intentions of keeping them safe."

"I know that, and you know that, but do they? Leverage, baby, leverage." Toni laughed.

CHAPTER SIX

Not wanting to allow herself to be distracted, Joy decided not to jump back on her laptop after Alina left the room to take her call. Joy doubted the call was from Alina's moms because Mama T or Mama C would have told her the previous evening if there was a new mission. She heard stirrings in Randi's room, but she hadn't appeared yet. When Alina didn't return after a few minutes, Joy looked longingly at her laptop. She didn't do idle. Joy had over an hour before needing to jump in the shower and get ready for her date. If she returned to the dark web, she knew she'd get sidetracked and wouldn't want to stop. That left fixing the tiny drone an eagle had attacked on their last mission. Joy had flown too close to an eagle's nest and discovered how protective the regal bird could be. Repairing the drone should take a little under an hour. Perfect.

Deep into her project, Joy lifted her head and barely acknowledged Alina and Maria rushing out of the house. It was a little strange because Alina had two speeds, sloth and cheetah. Cheetah was generally reserved for when a mission was going sideways.

"Going to breakfast. We'll be back to give you final words of encouragement before your date," Alina mumbled before leaving.

Joy opened her mouth to say something, but they were already gone.

"Where are they going in such a hurry?" Randi asked while stretching her arms above her head as she ambled into the kitchen.

"Breakfast," Joy answered.

"You sure she's not on a mission? Why would she be practically running out the door? She hungover or something and needs food to soak up the alcohol?"

Joy shrugged. "No clue. I haven't gotten a call, so I doubt it's a mission."

"Maybe they sent her solo because you have your epic date today," Randi teased. "Speaking of that, shouldn't you be agonizing over what to wear right about now?"

"That's the whole point of fixing the drone, so I won't brood over any aspect of the date, including what to wear, makeup or not, and how to fix my mop of hair." Joy gently tightened one of the tiny screws to affix the specially designed computer chip cover.

Randi poured herself a cup of coffee and leaned on the counter. "Too bad they already left. I'm starved." She yanked her phone from her sweatpants. "I'm calling them to bring me back something. You want a breakfast sandwich or pastry?"

47

Joy shook her head. "Nah, I'm too nervous to eat. Hopefully, by the time we get to wherever we're going for lunch, I'll be so hungry I'll be able to eat and not act like a noob."

Randi hit a button on her phone. "Yo, Alina, can you pick me up an egg and cheese sandwich, egg burrito, or anything that works as a quick to-go item? Not sure where y'all went for breakfast."

"Are we on speaker?" Alina asked.

"Yeah, why? It's just Joy and me. Are you on a mission and didn't tell her?"

"No. She's probably working on something and doesn't need us to disturb her focus," Alina answered.

Joy had been around Alina enough to know that she was lying. Alina was up to something. She would kill her if the moms sent her on a mission, no matter how small, and didn't tell Joy about it. Joy was always tech support.

"All right." Randi pressed the button and listened for a few seconds. "Oh, okay. Got it." Randi side-eyed Joy and then turned her back to Joy as she headed to her bedroom.

Something was definitely going on, and Joy wasn't about to let Randi off the hook. She'd wait for Randi to return, then pounce on her for information. Although, of the two, Alina was the easier person to break.

Continuing to work on her drone, Joy heard Randi return. She narrowed her eyes and asked, "What the hell was that all about? And don't lie to me. You two are up to something."

"Nope. Just the opposite. We aren't going to meddle in your date." Randi made the sign of a cross over her heart. "Promise. She told me how mad you were at her. Don't be so hard on Alina. You know she loves you and would do

48

anything to ensure your happiness. Just remember that. Me, too."

"I'm going to find out. You know that, right? Alina can't lie to save her life," Joy answered.

"So, not that I'm interfering, but you want my help picking out an outfit?"

Joy sighed. "Sure. It would be good to get an outside opinion because clearly, when it comes to my nonexistent love life, I need all the help I can get," Joy answered with a fair amount of bite.

"We love you, remember?" Randi smiled.

Joy set down her drone and stood. "Let's go survey my closet."

Randi rubbed her hands together. "Bangin'. We'll get you looking so hot, Sadie won't be able to keep her hands off you."

Joy chuckled. "Doubtful."

"Hey, if you weren't like an older sister to me, I'd totally hit on you." Randi followed Joy to her bedroom. "Grab that green shirt. It brings out your eyes. That will definitely have to be one option to choose from."

†

Toni began biting on the end of her pen, twirling in her chair, while she waited not too patiently for the bot to activate in Sadie. Char had disappeared a couple of hours ago, taking care of some other business for their legitimate wing of The Organization. Toni stopped spinning and grinned at her wife, who had a croissant sandwich and bag of chips in her hands.

Char pointed to Toni's mouth. "Blue ink, babe. I can't believe you never overcame that habit of biting the end of a pen."

Toni grinned. "I think I made it worse when I invented a pen that contains edible organic ink in all my favorite flavors. This one is blueberry."

"It still stains like ink," Char noted.

Toni grabbed a Kleenex from her desk and wiped her mouth. "Maybe, but it cleans up a whole lot easier than traditional ink." A ding from her computer distracted Toni from the conversation as her eyes tracked onto the monitor. "Yes! Good job, Alina."

Char set the sandwich and chips on Toni's desk, peered around to look at the monitor, and pursed her lips. "Please tell me you're not spying on Joy and Sadie. Can't you wait to do surveillance until after Sadie drops Joy off?"

"Spying is such an ugly term," Toni answered.

Char shook her head and moved to the keyboard, pressing one of the function keys, which turned all three monitors black.

"Hey, what if she reveals something important?" Toni asked.

"Then our brilliant daughter will relay the information. I know you have your bot recording everything, so Joy can review it later if there is something that requires jogging her memory. Speaking of which, when are you planning on telling her about the surveillance?"

"Never?" Toni suggested, glancing up with an expectant look.

"Nope. Wrong answer. We don't lie to our daughter. Never have, and we aren't going to start now. Delaying information is one thing, never sharing it is another," Char gently chastised. "Come have lunch with me. It's a nice day. Let's enjoy the sunshine. You need to get out of the lab and soak up a little vitamin D. In two hours, you can check your monitors."

"Fine." Toni stood and took Char's outstretched hand after grabbing her plate. "Can you tell Joy what we did when she comes to visit? By then, I should have enough data to assess whether Sadie is friend or foe."

Char laughed and led Toni to the expansive gardens in the compound. "Oh, no, there is no we in this. You're going to tell our daughter you put bots into her girlfriend."

"That's so not fair. First, one date does not mean Sadie is Joy's girlfriend, and second, you didn't raise a fuss when I suggested we inject Sadie with the tracking bots."

Char laughed. "True, but I'm not the one who called Alina to make it happen. No sense in her being mad at both of us."

"Outplayed again," Toni grumbled. "What good is being a genius if my wife outmaneuvers me at every turn?"

"Never forget, darling, there are multiple ways to be cunning. You have your strengths, and I have mine." Char smirked before sitting at the table where several sandwiches and a fruit and cheese plate sat.

Toni plunked her plate on the table and slumped into the other chair.

"Don't pout. You'll cause more wrinkles," Char teased.

†

Sadie was grateful that none of her alerts came through this morning. Since the hacker kept trying to penetrate her group and had probably seen a few things she shouldn't have before she put the alerts in place, Sadie had decided to shut down the group. She'd promised to stay in touch and create something new in the next few days, but it was too risky for now. Erasure wasn't her strong point because she was better at hacking into secure sites or interrupting hackers. Sadie had asked another group member to do that for her. She had no idea how long that would take. Removing all evidence wasn't easy because there was almost always residual data to reconstruct. She'd need to spend time on a preprogrammed fast acting demolition code to remove all evidence of her new group. Maybe Joy could help her with that. No time for that now. After having what she hoped was a secure conversation this morning to have the group shut down, she snuck into the NSA to see if anything was happening there. She found an odd string of code but didn't have time to check it out, so she reluctantly left that alone. Being late for her lunch date was not an option.

As she stood on the doorstep, waiting for someone to answer, Sadie wiped her sweaty hands over her jeans. She hadn't wanted to dress too formally, guessing that might scare Joy away. Sadie reflected on her nervousness, which she hadn't experienced since reinventing herself all those years ago. Of course, a beautiful woman would do that to her.

The door flung open, and Alina grinned at her. She thought it odd when Alina touched her back, directing her inside the brownstone. Even stranger was the odd sensation at the touch. She couldn't quite pinpoint what she felt. It wasn't exactly like an electrical impulse or even what she felt when she had consoled Joy during her panic attack, but she felt something. All thoughts flew out the window when she saw Joy, who greeted her shyly. She'd seen Joy in her green blouse before and always loved it, but Joy looked incredible paired with a snug pair of jeans.

Joy lifted her hand in an adorable wave. "Hi." She glanced at her shirt and smoothed invisible wrinkles with her hands.

"Hey. You ready to go?" Sadie asked while her eyes tracked to the table with a large assortment of electronics and strange gadgets. She wondered if this was a hobby of Joy's or one of her roommates.

"You kids have fun and be home by midnight, or not," Alina teased.

Sadie led Joy to her solar-powered car and opened the passenger door for Joy. "You look amazing, by the way. I love the color of your shirt." She shut the door and quickly went to the driver's side, climbing inside.

"Thanks. You look really nice, too. But you always look good. You could probably wear a ratty T-shirt and baggy shorts and make it look like that's the latest fashion trend," Joy answered, then immediately blushed.

"So, are you guys renting the brownstone until Maria, Randi, and Alina finish school?" Sadie asked, thinking it would be a safe question. "It's a really nice place for college kids." She started her car and checked her mirrors before rolling slowly out of the driveway.

"No, not renting," Joy mumbled, almost sounding embarrassed. "The moms bought the place so we would all have somewhere to live while everyone completed their schooling. I tried the dormitory route, wanting to have the full college experience. It didn't work well for me. I'm too odd to fit in. I was always escaping to Pepper's place. When the moms found out how miserable I was, they bought this home for us to live in. How about you? Did you buy your house? This is kind of an expensive area. The NSA must pay a hefty salary for you to afford a home in this neighborhood, or you're independently wealthy."

"The latter, but not because I was born with a silver spoon in my mouth. Not that there's anything wrong with being born into a wealthy family," Sadie quickly added, suspecting that Joy came from great wealth. She wanted to follow up on Joy's miserable college experience, but it sounded like a topic Joy wouldn't want to explore until they got to know each other better. She especially wanted to ask about Pepper because of her connection to Grace, but Sadie didn't want Joy to think she'd only asked her out because of her link to Pepper and Grace.

"So, how did you come by your wealth?" Joy asked.

Sadie could give her the basics. Surely that wouldn't hurt. "I used to spend hours as a gamer and then got interested in the tech behind the games, including how to create realistic avatars. That led to me developing a relatively popular game. A few years ago, Sony made me an offer, and I took it. I figured I had plenty of money to buy a place, and so I closed on my house about three months ago."

"You sold your game to Sony? Wow! Impressive. Is that what your undergraduate degree is in? There are schools for game development, right? A master's in Strategic Security Studies is kind of at the other end of the tech spectrum."

"I didn't even ask you what kind of food you like. I hope you enjoy farm-to-table restaurants. There are some great vegan dishes at Healthy Bites, but they also have other choices." Sadie glanced at Joy to gauge her interest, avoiding answering Joy's question. She had her reasons, but they weren't something a person shared on a first date. Especially when you threw in words like revenge.

"Oh, I'm not picky at all. Healthy Bites has exceptional organic food. Plus, they use local growers. I wouldn't say I'm a hard-core gamer, but I like a few of them. Would I know yours?" Joy asked.

Sadie spied an open parking space a few blocks from the restaurant and snuck into it before anyone else could nab the primo spot. "I hope you don't mind walking a couple of blocks. I honestly don't think we'll find anything closer. We got lucky with this spot."

Joy unclipped her seatbelt and squinted at Sadie, looking like she was trying to figure out a complicated code. "You don't like to talk about your game, do you?"

Sadie shrugged, pushed the button on the dash to unclip her belt, and answered, "It's not exactly something to be proud of. It isn't like I made a difference in the world by creating a stupid game. Probably did more harm than good. Games are addictive and keep people from interacting with the world in positive and productive ways. Ready?" Exiting the car, she put her phone against the meter and followed the instructions to pay for parking.

Joy stood awkwardly next to her as she completed the transaction. Sadie held out her hand for Joy, who looked at it and swallowed hard.

"It's only a hand, Joy. I believe that's about as low-level as one can get on the affection spectrum. I promise not to kiss you without your permission."

Joy accepted Sadie's hand, and Sadie threaded their fingers together. "You're probably going to regret asking someone like me out. At least I've managed to overcome my tongue-tied phase. There are very few people I can have a normal conversation with."

Sadie furrowed her brow. "Someone like you? What does that mean?"

"Oh, you know, socially awkward and inexperienced," Joy answered.

Sadie squeezed Joy's hand. "I don't regret a single thing. I mean that. Just because I reinvented myself many years ago doesn't mean I don't get nervous or revert to old habits. We're going to stumble through this date. But we'll do it together. And when we have a second and third date, it'll get easier. I promise."

Joy chuckled nervously. "That doesn't sound all that convincing. Dating shouldn't be hard. Should it? I mean, stumbling through a first date doesn't sound very encouraging. If you have to work hard to get through the date, that means it wasn't good."

"Everything in life worth having or experiencing comes with challenges. Dating is hard. Who told you first dates should be smooth and natural? Particularly with two computer geeks. We aren't exactly known for our velvety approach to dating. I actually believe this one is going much better than any I've ever been on before."

"You…you mentioned second and third dates. Uh, how do you know we'll have a second date?" Joy tentatively asked.

"Because I'm an optimist. Can't blame me for hoping." Sadie smiled as she released Joy's hand and opened the door to the restaurant, gesturing for Joy to go inside.

†

When Sadie mentioned a second and third date, Joy's heart began beating rapidly. She tried to take in several deep breaths. Alina always used humor to deflect or cover up any nervousness, but Joy wasn't naturally funny. Instead, she attempted to explore the topic of dating honestly. She'd been surprised at her ability to converse as naturally as she'd managed thus far. She wondered whether she should confess that she had nothing to compare to since this was the first time Joy had ever been on a date. Would that make her seem even more pathetic? Wasn't honesty the best policy? Because she was part of The Organization now, so much of her life had to be hidden. Maybe this was all she had to offer in the honesty department.

"I've never been on a date before," Joy blurted as they approached the host. "I won't have any knowledge to compare. No data to determine if this is a good or bad first date."

"Table for two?" the host asked.

Sadie nodded, and the host led them to a table. She turned her attention to Joy. "Perfect. Then I won't have to live up to some epic previous first date. How lucky can I get?" She pulled out the chair for Joy.

"You're like old school, huh?" A genuine smile spread across Joy's face. "Opening doors, pulling out my chair for me. It makes me feel special."

"You *are* special, Joy." Sadie looked so serious Joy almost believed her. "Can I ask you something?"

"Um, sure." Joy could almost feel her body stiffen.

She wondered if Sadie could pick up on the change in her countenance, regardless of how fleeting it was. After years of hiding a significant part of her life from the outside world,

Joy was adept at answering questions with enough detail to satisfy the curious outsider without offering any information of significance. However, over the years, having a reputation as the quiet one had its advantages. People stop asking questions when you're the shy and standoffish friend.

A waitress approached and pointed to the scan code under the glass on the table. "Please scan the menu, and I'll be back to take your order."

"Thanks. Give us a few minutes," Sadie answered. "Everything is wonderful here, but I especially love their portobello mushroom sandwich." She pulled her phone from her pocket to access the menu with the scan code. Joy did the same and started reviewing her choices.

After less than a minute, Sadie set her phone on the table and asked, "What made you choose Strategic Security Studies?" She held up her hand. "Before you jump to the conclusion that this is some kind of lead-in to a pitch to get you to join the NSA. It's not. I honestly want to know what attracted you to the program."

Joy wracked her brain for an acceptable answer. She should have predicted that Sadie would ask her that. It was a typical first-date question. She'd stick with as close to the truth as possible. "I thought it was a better way to use my skills versus corporate America. There are a lot of terrifying people out there waiting to create havoc in the world. I wanted to be part of the solution and not contribute to the problem."

"How in the world would you be part of the problem? You aren't some kind of mercenary hacker chasing wealth, are you?" Sadie grinned.

"No, of course not, but corporate America isn't exactly squeaky clean. A lot of shitty stuff happens when people chase the dollar, and that causes them to discard their scruples."

"You mean like selling a game to Sony?" Sadie teased.

"Oh, no. I didn't mean that at all. I don't know anything about Sony. I just meant some industries have horrific practices," Joy sputtered.

"Well, the government isn't exactly the pinnacle of ethics and honesty." Sadie frowned.

"Oh, I know that. I'm not naïve. But at least there are whistleblower laws to protect government employees. Private industries get away with far worse."

"Maybe, but I wouldn't be too sure of that. Certainly, there have been a few successful whistleblowers, but I assume the government has silenced an equal number under the guise of protecting our freedoms. There are unfortunate ties between the government and corporate America. Politicians are never free from influence."

"If you believe that, why do you work for the NSA?" Joy asked.

"Because I trust a person can change things from the inside. And there are far scarier forces out there than the United States government. I'd like to think I can play a role in keeping those daunting powers far away."

Joy nodded. "You *are* an optimist, aren't you?"

"Yup. And I finally have the confidence required to work at the NSA and truly make a difference. This is the only time I'm going to say anything about you working for the NSA because I promised my bosses I would talk to you, but I don't want this to ruin our date. I honestly believe the NSA is the right place for you. And I'd love to work with you. I think you could teach me a lot." Sadie grinned as she dusted her hands. "Whew. That's out of the way now. I never break a promise."

Joy smiled. "I swear I'll give it serious consideration. What were you going to do if you hadn't run into me at Pete's?"

"Take a chance that you wouldn't peg me as some kind of stalker when I walked to your house and knocked on your door," Sadie answered. "At least I would have a ready-made excuse to ask you to lunch without revealing my true motive."

"True motive?" Joy hated the fact that her first instinct was suspicion.

"Yeah, asking you out. I hoped you would recognize my wit and charm after I abandoned the pretense of recruitment, and that would earn me a second date."

Joy relaxed in her seat and smiled. "I think I'd like a second date."

Sadie playfully pounded her fist against her heart. "You think? I'm wounded. I haven't managed to lock that down yet? Clearly, I'm losing my touch."

"Losing your touch? So, um, you've dated a lot of different, uh, people?" Joy settled on a generic term because she didn't want to assume Sadie was a lesbian.

"Are you ready to order?" The waitress had returned.

Sadie winked. "Whew. Saved by the bell." She turned her gaze to the waitress. "I'll have the portobello sandwich with truffle fries, please. And water is fine for me."

"And for you?" the waitress asked.

"I'll have the same," Joy answered.

After the waitress left, Joy remained silent, hoping to get an answer to her question.

"Hmm. How to answer your question without you thinking poorly of me?"

"It's okay. I'm an anomaly. Most people have dated by our age. A lot if I'm to go by Alina and Randi's experiences. At least Pepper was more like me, so I didn't have to feel like such an oddball. But now she's practically married to Grace." Joy nervously rearranged the cloth napkin on her lap.

"You're not an oddball," Sadie insisted. "I might have gone on a few outings while in college, but I haven't dated anyone this past year. So, you're friends with Pepper Maggio and Grace Turner? That's impressive. They're extraordinary." Something about the way she asked about Pepper and Grace had tiny alarm bells ringing in Joy's ears, but Joy didn't want to act paranoid. She'd learned a healthy dose of self-protection living at the organization and didn't want any of that influencing her date.

"Yeah. Even though we're all different ages, Pepper, Alina, and I kind of grew up together. When Pepper started dating Grace, I got to know her. How do you know Pepper and Grace?"

"Oh, I don't, but I follow them and what they're trying to do to bring more awareness around the price of our gadgets. You know, with the exploitation in the mines. I have great admiration for their crusade. Are the rumors about them being targeted and almost losing their lives true?"

Don't react. Don't react. "You mean that story Politico did on Grace about the ongoing threats? I know we should all take threats from those fringe groups seriously, but so many people have been targeted that it loses its impact after a while." Joy chuckled nervously. "I've never seen any bullet wounds on either of them."

Sadie smiled. "I try not to pay too much attention to the conspiracy theorists, but I admit I have a gruesome fascination with the dark web where most of that shit grows wild. I know the majority of it is crap, but there are rare occasions when something on the dark web has a grain of truth to it. Plus, those groups are challenging to hack. I don't know about you, but I love a good hacking competition."

"Aren't you supposed to keep hackers out of the NSA? Did they hire you because you know all the hacking secrets? Or maybe you got in trouble with the NSA, and instead of tossing you in jail, they offered you a deal?" Joy teased.

Joy watched as Sadie's face lost a little bit of its color before she pasted on a smile and redirected, "Haven't you ever tried to hack into any high-security sites to test your skills?"

Joy wrestled with how much to share about herself. If she'd read the situation correctly, Sadie more than likely did her fair share of poking into places she should stay far away from. What could it hurt to admit that she'd done the same thing? Most accomplished hackers had made at least a few attempts at breaking into impossible sites just to prove their tech acumen. However, Joy was only aware of a handful of people who were actually successful, and most of them worked for The Organization. Joy must have taken too long to answer, because Sadie interrupted her internal dialogue.

"I can almost see those wheels of yours turning inside your head. You aren't sure whether you should admit this." Sadie laughed. "That's all the answer I need. Unfortunately, I'm the one responsible for keeping you out of the NSA.

Now, that would be a challenge that would make my work less boring. Although recently, I had a lot of fun with someone who was quite proficient. She almost got in."

Joy focused on slowing her breathing and acting normal. "What makes you think this hacker is a woman?"

Sadie shrugged. "Years of experience. How a person interacts. There are usually clues. Sometimes they use avatars that are dead giveaways."

Joy swallowed, trying hard to slow her beating heart. She wasn't sure if she wanted to know if Sadie was Dragonfire. But she needed to learn if someone successfully broke into the NSA, would Sadie lose her job? "I guess it's good that you have challenges. What happens if one of those hackers gets through the security protections? Would you get in trouble?"

Sadie waved her hand in the air. "Nah, I'm only the first level of defense. I can't tell you everything that is in place, but I wouldn't want to be the hacker who makes it past my level of security. If you come to work for the NSA, you'll get an up close and personal look at their systems, which are impressive. Although sometimes it can be boring, there's enough excitement with hackers constantly trying to get inside that it's a fun job most days."

"I promise to give it serious consideration." Joy wanted to pivot from talking about the NSA, regardless of how helpful it would be to know their higher levels of security. Instead, she wracked her brain for a safe question to ask that would take the conversation in a new direction.

"Um, did you grow up in the DC area? Any siblings?" Joy asked.

"No to both questions," Sadie answered without providing additional detail. A forced smile formed as Sadie volleyed back with her own more personal question. "What was it like growing up in DC? I get the sense that not only are your moms extremely wealthy, but they're also influential in this town."

Joy wondered why either of her questions hit a sore spot. "Did I do something wrong? Seems like you clammed up when I asked about your family. Is that a touchy subject?"

Sadie sighed. "Sorry. My parents are both dead. Mom couldn't have more children after me. I grew up in a small town in Idaho but moved in with relatives after they passed. So my childhood is an uninteresting tale. Although there is a lot to appreciate about growing up in a small town versus a big city. What was it like growing up in a big city?" Sadie redirected. "You grew up in DC, right?"

"Mmhm," Joy answered. She could have kicked herself for opening this line of questioning when she'd asked Sadie about siblings and where she'd grown up.

Sadie leaned forward and grinned. "Now, look who slammed a door shut."

"What?" Joy asked innocently, desperately trying to find a way out of the corner she had painted herself into.

Sadie held up her hand. "Don't worry. Message received. I can stay away from asking about your childhood for now. Although I am curious."

"Not much to share. My childhood is probably more tedious than yours." Joy placed her index finger on her lips in an exaggerated thinking gesture. "Hmm, how did you put it? Ah, yes, uninteresting tale are the words I believe you used," Joy teased.

"Okay, both our adolescent lives are off the table for now. That's a fair deal. But I do have to ask what it was like to have two moms. Weren't you born in the second dark ages, like me?" Sadie asked. "Even places like DC had their fair share of cult followers."

Joy laughed. "Yeah, but my moms are both bad asses. Plus, they always had the financial resources to give the finger to anyone who dared to say a word. Then, when I was old enough to understand most people didn't have two moms and a bunch of aunts, I had Pepper and Alina to play with. Pepper was like my big sister, and she performed that role well, always looking out for me. Alina was like the bratty little sister. I'm sure you can see that already about her. I guess that makes me the middle child."

"Sounds like you grew up in a lesbian commune," Sadie began.

The waitress approached the table and set down their meals. "Can I get you anything else?"

"I think we're good for now, thank you." Sadie glanced at Joy, who nodded her agreement.

"Lesbian commune. That's hilarious. I'll have to tell the moms that. Of course, Uncle Hank and Uncle Steve might not want to be lumped into that descriptor." Joy grinned. "Dang, you're good. I thought childhoods were off limits."

"Yours seems idyllic compared to mine. I can't imagine why you'd want to keep that hidden."

"Was it tough growing up in a small town in Idaho? Were you out?" Joy redirected. "Um, I guess I'm assuming you're a lesbian. Maybe you're bi or pan and didn't have to endure anything until you started dating girls. Sorry, I'm rambling."

"If that's your way to ask if I'm a lesbian, I am. I moved from Idaho before being a lesbian was an issue for me. Besides, I was a different person when I lived there. This looks great." Sadie pointed to the burgers and picked up a fry, shoving it into her mouth.

Both women seemed thankful the food had arrived to provide a distraction. As if they'd been reminded of an unspoken rule, they soon pursued other lines of conversation. As the afternoon progressed, Joy managed to relax, and by the time they'd finished their meal and had dessert, Joy didn't want the date to end. Never in her life had she talked so easily with another person who wasn't in her small, tight-knit group of friends.

CHAPTER SEVEN

Sadie couldn't think of an excuse to extend the date, so she reluctantly led Joy to her car after they'd taken a long walk. Standing in front of Joy's home, Sadie lost her confidence, not knowing if she should leave Joy with a chaste kiss on her cheek. It wasn't what Sadie wanted to do, but Joy had confessed she didn't date, so taking things slow was probably the way to go. She had already put out her desire to have a second date. A lot more than that if Joy had picked up on her overtures.

"Thank you for lunch. I know it sounds cliche to say this, but I honestly had a really good time." Joy looked at her feet.

"I'm going to be perfectly honest—"

"You don't want to go out again," Joy guessed

"What? No! Is that what you thought I was going to say?" Sadie asked.

"Um, yeah, because you're, well, you, and I'm me—inexperienced and insanely awkward."

"Goddess, I thought I was being obvious and clear about my intentions. I was going to confess to wanting to kiss you, but I wasn't sure how you would react." Sadie used her finger to lift Joy's chin so she was meeting her eyes.

"Oh. Oooh. That would be nice. Better than nice." Joy's smile grew slowly until Sadie thought she'd never seen a more beautiful sight.

"You have the most glorious smile. You should smile more." Sadie tentatively placed her hand on Joy's hip and took a step closer. Their lips were mere inches apart as she slowly closed the gap. Sadie let her lips graze lightly against Joy's. She resisted the urge to lengthen the kiss.

A satisfied sigh escaped from Joy's mouth as Sadie touched her lips. "Thank you."

She caressed the side of Joy's face. "It was my pleasure. Is it too soon to ask what you're doing tomorrow? I'm not really a churchgoer, but I'll tag along if that's something you do on Sundays."

Joy laughed. "Goodness, no. I've never stepped foot in a church. My beliefs don't exactly coincide with religion. I've always been a science geek, which seems incompatible with organized religion."

Sadie wiped her brow. "Whew, me, too. I believe more in aliens than some vague higher being that created Earth. So, are you free tomorrow?"

Joy nodded, sticking her hands in her pockets. "I could make us a picnic lunch or something. I'm not really a great cook, but Maria is, and I can ask her to help me put something together. You said you live a couple of blocks away. I'll come to get you at 11:30, and we could walk down to the park."

"Sounds perfect. Do you need my address?" Sadie asked.

Joy grinned. "Nah. I have my ways to find out your address."

Sadie chuckled. "Why, you little hacker. I'm not sure I enjoy dating someone with your skills. You'll have my entire life story by the time you pick me up tomorrow."

"Isn't that how you knew where I live?" Joy asked.

Sadie chuckled nervously. "No matter how I answer this question, I'm going to come across as some unhinged stalker. Let's just say I make it a point of learning everything I can about the women I'm interested in, but I promise I didn't hack the DMV to find your address." Sadie couldn't resist leaning in for one more kiss, this time letting her lips linger on Joy's a tad longer. "See you tomorrow."

Practically skipping to her car, Sadie was pleased the date had gone so well. She'd been amazed at how engaging Joy had been, even though she held some of her cards very close to her vest. Sadie couldn't fault her for that. She wasn't any better, but she couldn't very well spill the beans on certain aspects of her life. Being so guarded was a necessity. She sighed, wishing she could be completely open and honest with Joy. Maybe someday. She'd taken the chance with Carson, but Carson wasn't someone she wanted to date anymore. That ship had sailed long ago after they'd both determined they made better friends than lovers.

†

Toni had waited three hours. Surely that was enough time for the date to reach its conclusion. She must have been fidgeting in her seat because Char interrupted her scheming thoughts of how to get back to her lab.

"Go. But later tonight, I want those hands of yours to touch my body as much as you've been putting them on your keyboard. I can't believe I'm jealous of your computers."

"They're not computers. They are the next level artificial intelligence, supercharged technical maestros," Toni answered with a touch of haute in her voice.

Char chuckled. "Whatever."

Toni jogged into her lab and activated the machine. She only felt remotely guilty for watching as Sadie chastely kissed her daughter. It was a sweet scene to watch. Toni sincerely hoped that Sadie was a good person and not working against The Organization's primary mission. Sometimes the government's priorities aligned, but more often than not, they didn't. Depending on the administration in charge, their relationship with the US Government had waxed and waned over the years, despite the fact that only President Sandra Murphy, and a few handpicked FBI or intelligence agents that moonlighted for The Organization, knew they existed.

Toni had already discovered that Sadie only lived a few blocks from Joy but hadn't quite placed the exact location in relation to her daughter. She wasn't sure if this boded well for Sadie. Did she move close to Joy for nefarious reasons? Was Joy a mark that Sadie was tasked with getting close to? Toni wanted to give Sadie the benefit of the doubt because the look on Joy's face was pure bliss when Sadie delivered a chaste kiss. Her daughter was clearly besotted with Sadie, and the last thing Toni wanted was for Sadie to break Joy's heart.

Sadie burst through what Toni assumed was the front door of her house. The young woman sprawled on the couch turned her head.

"Well fuck me," Toni exclaimed. "Carson is Sadie's housemate?"

Char poked her head inside the lab. "Talking to yourself again? What was that about Carson?" She walked into the room and took a seat next to Toni.

"She's Sadie's roommate. Sshh… they're talking about the date. I want to hear what she has to say."

"Well, don't you look satiated," Carson teased. "I thought Joy was shy."

Sadie tossed a stuffed animal she picked up from the floor at Carson. Carson batted the toy away and it landed on the floor again.

"Don't be an ass. Whatever you're suggesting happened, did not. I really like her, Carson."

"I know you do. But don't throw Beta's toys at me. Who knows where this gross little frog has been? So, tell me all about your date."

Sadie smacked Carson's feet, and she moved them from the couch before Sadie sat. "She was like a whole different person. I thought for sure she would clam up, and I'd have to hold up both ends of the conversation, but it wasn't like that at all. The only thing we mutually agreed to stay far away from was our childhoods."

An enormous male tabby, that Toni assumed was Beta, strolled into the room, meowed and then picked up the frog, dropping it at Sadie's feet. He jumped into her lap and settled. After he got comfortable, she began petting his head as he purred loudly.

71

Carson arched a brow. "I know why you don't want to talk about where you grew up and the rest of it, but why do you think Joy doesn't like talking about hers?"

"No clue," Sadie answered.

"Speaking of secrets, how's it going at the NSA. Did you learn anything else?"

"No, only that they're still fixated on finding out who is behind the sabotage of the mines. What about you? Any more clues about the guest trainer that sends your spidey sense up a wall? She's a total badass, right? Do you think she could be a Crusader?" Sadie asked.

Carson shrugged. "She's not exactly chatty with us, other than barking commands. I think I surprised her the other day when I knocked her on her ass. Are you going out again with Joy?"

"Yeah. We talked about a second date." Sadie smiled. "She's going to make a picnic lunch and pick me up tomorrow."

"Cool. I'm thrilled for you, Sadie. She seems genuinely nice and drop-dead gorgeous. I would have given it a go if I'd met her first." Carson grinned.

"Oh, right, and that would have gone just as well as your efforts to seduce me." Sadie laughed.

"It worked, didn't it?"

"Until we both discovered that the whole opposites attract thing can go a bit too far. You need someone who has at least a few shared interests. Plus, with that adrenaline junkie gene of yours, you require someone more stimulating to share those adventures with. I could never fit that description. It's okay. We're much better as friends."

"True. I always seem to go for the sexy librarian types. Brainy women are a total turn-on, but yeah, I do need that physical stimulation. Maybe I'll ask out her roommate. She looks like someone who could keep up with me," Carson said.

"Randi sure hung onto every word you uttered. She's a little young, though, isn't she?"

"She's not jailbait. So, will you tell Joy about your obsession? Didn't you say she was some kind of tech-savant? Maybe she can help you," Carson suggested.

"She probably could, but I don't want to drag her into this. It isn't her fight, and we know how dangerous it could be. He's got endless resources and the kind of connections to make people disappear that cause him grief. I'm still unraveling those allegiances. That's why I need the help of The Crusaders. This is way too big for us. No way will we be able to bring down his vast network, and that's just in the US. I know I should care about other countries like Grace Turner, but I'm only concerned about what that asswipe is doing here." Sadie rested her head against the couch and sighed.

"Okay, Joy's out as an ally. What about that hacker you've been fighting with? You said she's better than anyone else in the group." Carson stretched her arms and stood. "I'm restless. You want to go for a run?"

"Nah. I'm going to work on a new dark website and a fast-acting demolition code in case I need to erase the new site quickly. I had another member shut down the old site for me. If the mystery hacker finds the new group, I'll work on discovering more about her. She's good, though. Better than me. I got lucky when I found her poking around. Right place at the right time. It's a long shot that I'll uncover her identity, though. I may have caught her snooping, but tracking her is a whole new ballgame." Sadie gently placed the tabby on the couch next to her, then grabbed her laptop, pulling it close. Beta grumbled and let out a pitiful meow before jumping from the sofa and swishing his tail in aggravation.

Toni turned to her wife. "Well, what do you think?"

"I want to know more about the guy with all the resources. He sounds like someone we'd be very interested in taking on. It certainly appears as though Sadie's goals and ours align. I know you have the broad strokes on her childhood, but perhaps there's more to learn. Keep on it. Let me think more about how to approach our daughter. I am delighted to learn that Sadie is genuinely interested in Joy and doesn't have an ulterior motive to drag her into this. Still, I'd like to learn more about this dark web group she started."

"Ironic, huh? Hard to know how either will react once they discover they have far more shared interests than their love of technology. When do you want to tell Joy?" Toni asked.

"Soon. We have another decision to make on Carson. No wonder Sophie has her eye on the young woman. Not too many people get the jump on Soph. If Carson put her on her ass, that is impressive. It's also notable that Carson sensed something about Soph. I don't suppose I'll see you for the rest of the afternoon, will I?" Char asked.

"Nope. I have the perfect opportunity to dig into this dark web group and see everything they have on us. It will be interesting to discover how accurate their information is. Plus, you know I need to call Soph and tease her. I'll let her know about the latest developments, too. As soon as you decide what to do about Carson, we can inform Sophie. I would imagine that you'd like to time everything perfectly."

"Yes, I would. Sadie and Carson being roommates adds another wrinkle. They seem close, so approaching one before the other will not work. Don't toil on this too long. I'll be back later to make sure you take a break for dinner." Char massaged Toni's shoulders for a few seconds and then left the lab.

†

Joy was in a bit of a panic. What was she thinking, offering to make a picnic lunch? She didn't have the first clue what to pack, much less have something to carry the food in. A picnic lunch sounded romantic and was the first thing to pop into her head, but now Joy had to execute those plans.

Alina must have seen Joy's panicked face and remarked, "That bad, huh? I'm sorry, Joy. I really thought you two were hitting it off. You actually talked last night. You never do that unless you feel comfortable around someone."

Maria sat next to Alina and shot Joy a sympathetic look. "There are plenty of fishes in the sea. You will find the right salmon, *si*?"

Alina chuckled. "I don't think I've heard anyone ever add to that saying. Why a salmon?"

"Because they are tasty and beautiful fish. When they spawn and reach the end of their life, they turn those spectacular colors. Sure, it is sad they must die after spawning, but it is like a tragic fairytale," Maria answered.

75

Joy hurried to a chair, dropping into it like a dejected rag doll. "Forget the fish thing. The date went well. Then I had to open my big mouth and offer to pack a picnic lunch for tomorrow."

"Oh, that is very romantic. I will help you prepare the food," Maria offered.

Joy leaned forward in the chair. "I was hoping you would say that. Should I go out and get a picnic basket? I don't even know if there is a store that has those things. It's not as if a picnic basket is a last-minute item to purchase in a brick-and-mortar store. And wine? I don't have a clue what wine to buy."

Alina shrugged. "Beats me. I hate wine. Why don't you ask the moms? Can't you just put the food in a backpack or something?"

Maria shook her head. "I love you, Alina, but you are not good at this. No, Joy should get a proper picnic basket. Go to your laptop and order now, and I'll bet the delivery drone can drop it off before tomorrow. Of course, you might have to pay more for a rush delivery. It is a good idea to call your moms, though. I do not know about wines, either."

Joy pulled her phone from her pocket and dialed the moms.

"Joy, how did your date go?" Char answered.

She couldn't put her finger on it, but something in the inflection of her mother's voice led her to believe something was up.

"Good, Mama C. Why did you sound so weird just now? Never mind. I need some help. I offered to make a picnic basket, and I don't know what wine to buy."

"Swing by the complex, and we can go to the wine cellar to pick something out before tomorrow. Is Maria making the food?" Char asked.

Bingo. Joy knew something was off. The only way her mother could have known her date was for tomorrow was if Toni had arranged for surveillance. How could Mama T have done that?

"What did Mama T do?" Joy could barely get the question out.

"What do you mean, honey?" Char answered.

"I knew there was something off. Did you send someone to spy on us? How did you know the picnic lunch was tomorrow?" Joy put her palm on her forehead. "Oh, no, no, no, please tell me you didn't arrange for someone to put bots in Sadie."

Char sighed. "We'll explain everything. You don't know all the facts. Just come to the complex, hon, and don't be angry until you hear us out."

Joy glanced at Alina, who wouldn't meet her eyes. She pointed a finger at Alina and mouthed, *I will deal with you later.* "Fine, I'll swing by right now after I've reamed my roommate out."

"Now, honey, don't blame Alina. I promise there was a good reason for the order."

"Thanks for the confirmation that it was Alina, but this is between her and me. You can't expect me not to be hot about this. You know this is a total invasion of our privacy. Alina knows it isn't cool to violate the friend code. I'll see you soon, and, Mom, your explanation better be flawless," Joy warned.

"We love you," Char responded before Joy ended the call.

Joy narrowed her eyes at Alina. "Spill. Right now, or you and I are done."

Alina held her hands up. "I only agreed because I love you, Joy. You know that. I would never put our friendship at risk unless it was absolutely necessary. I told Aunt Toni that this was going to blow up in our faces," Alina grumbled.

"That doesn't tell me squat. So why was it vital?" Joy asked.

"I don't have all the details, but Sadie isn't exactly who she presents to the outside world," Alina confessed. "First, we had to know if she was a friend or foe. That's all I know. Your moms have more information. Aunt Toni is probably collecting more data as we speak. Please don't be mad at me."

Joy sighed. "I reserve the right to continue this discussion and pass a final judgment."

"Okay, that's fair. I'll help Maria with preparing food for your date tomorrow. I promise we'll put together something so spectacular, you'll have to forgive me." Alina grinned.

"We'll see." Joy stood, grabbed the keys from the hook, and stalked out of the house.

CHAPTER EIGHT

Sadie leaned back and moved her head from side to side, stretching her neck, which had started screaming at her. Then, rolling her shoulders, she hoped to address the other equally disturbing message from her body. She really should have moved to her tiny office much earlier. Unfortunately, it was too late because the muscle was already pinching the nerve and sending sharp pain across her shoulder and down her arm.

At least a fellow hacker had shut down the old site and she'd finished creating the new one. Even if it didn't keep out the unknown hacker, maybe the new security gates she'd established would, and Sadie might get lucky and find an originating address. Onward to hacking Alvin Marks' front-facing business, the one he showed the world.

Grabbing her laptop, she walked into her office, sitting heavily in her Ergocloud chair. She'd be at this for several hours, and there was no sense in aggravating her already displeased body. Beta kept putting his paw on the keyboard, begging for her attention, which she distractedly offered until his paw kept messing up her code. Finally, she set him down on the floor, receiving an irritated meow in response.

"I know, I know. How dare I send you packing, but Mama has work to do," Sadie declared. Beta swished his tail in irritation, but left the room, undoubtedly looking for Carson, who gave him attention when Sadie was preoccupied.

Sadie had already tried hacking Marks' social media empire and the multibillion-dollar business she was most interested in. So far, she'd been unable to definitively tie the slimy businessman to the mines, but she knew the evidence was there. No way was he a trillionaire with the failing social media site, SoBites, and his overpriced solar cars. Don't even get Sadie started on her derision for his pretentious shuttle space service that was nothing more than a gimmick for the rich and famous—a glorified carnival ride. On principle, she'd bought her solar-powered car from Marks' biggest competitor.

After looking closely at the code the unknown hacker used, Sadie tweaked it a little, gaining a new way to penetrate Marks' security wall. All her senses erupted to the surface, and she felt a chill travel through her body, not unlike a cold shower. Finally, Sadie was getting somewhere. Mumbling to herself, she declared, "I just need a tiny sliver of confirmation."

"Talking to yourself again?" Carson poked her head inside Sadie's office.

"I've almost got him."

"Marks?" Carson asked.

Sadie absently nodded as she continued to type. "Uh-huh."

"What good will that do? Even if you can prove he owns the company, it's not like you're able to tie him to the Russians and Chinese." Carson leaned against the door frame.

"It's a start. The NSA hasn't even been able to link Marks to Metalico Inc. They continue to monitor that other bozo." Sadie grabbed her left shoulder and rubbed it.

"Did you ever consider that maybe Marks is in bed with the US Government, and that's why they aren't tracking him at the NSA?"

"Hmm, that would align with their hyper-focus on The Crusaders and relatively obvious disinterest in Marks." Sadie rolled her shoulders and grimaced.

"Why don't you take a break? I can tell your shoulder is bothering you again. You have to stop these marathon sessions. I predict you won't even make it to thirty at this rate before you're slumped over like an old woman in her nineties. Now that you finally got Joy to go out with you, maintaining prime flexibility should be your first priority. It's always the quiet ones who are wildest in bed."

"Don't be rude, Carson. And don't joke about Joy like that. She isn't some random bimbo to take to bed. I told you I really like her, and I meant it."

Carson held her hands in the air. "Sorry, sorry. I didn't realize you'd be so touchy about her. You're right. I'm an ass sometimes. Probably why we didn't work out."

"You have your own charm and redeeming qualities, but yes, you really should adjust how you talk about women. You're better than that, and I know deep down you have the utmost respect for the women you date. Have that same regard for the ones I'm interested in." Sadie lifted her arms above her head and stretched. "I guess I could take a quick dinner break. It's not like the data is going to disappear. The asshole thinks he's untouchable. I just wish we were further along in finding The Crusaders. No way the two of us are capable of taking Marks and his associates down, especially those tied to the Russian and Chinese governments."

"Pizza?" Carson asked.

"Again? Aren't you tired of pizza and beer? It's like you never graduated from college and are perpetually living your glory days as a student. How about takeout that isn't pizza?" Sadie suggested.

Carson shrugged. "Fine, but for the record, pizza never goes out of style. My grandma still loves to order pizza from Pete's. Thai?" she suggested.

"Sure. Order me some Chicken Pad Thai. Wimp-level spice, please. I think it's my turn to buy."

"It sure is, so I'm ordering a feast." Carson grinned. "Who else is going to help you spend your fortune? Joy has wealthy parents, right? She sure doesn't need your money. I'd say that's another reason I like her. She obviously isn't after your fortune." Carson turned uncharacteristically serious. "Can I ask you something?"

"Sure."

"Did it ever bother you I never had the money to take you somewhere nice? Was that a factor in us breaking up?" Carson asked.

"Don't be a noob. Of course not. I appreciate not having to struggle like Mom after Dad died, and she got sick, but having a healthy bank account is the least important thing to me. Money corrupts. If anything, I'm more wary of rich people."

"What about Joy? She's wealthy, and you don't seem guarded with her," Carson noted.

"Joy doesn't act like some entitled prig." Sadie closed her laptop. "That's the difference. It's almost like she's embarrassed by her mothers' standing in the community. She won't even talk about her childhood. I think Pepper and Alina are well off, too, and they act a lot like Joy. So, either they were raised to be humble and kind, or all three have rebelled against their privilege. I'm unsure about Randi, but Maria has a scholarship from the foundation that Pepper works with, so she's definitely not well off. Regardless, none of them are typical rich kids. Are we ordering food or not?" Sadie stood and made her way to the door.

Carson laughed. "*Hangry*, huh?" She followed Sadie to the living room.

"You poked the bear, so now you have to deal with the consequences of influencing my mood." Sadie settled on the couch while Carson made the call to order food.

†

The middle-aged man with thinning, mousy brown hair and an unremarkable shade of brown eyes sat in his rich leather chair, drinking his Macallan forty-year-old single malt scotch. He was stewing over the fact that he'd fallen in the ranks to the number five position in the world. Seething, Alvin Marks vowed to eliminate his competition. Although solar vehicles weren't his only business, Solio was the company that had propelled him into the spotlight and helped him make his initial fortune. Now, because of Solar Flair and all the recent attacks on his mines, Marks had fallen to the fifth richest man in the world. Actually, if the unverified rumors were correct, a woman had moved into a higher position than his. The top ten wealthiest people in the world were no longer all men. Toni McFarland didn't give interviews or verify her wealth to anyone. It's not like the woman volunteered information about her company or any other businesses she might be involved in.

Marks couldn't believe how the blasted woman had managed to turn trash into profit and almost bankrupted Solio. The US had evolved into the largest contributor to the growing heap of solid waste. US consumers insisted on the latest, greatest marvel of technology. For most, the recycling programs were simply not worth it. Even trading in one's old video phone for a new one went out of fashion. Then McFarland came along and developed manufacturing processes that turned refuse into solar cars. The cherry on the top was her new solar cell, ten times more efficient than his own.

He continued to stew as he took another sip from the tumbler. There had to be a way to get to McFarland, but the woman never seemed to pop her head up long enough to take a shot. No one knew where she lived, and sabotaging any of the Solar Flair manufacturing sites had proved futile. He'd tried that and learned that the sprawling complex had an innovative security system that made it harder to breach than the White House. Perhaps he could give another nudge to his allies in the government. Surely, they'd learned something more about the mysterious group that continued to launch successful attacks on his mines. How hard would it be to track down McFarland's location? She couldn't stay locked in her castle twenty-four-seven. Without the CEO of Solar Flair and maybe her top engineers, the company would fold faster than a cheap laptop.

Marks grabbed his secure phone and barked a voice command. It was worth a shot. Maybe this time she would accept the invitation. "Call Ronald Dawson."

†

"Alvin Marks!" Toni exclaimed. She knew he was a douche of the first order, but this was an interesting new piece of information. Toni didn't like admitting that Sadie had uncovered this vital fact, and none of her digging had resulted in this surprising new wrinkle. She supposed she should be grateful, but her pride would not allow her to let this go.

Char barreled into the lab like something was on fire. "Joy is coming by soon, and she knows," Char revealed.

"Knows what?" Toni was genuinely perplexed. Normally, she could almost read her wife's thoughts.

"That Alina put bots in Sadie."

"Oh. Fuck me. How mad is she?" Toni slumped in her chair.

"You know how even-keeled Joy is normally, well, not anymore. I'd say off the charts. I've never heard her this upset before. Do you think we made an error in judgment?"

Toni scratched her head. "Maybe. But, get this, I know who the guy is now. I can't believe Sadie discovered this, and we haven't. I'm relatively confident that Sadie's agenda aligns with ours. She definitely has an ax to grind. I think we should bring her into the fold. I've seriously underestimated the girl's skills. One more thing." Toni cringed.

"What now?" Char began pacing.

"I think Carson still has feelings for Sadie. Could be she is still in love with her."

Char stopped pacing and turned her focus to Toni. "Shit. Does Sadie still have feelings for Carson?"

"I don't think so. At least not those sorts of feelings. Sadie loves Carson as a friend and would probably do anything for her, but I don't think she's in love with her. Remember when Ronda pined after you, and we thought she might be the mole?"

"Yeah, but it all worked out in the end. Ronda and Cindy are a perfect match. Although it was uncomfortable for a bit. I hated second-guessing a good friend. Are you telling me we should be cautious with Carson?" Char took a chair beside Toni, a frown marring her beautiful face.

"Caution is never a bad thing, but it won't exactly go over well if we put bots in her, too. Nevertheless, that's my recommendation. But if we have any chance of repairing whatever damage we've done to our relationship with our daughter, we need to come completely clean with Sadie, including sharing our plan to track Carson before Sophie approaches her."

Char nodded. "Agreed. Sadie's reaction and her ability to keep The Organization's existence under wraps will be her first test. Now, what to do about the bots already inside her?"

"You take them out." Joy pushed open the door and glared at her parents.

"Shit," Toni murmured under her breath. "How much of our conversation did you hear? Has Val been teaching you a few things about stealth? Damn, that was good. We didn't hear you come in." Toni felt a sense of pride. She'd never mastered any skill except those related to tech support.

"I want you to spill. Right now. You're going to tell me everything. And I swear, if you leave out even the tiniest bit, I will never forgive you. I'll take a job with the NSA and divorce myself from The Organization."

Char pulled out a chair. "Come and sit, and I promise, we'll tell you everything."

"Let me give you the crib notes' version first. Sadie is the lizard. Your mysterious hacker," Toni added.

Joy looked between Char and Toni. Her mouth opened, then promptly closed as she took the offered chair.

"We weren't sure at first about Sadie's motives for asking you out. She's very good, and we needed to be sure. Sadie has a lot of reasons for hating Metalico Inc. and the entire mining industry. Her parents died either as a direct or indirect result of working for a mine in Idaho. Revenge is her primary motive. She has a vague awareness of The Organization and calls us The Crusaders."

"So, she knows who I am and is just using me. That makes perfect sense now. Of course, Sadie wouldn't be interested in someone like me." Tears fell down Joy's cheeks.

"No, no, no. That isn't true at all. Sadie is genuinely interested in dating you. In fact, she most definitely cares about getting to know you better. That was evident in her discussions with Carson. And she doesn't know who you are. Not yet, anyway," Toni added.

"What do you mean, not yet?" Joy looked up and absently brushed away her tears.

"We want to bring her into the fold," Char answered. "She's discovered a crucial piece of information that even your mother hasn't uncovered. One head of the snake is the trillionaire, Alvin Marks. But our strategy has a tiny wrinkle that neither you nor Sadie will like." Char glanced at Toni.

"That would certainly make dating Sadie a lot easier if I could talk about The Organization. So what's the wrinkle?" Joy asked.

"Carson is someone Sophie had her eye on to recruit, but she still has feelings for Sadie. We're hesitant to approach Carson. Given how close Sadie is with Carson, we want to be sure that Carson won't bring hell down on our heads as a means of coming between the two of you. We want to put bots in her as a cautionary measure. And, Sadie can't say a word until we're sure Carson won't act against us," Toni explained.

"I don't like it. Isn't there another way?" Joy asked.

Char shook her head. "I'm afraid not. If we're not one hundred percent sure, every member of The Organization is at risk. I'm sorry, but Carson and Sadie's privacy is a small price to pay for that assurance. We will, of course, come clean with Sadie. We owe her that."

"And you'll remove the bots?" Joy bargained.

"It would be better to let them run their course..." Toni had the good sense to look guilty. "I have something that will expel the bots, but it isn't pleasant."

"Define isn't pleasant, please," Joy demanded.

"Think twenty-four-hour stomach flu on steroids," Toni answered.

Joy scrunched her face. "We should give her the option. And, Mama T, if she chooses to keep the bots inside, I want your word that you will not monitor her anymore."

Toni held up her hand. "You have my word. I swear on both your mother's life and yours. I will shut down my surveillance right now. You can watch me."

Joy stood behind Toni as Toni rapidly typed commands, shutting down the link to Sadie's bots. "Are these the new long-lasting bots?"

Toni nodded. "Uh-huh. They should be out in about a month. Do you want to be the one to explain everything tomorrow on your date?"

"Nope. No way. I'll bring Sadie by tomorrow for you to meet her. You're going to have to fess up because I want her to know I had absolutely nothing to do with this egregious breach of her privacy."

"Oh, don't be so dramatic. Both of you desecrate privacy every time you hack into different sites. So neither of you can claim total innocence," Toni argued.

Char subtly shook her head. "Hon, I don't think you should go the righteous route. We're sorry, Joy. I know this was a total fracture of ethics, but we did not see another way. Sometimes the ends do justify the means. I believe even Sadie would agree with that."

"Perhaps. I guess we'll see when you explain everything tomorrow. You better have the good alcohol ready," Joy noted with a tiny smile. "Now, who's going to help me pick out a bottle of wine?"

Toni breathed a sigh of relief. She could tell their kind and loving daughter had already forgiven them.

CHAPTER NINE

Joy was grateful for one thing. The weather had participated, and it was a glorious day. Early summer in DC was a crapshoot. One day it would be eighty degrees; the next day, thunderstorms darkened the sky and drenched the earth. Carrying the newly purchased deluxe picnic basket that the drone had delivered in the morning, Joy walked along the sidewalk, passing the carefully manicured lawns. The hydrangeas and rose bushes were in full bloom, adding brilliant colors as they dotted the beautifully landscaped yards. Joy often wondered if there was some unwritten competition in the neighborhood, pitting all the owners against one another for who could create the most appealing designs. Thank goodness for Maria, who enjoyed gardening; otherwise, their home would fall to the bottom of the pecking order.

As she walked the stone path, Joy noted that Sadie's home adhered to the neighborhood standards but contained a simplistic flair that fit Sadie's personality. Joy tugged on her tank top, smoothing the nonexistent wrinkles, before pushing the doorbell. Walking to Sadie's house took less time, so she was a few minutes early. Joy hoped her eagerness would not come across as desperation.

Carson answered the door, waving Joy inside. She wasn't exactly rude, but she wasn't overly friendly, either. "Come on in. Sadie is doing some last-minute primping."

Joy followed Carson inside and awkwardly waited in the living room. She didn't know whether she should sit and was grateful when Sadie arrived, making it less clumsy for her to remain standing.

As Sadie glided into the room, a broad smile quickly blossomed on her face. "You're early."

"Uh, yeah, sorry, your home is much closer than I thought it would be. It took less time to walk here. I debated whether to take my car."

Sadie laughed. "Why on earth would you want to do that? It's a beautiful day, and the park is so close." She slipped her arm inside Joy's free arm and led her to the door, waving her other hand at Carson. "You should call Randi and see if she wants to do something. It's such a beautiful day."

Carson leaned against the wall and said, "Yeah, maybe I will. It's too hot for a run, but perhaps a bike ride or a hike. It's late, though, so she's probably already out and about."

"No, she isn't. She was moping around the house because her softball team canceled practice, and Randi doesn't do idle."

A small smile appeared on Carson's face. "Thanks. Have fun."

As they began their trek to the park, Sadie let her hand fall, smoothly threading her fingers with Joy's. "So, what delicious foods did Maria prepare for us?" Sadie teased.

"I forgot to ask if you were vegan, so she made two different pasta salads. A chicken Caesar and chickpea arugula. There's also fruit, cheese, olives, crackers, and nuts."

"Yum. No, I'm not vegan. I thought Maria would make something like tamales or another Mexican specialty, not that I'm complaining, because what she made sounds wonderful."

"Maria didn't want us getting bored with Mexican food, so she's branched out. She often watches those streaming food shows so she can try new recipes on us. Alina thinks she should go to a culinary institute rather than finish college, but Maria's dream has always been to get a college degree. It hasn't been easy for her because English is a second language. She's struggled, but after two years, she's finally getting better grades, and she isn't about to quit now," Joy explained.

That was all true about Maria, but Joy failed to share that Maria had also found she had a knack for languages, which served the organization well, considering there were kids from all different nationalities, and communicating with them was difficult for the rest of the agents. She'd even managed to learn Mandarin. Whenever there was a suspected need in a particular mission, Maria tagged along to assist with communications.

"Good for her. If she wants to combine her cooking talents, she could get a business degree and open a restaurant," Sadie suggested.

"That's what I said, too. She's thinking about it. Um, the reason I debated bringing my car was because I promised my moms that I would take you to meet them after lunch. They can be rather insistent about some things. Is that okay?" Joy asked.

Sadie slowed her walk and tilted her head. "Will I have to pass some test?"

Joy coughed. Although she knew Sadie was teasing her, that was precisely what her moms had done when putting the bots inside Sadie, as well as what they were about to do with Carson. "Not exactly."

Sadie's brow furrowed. "I was joking. I didn't know that old-fashioned ritual still happened, especially with lesbians."

"Uh, yeah, my moms are unique. They'll explain everything." Joy cringed at how it sounded. She wasn't sure how to wiggle out of the conversation and was grateful when she heard Sadie chuckle.

"Well, you're worth it. If I have to jump through a few hoops to date you, I'm up for it." Sadie grinned.

†

Joy fidgeted the entire time they ate lunch and barely sipped on the expensive wine she brought. Sadie hesitated to drink more than Joy because she didn't want to appear to be a lush. But the wine was so good she couldn't help herself and capitulated when Joy lifted the bottle, gesturing to her glass. As they walked along the sidewalk on their way to Joy's home, Sadie could almost feel the vibrations from Joy's nervous energy.

Before sliding into the passenger seat of Joy's car, she touched Joy's arm. "Hey, relax. I'm perfectly fine with meeting your moms. I tend to make a good first impression with parents," Sadie declared.

Sadie noticed the LCD panel on the car, and before Joy switched the screen, she caught of glimpse of odd tech she wasn't familiar with. Although there were clearly solar panels that powered the vehicle, the oddities were unlike anything she'd seen before. Moreover, this sleek vehicle wasn't manufactured by any major company that had entered the new green revolution.

"Nice ride," Sadie remarked. "I don't recognize the manufacturer. Not that I'm a car expert. This is fancy."

"Um, it isn't from any manufacturer because, except for Solar Flair, the components most companies use come from places with atrocious work practices, and we don't want to support that. Mama T and I built this on the weekends and after school. We scoured the wrecking yards for certain items and then adapted other components to make it work. It's like a souped-up version of a recycled car. Practically everything I own comes from recycled materials, including computers and other tech. The car has sentimental value to me. I'm reluctant to give it up. So I keep it in top shape using the workshop on the complex. Although I now have a steady source of raw materials, I don't need them anymore. If something breaks, we don't toss it away. We fix it."

Sadie arched her eyebrow. "Wow! Impressive. That's like the Solar Flair cars."

Joy appeared uncomfortable. "Um, yeah. I told you my mom is a genius. You'll discover that soon enough when you meet her today," Joy answered.

"Well, in that case, you have nothing to worry about because I can't wait to meet her. Maybe she can teach me a few things. I'm always up for learning something new."

The conversation was stilted for the rest of the journey until Joy's car rolled to a sprawling estate. The driveway alone had to be close to a quarter of a mile. Sadie had seen nothing quite this large before. She couldn't detect the gate or the multiple residences from the road, as the dense copse of trees and other foliage completely hid the complex. The place was a fortress.

"Holy shit. How rich are you?" Sadie asked. "Your parents live here?"

Joy nodded. "Some of my aunts, too."

"Like an upscale lesbian commune?" Sadie attempted to joke to hide how overwhelmed she was.

"Yeah, something like that," Joy answered.

Rolling up to a massive brick house, she pressed a button on her LCD screen. What appeared to be a large garage door opened, and Joy rolled her car into an open space. She sucked in air and turned to Sadie after selecting an icon on the LCD that unclipped both seatbelts. "Ready?"

"Not really, but you'll protect me, right?" Sadie teased.

"I will," Joy answered seriously.

Sadie was grateful when Joy took her hand as the two women entered the large mansion. The door appeared to have biometric access because Sadie heard the lock click open when Joy touched the doorknob.

"Remarkable." Sadie glanced at the doorknob, looking for how the biometric access worked.

"My DNA is encoded. Mama T designed the doorknob with a special material that absorbs my DNA and activates the lock."

"Joy, Sadie, we're so happy you could make it on such short notice," a tall woman who looked like a slightly older version of Joy said. She held out her hand. "I'm Char."

Sadie eagerly shook it. "Joy could almost be your twin. I'm so happy to meet both of you."

By her side was a lanky woman with long dark hair streaked with silver. An impish grin appeared on her face. "Toni." She offered her hand.

"I've heard so much about you, Toni. I'd love to pick your brain. I think you could teach me so much."

Char motioned for them to follow her to a large, comfortable sitting area. "Would you like something to drink?" she asked.

Sadie shook her head. "No, I'm good."

"Sit, relax," Char directed.

Joy sat on the empty loveseat and rolled her eyes. "Can we just get this over with?"

Sadie surveyed their faces before joining Joy on the loveseat and waited patiently for one of them to explain.

Char gracefully sat in a chair to the right of the loveseat. "I've been pondering how to do this, and I suppose the best approach is to simply rip off the bandage. You might know us as The Crusaders, but we prefer to be called The Organization. Our daughter is the hacker you've been trading taunts with." Char held up her hand. "Joy was completely in the dark about that until yesterday."

Sadie was too shocked to speak. She wanted to respond, but the words wouldn't come out. She barely managed her one-word response. "Wow!"

"You better tell her the rest." Joy squirmed in her seat.

"While some may debate the ethics of how we operate, we hope you can understand that caution is essential to our continued existence. As a result, Toni felt it necessary to learn everything there is to know about you, Sadie. You have every right to feel angry at our blatant disregard for your privacy, but I hope you understand our reasoning," Char explained.

"The bots," Joy prompted.

Char glanced at Toni, who had yet to sit, standing to the side of Char with her hand on top of Char's shoulder. "Honey, will you explain?"

Toni nodded and moved to sit in the chair on the other side of the room. "Before I tell you about the bots, I want you to know that we believe you can be an asset to The Organization, and we'd like you to join us. We aren't your enemy. Since I'm relatively sure I understand what you'd like to accomplish, joining forces is the best way to achieve your goals. After discovering your background, including how you came to work for the NSA, we had Alina inject a tracking bot into you before your date yesterday. We had to make sure our missions aligned, and you weren't someone who was using our daughter to get to us."

Sadie's heart started racing. She used every trick in the book to keep her voice steady. "Can you please explain exactly what a tracking bot is?"

Toni's face adopted a slightly sheepish expression. "Technically, it's hundreds of tiny nanobots, but it only takes one to do the job. The rest just float around in your body until they're expelled. They don't cause any harm. The first one to find an opening, usually in an eye or an ear, transmits video and audio to whatever device I choose to send it to. In this case, the bot sent information to my computer in the lab.

Yours went to the eye. Basically, it works like a tiny camera recording everything you see and hear."

Containing her anger, Sadie responded, "So, you've been eavesdropping on me since yesterday? Did you have fun posing as an unwelcome voyeur during your daughter's date with me?"

"Toni didn't monitor the date. I made sure of that," Char interjected.

"Well, that was nice of you," Sadie sniped.

Toni cringed. "I only observed you long enough to determine if your motives regarding our daughter were pure. Your conversations with Carson were enough to decide we could offer you an opportunity to join us. For nearly thirty years, various people have tried to discover our identities. None of them honorable. Although I am sorry we had to resort to what I know is a supreme violation, protecting our sisters in The Organization is a top priority. We couldn't take the risk when I learned you were poking around. I hope you understand that, literally, lives are at stake here. What we do is dangerous."

Sadie didn't know how to absorb the information. It was a lot to take in. She felt a little defeated, and if she were completely honest, disappointed and sad. Of course, Joy was too good to be true. She had to know if Joy's feelings for her were all an elaborate set-up. "So, everything was a huge ruse. I'm just another mission to you." Sadie glared at Joy.

"No, no, honest. I didn't know you were Dragonfire, and I wanted my moms to explain everything because I'm not very good at that. I thought the same thing when they first told me who you were. Surely someone like you wouldn't be interested in me. You have to know I don't have the skills to be deceitful. If you only knew how pissed I was. While Mama T teases us sometimes and threatens to put bots in us, she's never done that before. It's a massive intrusion." Joy glared at her mother. "I don't defend their perspective, but I get they made that tough decision out of love and concern."

Sadie clasped her hands in her lap. She tried hard to put herself in Char and Toni's place. It wasn't like she was a saint. No hacker was. For now, she would stick with asking practical questions and learning everything she could about this organization. After all, wasn't that what she'd been doing for years? Anger served no good purpose. "How long do these bots stay in my body?"

Toni's face distorted again, and Sadie knew she was about to hear more troubling news.

"A month. Give or take a few days," Toni answered.

"A month!" Sadie exclaimed.

"Toni has a way to expel the bots, but it isn't a pleasant experience," Char interjected. "It's your decision whether to have her give you the serum. Whichever you choose, you have my word that no one in The Organization will monitor you from this point forward. We stopped when we were convinced you weren't a threat to us. Joy watched Toni shut down her surveillance of you."

"How unpleasant?" Sadie asked.

"Like the worst twenty-four-hour flu you've ever had," Toni answered.

Sadie caught a look passed between Toni and Char and knew she wouldn't like the answer to her next question. "There's more you aren't telling me that I need to know. Isn't there?"

Char nodded. "There's a lot more about us and our missions that you'll need to learn, especially if you choose to join."

"I haven't committed to joining yet. However, that is not what I'm sensing."

Char smiled. "You're very perceptive. That will serve you well. Yes, you're spot on about something crucial we need to share. We're aware of how close you and Carson are. You've been working together to take down Marks, and we want to combine forces. But, for right now, we need to monitor Carson. Before learning about your agenda and the connection to our missions, we had focused on Carson. She has the kind of skills that are useful to us. Many of our agents are older and on the cusp of retirement. It's time to let the next generation slowly take over. For that, we need to recruit younger agents."

"Okay," Sadie answered hesitantly. "I don't see an issue in that. Carson will jump at the chance to join, especially if she learns I've already been approached."

"Initially, we were going to provide this information to you and Carson simultaneously. After observing Carson interact with you, we had concerns. Carson is still in love with you. That makes her an unknown quantity. People in love sometimes do strange things. We've determined the prudent course of action is to monitor Carson until we're sure she won't be an issue. That will require your discretion with the information we've already shared."

"You want to put the bots in Carson," Sadie stated, her horror apparent.

Toni and Char nodded.

"Look, I know Carson better than anyone. If I join your organization, will you let me worry about Carson?" Sadie pleaded. "You said I was perceptive. Let me be the one to assess the situation without your draconian measures. Nostalgia sometimes presents in different ways. Carson and I still care a great deal for one another, but what you saw is more about her yearning for someone compatible to share her life with. Deep down, Carson knows that isn't me. Been there, done that, and it clearly did not work."

Toni and Char shared another look. "All right. If we're going to establish mutual trust, we may as well start now. You have a week to evaluate Carson. Shall we assume you want to join forces to take Alvin Marks down?"

Sadie nodded. "Yes." She held out her hand. "I'll take that serum now. And I want a tour, complete with detailed explanations of all the tech at your disposal."

Toni grinned. "Joy can be your personal tour guide. Follow me to the lab, then we'll go to medical, and I'll get the serum for you."

The group stood, and Toni led them through the large house.

"Will you come and stay with me today and tonight? I feel like it's all my fault that Mama T put the bots in you. I'd like to be the one to help you through the effects of the serum," Joy hesitantly asked as they walked through a long corridor.

Toni turned her head and added, "It would be better to have someone with you while the serum expels the bots. You both are welcome to stay here at the compound. In fact, that is preferable."

Char pulled a video phone from her pocket and stated, "I'll call Cindy and have her available to monitor the effects of the serum in case it's worse than Toni suspects. We promised our daughter we would let you decide, but we'd like to take every precautionary measure to ensure you return to optimal health as soon as possible. Cindy is very good at her job and may help you diminish the side effects."

"Cindy?" Sadie asked.

"The Organization's head of medical. She patches us up when a mission goes awry. Cindy is a little gruff sometimes, but she's saved several agents' lives, including mine and Joy's," Char explained, following Toni inside a massive room filled with computers and strange items she'd never seen. There were parts littered on top of a long table, some so tiny Sadie couldn't decipher their purpose.

She was sure her eyes widened to the size of large dinner plates. "Tech support is at risk for bodily harm?"

"Not usually." Char glanced at her wife. "I was pregnant at the time. I lost a lot of blood, and the stress on my body nearly caused a miscarriage."

Toni frowned. "You never told me that. Neither did Cindy. She said the baby was fine."

Char shrugged. "And she was, but only after Cindy did her magic. It would not have served any useful purpose to share how close I was to losing Joy. We needed your focus on the mission. We can talk about this later." Char stepped out of the room with her phone in her hand, presumably making a call to Cindy.

Sadie didn't feel so bad anymore. Apparently, even married couples had secrets. She had to admit that both Char and Toni had been extremely transparent. Their willingness to show her all the gadgets in the lab, which she was sure were unknown to the world, was a first step in building that trust. Besides, if she could join forces with The Organization, she could finally get the justice her parents deserved. Stopping the mining industry from its atrocities was worth everything to Sadie, including the previous violation of her privacy and the unpleasantness of expelling those damn bots.

Annette Mori

CHAPTER TEN

Joy observed Sadie as Toni patiently explained the tech available to the agents in The Organization, including the new prototypes she was working on. Ever since Joy had tinkered with the miniature drone, adding an electronic pulse that interrupted the signals and rendered anything with a chip useless, Toni had been on a nonstop mission to develop similar devices. Tiny was the operative word for what littered the long table. Toni had strewn every kind of rodent, arachnoid, bug, or other small living creature native to different parts of the world over nearly every inch of the lab. Unless a person closely inspected the pulse generating gadgets, the tiny metal creatures were indistinguishable from their live counterparts. Hacking a person's security systems to shut down the barriers while on a field mission was no longer required. That made sabotaging the mines infinitely

104

easier. The Organization was more than a small thorn in their side.

Joy was cautiously optimistic as Sadie seemed to have lost her previous anger. Even though it wasn't outwardly apparent, it could be more like a simmering boil. Sadie had even expressed a fair amount of reverence as Toni proudly expounded on her inventions.

"The rest of our tech is in the medical unit, including the serum to expel the bots. Cindy and I work together on anything with a biological component. You'll need to call in sick tomorrow," Toni said. "Our medical unit is on this campus, but in a different building. Follow me." Toni walked brusquely to the home's back entrance and started down the stone path to the medical facility.

The crease in the middle of Sadie's forehead deepened. "I'm sure it can't be that bad. Surely the worst of it will pass through by tomorrow morning."

Sadie and Joy quickly followed, with Char walking beside Toni as their hands naturally came together. Joy enjoyed seeing her parents continue to show affection for one another. She hoped she would have the same level of love and devotion one day.

Toni shook her head. "Nope, trust me, I used myself as a guinea pig. It will feel like you're releasing the demons from hell before they're gone. Don't forget, we gave you the option."

"Why haven't you perfected the serum to make it less debilitating?" Sadie asked. "Surely you have the knowledge and skill to accomplish that."

Toni shrugged. "It hasn't been a priority. We've never injected bots into someone and then offered to remove them."

Something wasn't adding up. Joy blurted the question without thinking, "If you've never offered to remove the bots, why the need to create a serum to test on yourself?"

Joy saw the split-second of guilt flitter over both her moms' faces. "Oh, no, you didn't. For fuck's sake, Mama T."

"We didn't actually go through with it. We sent Val instead. Then Char made me promise I would never put bots into any agent in The Organization, no matter what," Toni confessed.

Joy stopped walking and crossed her hands over her chest. "I can't believe you almost put bots in us. Are you telling me the serum is over two years old? How the hell do you know if it will work? Please tell me it won't be worse because it's been sitting there getting more potent or something."

"No, no, I made a new batch when you read me the riot act yesterday and insisted we give Sadie the option. Relax. I'm relatively confident she'll have the same reaction I did. Besides, Cindy will be there to monitor her, and because no one enjoys having the stomach flu, I already asked her to help me with something to offset extreme nausea and," Toni made a gagging gesture, "you know, purging the demon. Unfortunately, we haven't exactly tested that out yet. I was going to inject myself again and then have her inoculate me with the new anti-nausea antitoxin. But I didn't have time."

"You can't be serious. You're not going to use Sadie as a guinea pig for your experiments. That's reckless even for you, Mama T," Joy exclaimed.

"I have to agree with Joy, hon. You failed to share that fact with me." Char narrowed her eyes at Toni.

106

"Guess that makes us even." Toni grabbed the door to the medical facility and yanked it hard enough to bang against the wall.

"Oh, for shit's sake. I knew that would come back to bite me. I didn't tell you about the near miscarriage because it didn't happen, and the last thing you needed was unnecessary stress. You're acting like a child now. I suppose it's true what they say; when a person ages, they revert to their childhood."

"Low blow," Toni hissed.

Sadie kept looking between Toni and Char, and Joy could only imagine what she might be thinking.

"What the fuck is going on now?" Cindy asked. "I could hear you sniping at each other before you barreled into my clinic. I don't see any blood, so why are you here?"

"I tried to call to give you a heads up, but you weren't answering," Char stated. "This isn't an emergency, but we still need your expertise."

Cindy grabbed her phone and glanced at it. "Sorry, Ronda must have put my phone on silent. Who's this?" Cindy pointed to Sadie.

"Be nice, Aunt Cindy. This is Sadie. She's a new recruit. Mama T put bots in her, and we need you to administer the serum and monitor her as she expels them. I'm staying with her," Joy stated, leaving no room for argument.

Cindy arched an eyebrow. "All right. I'll prepare the IV." She pointed to a large leather recliner. "Sit."

"Go ahead and include whatever antitoxin you and Toni worked on. I don't mind being an experimental subject, especially if it lessens the side effects," Sadie stated. "Can you give me a minute? I need to call Carson and let her know I'm not coming home tonight. If I don't, she'll worry." Sadie

107

sighed. "Goddess, I hope this choice is worth the teasing I'm sure to receive when she makes assumptions about what I'm doing tonight. At least I can honestly tell her I'm spending the night with you." Sadie looked at Joy and smiled.

Joy's heart did a few flip-flops as Sadie walked outside to make her call. Maybe she still had a chance with Sadie. She sure hoped so.

Every once in a while, Cindy softened and showed another side, especially with Pepper, Alina, and Joy. After Sadie left to make her call, Cindy held up her thumbs and said, "She's cute, Joy. Don't worry. Between the two of us, we'll make this as comfortable as possible. Your mother is an idiot sometimes. Hopefully, the serum won't be as harsh on Sadie because we're not going to directly inject it into her veins like your mother did. Putting the serum in the IV should help. The antitoxin should also make a big difference, although it's untested."

"Thanks, Aunt Cindy."

"No problem, hon."

†

Sadie's head was spinning. If there was such a thing as information overload, she was there. It was sweet and a little sexy how Joy insisted she remain with Sadie. It was the most forceful Sadie had ever heard Joy be. Usually, she was so timid. Sadie sensed she would see a different side of Joy when they went on missions together. At least she hoped The Organization would let her join Joy on missions. Isn't that what they had insinuated when they indicated she could be an asset and wanted her to join? Of course, Sadie would have to clarify what exactly that meant and how they envisioned joining forces.

Taking a big breath before connecting with Carson on videophone, she pressed the button. She prepared herself for a ration of shit from Carson. Carson's smiling face appeared on the screen.

"Hey, Carson."

"Where are you? I thought you were at the park with Joy."

Shit. How could I forget how Carson never misses a single detail? "We were at the park, and then Joy wanted me to meet her parents," Sadie answered. It wasn't a lie. Just not the whole truth.

"The parents? Already? How serious is this? I mean, the two of you have been on exactly two dates. Fuck, Sadie. I never took you for a typical lesbian. Moving a little fast, isn't it?"

Sadie tried to keep from cringing. Carson knew her too well. She went on the offensive in an effort to toss Carson off her game. "I told you I really like Joy. You never listen to me. When things are right, they're right. I'm staying with her tonight, and I don't need any shit from you. I know what I'm doing."

Even on the small phone screen Carson had propped against something to keep her hands free, Sadie could clearly see her apologetic gesture as she held her hands in the air. "Whoa, sorry. I didn't mean to give you any grief." Carson crinkled her nose. "I didn't think either of you was the type to sleep together so soon."

"You do know that people can sleep together without having sex, right?"

Carson snorted. "Yeah, right. I told you, it's always the quiet ones," Carson joked. "Have fun, okay?"

Randi's head popped into the screen. "Wow! Joy actually asked you to stay the night? I'm so proud of her." Randi laughed. "I guess I'll see you later tonight."

"Um, we aren't coming back to your place. Neither of us wanted to get a ration of shit from our roommates, but we didn't want to worry you when we didn't come home. Maybe you can tell Alina and Maria." Sadie smoothly relayed the information.

Randi turned her head to Carson. "Awesome. I guess we have your place all to ourselves tonight. Oh, the trouble we can get into," Randi teased. "I promise we'll clean up all the sex toys before you return." Randi threw her head back and laughed.

Carson playfully nudged Randi's shoulder. "Have fun. I'll see you tomorrow night after work? That is, unless you've already scheduled the U-Haul to clean out your home and have decided to sell me the place for way below market."

"You wish. Nope, you're stuck with me for the time being, roomie. I better not come back to a mess, either," Sadie warned.

"Don't worry. We're just chilling. Having a few beers and bingeing that new show with all the hot lesbians." Carson waved and ended the call.

Sadie let out the air in her lungs and walked back inside. First, she needed to tell them Randi was at her place with Carson. She didn't know if Randi was also part of The Organization, but she planned to find out. That might make things easier. Then there would be two individuals assessing Carson's suitability. Sadie was convinced that Carson was a safe bet, but she supposed she understood The Organization's hesitancy. She hoped to learn as much as possible while suffering through the next twenty-four hours. Sadie would make the call to her boss in the morning. Considering she'd never called in sick before, even though she'd only been at the NSA for a few months, Sadie hoped they wouldn't blink an eye at her need to take the day off.

"Everything go okay with telling Carson?" Char asked.

"Sort of. Randi was there with her. I wasn't specific about where we were staying tonight, but I mentioned I was here because Joy wanted me to meet you. Carson is very observant and noticed I wasn't in the park, so I provided the truth without revealing any details. Does Randi know about The Organization?"

"She does," Char answered. "Her parents aren't crazy about her joining, but Randi is champing at the bit. The deal they made with her is she needs to complete her education before deciding what to do with her future, whether that be joining The Organization, going into the Army, or applying to some other law enforcement agency. She's an adrenaline junkie."

Sadie grabbed her chin in thought. "Hmm, so is Carson. They'd be perfect for one another. I think Carson is interested. Not sure about Randi, but she's there hanging out. How observant is Randi? Maybe she can also be another person to assess Carson's suitability."

"I'll call Alina and give her an update. Then, she can talk with Randi tonight. Good idea. Even better to have two people evaluating Carson," Char noted.

Sadie walked to the recliner and sat. "Okay, let's do this before I chicken out. I have a lot of questions. Hopefully, I'll be able to pass the time by getting answers to those questions. The first one is when are we going after Marks? I better be in on whatever mission you're planning for him."

"Don't worry. We wouldn't dream of cutting you out," Char assured. "I'll set a meeting for later this week. Does that work for you?"

Sadie smiled. "The sooner, the better. I've been waiting a long time for this."

Toni grinned. "Sophie and Kim are going to love this. Just like old times. I'm assuming we're going to attack his vast financial resources."

Char nodded. "That's exactly what we're going to do."

"Perfect. Now that we know Marks is intimately associated with the mines worldwide, I won't feel the least bit sorry about extricating his fortune from him. This will be the largest heist we've ever tried." Toni rubbed her hands together. "The kids are going to learn a whole new strategy."

Joy scowled. "Stop calling us kids."

†

Cindy dragged over a cart with materials for the IV and snapped on a pair of gloves. After palpating for the best vein, she cinched the rubber tourniquet and wiped the area where Sadie's vein showed prominently. "You're going to feel a little pinch."

Before inserting the needle, Cindy flawlessly released the elastic band. If Cindy's mastery with the needle was any indication of her skill, Sadie presumed she was in expert hands because she barely felt the needle go in.

Taping down the needle, Cindy fiddled with the bag before stating, "Let me know if you feel any discomfort

112

besides nausea. Hopefully, my new cocktail will make it less painful for you. I'm sorry you have to go through this."

Sadie smiled. "It's okay. You're not the one who put the bots into me."

"It's a good thing it's slow here," Cindy grumbled. "At least for now. I saw that glint in Toni's eyes. You are about to go on another mission, aren't you?" Cindy asked.

Joy pulled up a chair next to the recliner. "Yeah, but I don't think this one will put us in harm's way. We're going after their bank accounts. More hacking and less fighting."

"Don't be too sure about that. You should ask Toni and Char about when they first met. Some asshole drugged Kim, and if The Organization hadn't intervened, the powerful men they were targeting would have discovered Toni, Kim, and Sophie's identities. Trust me, those guys were not playing around. They wanted blood after those three kept stealing their money. When it comes to money, they all resort to violence to keep their fortunes. With all the biometric safeguards in place, you can be sure whomever you plan to target won't be an easy mark. No doubt it will require you to get up close and personal," Cindy explained.

"Fine with me," Sadie stated. "I've been wanting to get up close and personal for a long time." Sadie's stomach gurgled. "Um, I think I'm going to be sick."

Sadie started to get up, but Cindy gently held her back while Joy grabbed the yellow tub and placed it under her chin. The lovely lunch that Joy had brought landed in the barf bucket. Joy tenderly held back her hair, and Sadie tried not to feel embarrassed about Joy seeing her like this but then remembered why she had to endure this mortification. One thing that was for sure, she'd probably never eat another chicken Caesar or chickpea arugula salad ever again. Wine wouldn't be on the menu for a long time, either.

Cindy removed the yellow tub, carrying it into the closest bathroom. Sadie rested her head against the chair. Joy took her hand and began stroking it. "I'm so sorry about this. I don't know what I can do to make it up to you."

Sadie offered Joy an anemic smile. "Getting Marks will go a long way toward forgiveness. Besides, you had nothing to do with this. Although, if you do feel compelled to make it up to me, you'll agree to a third date."

"Anything you want. Anywhere you want to go. I'll make the arrangements. I was afraid you wouldn't want to have anything to do with me after…" Joy's voice trailed off.

"Not at all. So, you're the Amazon, huh? Even though I was irritated about you continuing to hack into my group and the NSA, which caused me a fair number of problems at work, I couldn't help but admire your skill. And if I were completely honest, I wanted to meet you. I would have eventually let you into my group."

"Well, it wasn't all me. Mama T helped with some code," Joy answered.

"So, is The Organization really a collection of high-powered thieves?" Sadie asked. "Is that how you obtained your fortune?" Sadie held up her hands in supplication. "No judgment. It sounds like your targets deserve it."

"It might be how they started out many years ago, but we have legitimate businesses that provide for our personal wealth. Everything else is anonymously given to charities or used to support The Organization's charity operations. It's more a matter of redistributing the wealth. The Organization learned long ago that the government would never establish fair policies to benefit all. Even when Sandra Murphy was president, she couldn't get everything through Congress because we were and still are so divided as a country. The Organization helps level the playing field. Lately, we've been concentrating more on breaking up the mines, with less focus on redistributing wealth. There was also a time when the principal focus was shutting down human trafficking. Those were dangerous times. The Russian mob is brutal when challenged," Joy explained.

Sadie's stomach roiled again. "Can I please have the bucket?" She grimaced, and Sadie barely managed to keep the remaining contents in the second bucket that Cindy had laid out for Sadie.

A concerned look crossed Cindy's face as she placed the cleaned bucket on the side table and removed the newly soiled yellow tub. When she returned, she said, "I'm going to add more medication to the bag. I don't like how minimal the antitoxin has been on reducing the side effects of the serum. Fucking irresponsible Toni," she griped.

"Cursing me again, Cindy?" Toni asked.

Sadie turned her head to see Toni and Char enter the medical facility. Neither was smiling, and Sadie thought she almost saw regret on both their faces.

"I did warn her," Toni defended. "I also meant what I said that we wouldn't continue to monitor her because I gave her my word; you know I would never break my oath."

"I know that, but Goddess, Toni, for someone so brilliant, you're an idiot. Why would a stranger trust your vow?" Cindy grumbled.

Toni nodded. "Good point."

"I want your word that you will never do this again. No more bots injected into anyone but confirmed enemies. Find another way to satisfy any potential concerns," Cindy insisted.

"How about if we perfect the antitoxin instead? I'll test it on myself."

Cindy shook her head. "Why do I even bother?"

Sadie watched the interaction and finally spoke up. "Do I have your word you won't inject Carson? You gave me a week, but considering I already trust Cindy more than you, and it seems like Cindy relies on your promise, I want to hear you say it."

"Fine. You have my ironclad guarantee. But you're responsible for the fallout if it all blows up in our faces." Toni glanced at her wife, who nodded.

"I hope you understand the ramifications. We will employ whatever means necessary to remain hidden, even if that means authorizing something you may personally find distasteful."

The horrified expression on Joy's face gave Sadie some pause.

"Aunt Val?"

Char nodded.

"Who the hell is that, and what does that mean?" Sadie asked.

"We can talk about it later," Joy placated.

CHAPTER ELEVEN

It was rare for Toni not to hover over her monitoring equipment or obsess over the next prototype, which was sure to give them an edge over their enemies. As she relaxed on the bed and turned toward her wife, Char spoke of her trepidation over what would surely be required of The Organization to take Marks down.

Char propped her head in her hand and looked at Toni. "This isn't going to be a walk in the park. It's not like we can don a few disguises at some political gala to obtain the biometric access needed to unlock his secret accounts. Even with adding Sadie to our ranks and having more tech experts than ever, our chance of success is limited. Besides, he's locked much of his wealth within his numerous companies. I doubt our attacks on his mines have made much more than a small dent."

"I'm not so sure of that. From what I hear, he keeps propping up those companies with personal funds. I'll know more when I get a chance to dig in. We should call Katrina," Toni suggested. "Bringing her back into the fold can't hurt. Maybe she's developed innovative ways to steal money in the past twenty years."

Char moved her hand down Toni's hip. "This is such a rare treat to have you relaxing with me and talking strategy. Have you kept tabs on Katrina?"

Toni smirked. "What do you think? Not that I don't trust her, but it's always good to make sure she isn't mucking around in our territory."

Char chuckled. "I suspect you would have already shut her down if she had."

"Oh, I don't know. Katrina was every bit as talented as me. I'm not too arrogant to admit she could give me a run for my money. Good thing we've always had a cautiously respectful relationship; deep down, Katrina's motives were pure. If someone had harmed you the way they broke Lyric, I might have gone rogue, too."

"So, how is Lyric doing?" Char asked.

"Good. Dr. Carmichael put her on the path to recovery." Toni trailed her fingertips down the middle of Char's cleavage. Even in her fifties, Char had an enticing body. "You know that Dani, Val, and Candy stay in touch. Occasionally, they have lunch with Lyric, just the four of them. No spouses allowed. They share a bond that none of us can relate to. Last I checked, Katrina and Lyric live on some island in the South Pacific in the fall and winter and return to DC for the spring and summer. Katrina hasn't pulled a heist in years, but that doesn't mean she doesn't have her own little tech fortress to tap into. Maybe she's bored and would welcome a little action and exercise for her brain."

"All right. Make the call. I'll set up a strategy session for sometime next week. We'll need Kim involved. In the meantime, our top priority is to discover Alvin Marks' schedule for the month. I want to know if he's attending any public events. Your little tech squad needs to follow the money. Find out where he's hiding his fortune, every shell company, every hidden account, and anything else there is to know about his vast assets. I'm counting on you, Joy, Dani, Sadie, and, hopefully, Katrina to get this done. Pronto."

"Ooh, I love it when you get all bossy." Toni skootched closer to Char and lifted the flimsy top over her head, then proceeded to take one of her nipples in her mouth. "Mmm," she moaned, talking around her light sucking, "I'll start on this tomorrow. We'll have to coordinate with Sadie's work schedule. She's already missing a day of work because of my bots."

Char fell onto the bed and let Toni crawl on top.

†

The additional antitoxin and anti-nausea medicine that Cindy added to the IV bag seemed to lessen the violence of Sadie's retching, but it was evident Sadie was still miserable. There was no chance that any of them were getting rest tonight. Although Cindy had moved Sadie to one of the infirmary beds, Joy took a comfortable recliner beside her.

Every time Joy heard Sadie stir, she put the bucket underneath her, smoothing her hair back and wiping her face with a cool washcloth. The times between her almost explosive vomiting were getting further apart. It had been

119

several hours, and Joy peeked out the window when she heard the birds chirping. Glancing at her watch, she noted the time. Usually, this was one of Joy's favorite times of the day, when the sun barely started shining through the clouds, creating a kaleidoscope of color.

Joy pushed a damp lock of honey-blonde hair back from Sadie's forehead. Although she looked a little pale, Joy still thought Sadie was one of the most beautiful women she'd ever laid her eyes on. She should have known Sadie was Dragonfire with those compelling amber eyes, the exact same shade as her avatar. Joy couldn't believe her luck. Even after what her moms did to Sadie, she still wanted to go out with Joy.

A weak smile appeared on Sadie's face as her eyes fluttered open. She'd been asleep now for a record two hours. "What time is it?" Sadie asked in a groggy voice.

"Around 5:30. How are you feeling?" Joy asked.

"A little better. I think the worst has passed. You should have left to get some sleep. You look a little rough."

"No way. It's kind of my fault you're in this condition. If I hadn't tried to hack your dark web group or the NSA, I never would have got Mama T involved, and she wouldn't have known anything about you," Joy stated miserably.

Sadie lifted her hand and reached for Joy, who eagerly clasped the offered hand. "I'm not sorry. I found The Crusaders. Well, technically, you found me. Once I'm on the other side of feeling crappy, I may even find it funny. I'll include it in the war stories I plan on telling my children."

Joy shook her head. "That's awfully generous of you to reframe this experience. I'm still mad at my folks."

"Don't be. I get it. I'm not sure what I would do to protect the ones I love, and I can be just as intense as your moms. That should be clear from the lengths I've gone to seek revenge on everyone associated with the abuses in the mines. Something you and your moms may not know is that I didn't get caught hacking into the NSA," Sadie stated.

Joy crinkled her nose. "I didn't think you did."

"Your mom probably had questions about why the NSA offered me a scholarship. And if I were her, I might guess that the NSA had caught me hacking and offered an opportunity instead of likely jail time. It makes more sense because I'd already sold my game and had plenty of money to do whatever I wanted. Developing games is a different skill set than hacking. So why would the NSA try to recruit a game developer?" Sadie posed the question as she rearranged her position in the bed and reached for the remote to bring the head of the bed up.

"Why are you sharing this with me?" Joy asked, perplexed about the reasons for Sadie bringing this topic up out of the blue.

"I don't want there to be any secrets between us. If you're going to trust me, and I'm going to trust you and The Organization, I want you to know everything."

"Okay, but I already trust you. And I think the moms do as well, or they wouldn't have invited you to join," Joy insisted.

"Can I have some water, please?" Sadie croaked. "I feel like I just sucked in all the sand in the Sahara Desert."

"Let me get some fresh water and ice for you. This has been sitting here all night." Joy hurried to the ice machine, and after tossing the old water, she put a scoop of ice into the cup and then filled it with water from the dispenser.

Grabbing a new straw, she stuck it into the cup and handed it to Sadie.

"Thanks." Sadie took a sip before continuing her explanation. "I purposely left a tiny breadcrumb for the NSA to find me. I wanted them to catch me and offer the scholarship, thinking they would be smart enough to recruit a valuable hacker." Sadie returned the cup to the side table. "I figured I could find out more from the inside, and I desperately wanted to learn more about your organization. As far as I knew, the NSA was the central repository for information about the group attacking the mines." Sadie laughed. "They've been at it for two years, and I can tell you they have *squatola* on The Organization, other than you're mostly women, with exceptional fighting skills. Now that I know who you are, I can laugh about it. But I'll admit, I was incredibly frustrated at the utter lack of information. I thought the US Government had much better spies."

"I've never met anyone better than Mama T. She has a knack for making information disappear." Even though her mother sometimes did things she disagreed with, like putting bots in Sadie, Joy was proud of her.

"I can't wait to work more closely with her. I'm sure she could teach me a few things."

"You're really not angry with her anymore?" Joy asked.

"Nah, I'm nothing if not pragmatic. It doesn't matter how I stumbled onto The Organization, my goal was met, and I can almost taste the inevitable justice I'll finally get," Sadie declared as she reached for the water again.

Joy helped her with the cup and turned the straw around to make it easier for Sadie. "Revenge can be a dangerous motive. Justice is essential, and we're clearly all about righting wrongs and protecting innocent people, but losing one's focus in a haze of anger can cause disastrous missteps. Growing up, hearing my moms' and aunts' stories, I absorbed this lesson. Aunt Val is one of the most stoic women I know, and she almost allowed her anger and revenge to take over to near-catastrophic consequences."

After sipping more water, Sadie nodded. "You're right, of course, but it's hard not to be excited about taking Marks down. Do you know when we'll start?"

"No doubt the moms are already plotting and planning. I'm sure they'll bring our best agents together to discuss the mission. In the meantime, they'll probably want your assessment of Carson sooner rather than later. Still feeling okay?"

"Yeah. I thought for sure that even the little bit of water I just had would come up again, but it seems to be staying put for now. I'm not gonna lie. I kind of wish I hadn't chosen this route. I think I can call the NSA to let them know I'm not coming in now without risking getting sick again. Although, that would surely sell it," Sadie joked.

Joy grabbed the phone sitting on the table and handed it to Sadie. Out of the corner of her eye, she saw Cindy enter the private space where she'd suggested Sadie ride out the remaining side effects of the serum. As Sadie made her call, Joy approached Cindy.

"How's she doing?" Cindy asked.

"Better. The last time she was sick was over two hours ago. I think the worst has passed. She still looks relatively peaked."

"Yeah. I don't like Sadie's pallor at all. I may have to put something in the IV to boost her ability to recover more quickly. You look like you could use some rest, too, kiddo.

After we're sure she's done throwing up, perhaps the two of you can retire to one of the guest rooms and get some sleep."

Joy could feel the rush of blood hit her face. "Oh, um, you mean like sleep in the same bed?"

Cindy chuckled. "Yes, sleep," she emphasized. "I doubt either of you is up for sexual calisthenics yet."

Joy was both excited and anxious at the prospect of taking a nap with Sadie.

†

Char and Toni sat on their back patio, enjoying the sun's warmth as they ate a leisurely breakfast. Toni popped a piece of croissant into her mouth and waggled her eyebrows at Char.

"Stop grinning at me like the cat who caught the canary," Char teasingly chastised.

"Canaries aren't nearly as beautiful as you, but being referred to as a cat works for me. They're sleek and sneaky. I'm okay with that." Toni smirked, bringing her coffee to her lips but continuing to stare at Char. "Besides, you must admit, it was particularly good last night, right? It's been too long. I'm sorry I've been neglecting you. I'll try not to do that. We should have more time with each other, not less. I thought letting the kids take over many of the missions would leave us more time, but frankly, their youth and vitality are killing me. Even relegating ourselves to backup is more work than if we were leading all the missions ourselves."

"The reality is that they're still too young to take over completely," Char noted. "Plus, you have a lot to teach Joy and now Sadie. Do you really want to stop tinkering? We can't fill all our hours with hot monkey sex."

Toni laughed. "You did not just say hot monkey sex. That is not a Char thing to say." She leaned back in her chair and looked up when she saw Cindy approach. It was clear Cindy was not in a good mood.

"Glad you two are having a grand old time this morning while that young woman puked her guts out all night. Honestly, Toni, you're as reckless as you were when you first joined The Organization. You should have been smart enough to know everyone's body chemistry differs. I tried everything to lessen the impact, but not much worked. You put her health in danger, and for what?"

Toni had the good sense to look sheepish and not respond. There wasn't much she could say in her defense other than to remind Cindy they'd given Sadie a choice.

Char frowned. "Is her health at risk? Will this cause permanent damage in any way?"

"I don't think so, but she had it worse than Toni. And I'm referring to the time Toni injected herself with the serum before we developed the antitoxin to diminish the impact." Cindy glared at Toni.

Toni cringed. "I should apologize to Sadie."

"We should apologize," Char interjected, then confessed, "Toni didn't make this decision alone."

"You will do no such thing. They're both napping right now. I put them in the guest house. I think the worst is over for Sadie, and Joy stayed up with her all night, so she's exhausted. I'll do a full work-up when they wake. Next time you decide to inject bots into someone, make sure they're the enemy," Cindy ordered, then stalked off.

"Wow, I've seen Cindy grumpy before, but not like this. We better steer clear of her for a few days. In hindsight, I suppose it wasn't the best decision," Toni acknowledged before gulping the rest of her coffee.

"As much as neither of us wants to admit, we're only human. Sometimes we make mistakes. I'm not too proud to admit this was a major gaffe. I won't wake them, but I want to check to make sure they're resting comfortably and don't need anything."

Toni pushed away from the table. "I'm coming with."

"Okay, but take off your shoes. You aren't as stealthy as you think. Years in the field as our tech specialist is not the same as a field agent that has to approach a target quietly." Char grinned.

"Hey, I hold my own in the field. It's not like I'm completely helpless. Yes, you're a better fighter than me, but I can sneak around like the best of them."

Char chuckled. "Sure you can. Come on, Catwoman."

Toni followed Char down the path and tried her best to step lightly behind Char after she carefully opened the door and peeked into the bedroom. Joy had her arms protectively wrapped around Sadie, spooning her from behind. Toni noticed how pale Sadie was in the dim light of the room. Cindy had probably closed the blinds tight to keep out the morning light, but Toni could still make out the tiny dark, nearly purple circles underneath her daughter's eyes. Light snoring sounds, barely noticeable, came from both young women. Char carefully shut the door.

"They look adorable together," Toni said. "But I feel worse now. Did you see how much last night took a toll on both of them?"

Love Hacks

Char nodded. "I hope they'll look a little better after they've slept for a while. Perhaps Sadie will regain some color in her face, and Joy's dark circles won't seem so prominent. Any idea how we can make it up to them?"

Toni shrugged. "I have a feeling that getting Marks will go a long way toward Sadie forgiving us. As for Joy, no clue."

"Joy is clearly beyond smitten with Sadie. I wish there was a way to ensure that Sadie falls madly in love with Joy. I want Joy to experience the magic we have. Any chance you can develop a love potion?" Char joked.

"Even if I could, there's probably unimaginable side effects. You know there's always a catch to things like that. Better to let nature take its course. Somehow, I think it just might."

†

Sadie wasn't sure how long they'd slept, but she didn't want to move from her current position. Joy had her arm draped over Sadie's stomach, and she felt a rush of emotion. It wasn't sexual, more like a feeling of contentment or rightness. The fact that Joy had stayed with her throughout the unbelievably vile day and well into the night said a lot about Joy's character and kindness. Sure, guilt might have been a part of it, but Joy wasn't responsible for the decision to put bots into her, and Toni had warned Sadie.

Moreover, Joy hadn't hesitated to jump up and grab the garbage can in the bathroom adjacent to the guest room. They all thought she was done purging the demon, but no such luck. Sadie ended up getting sick several more times before she succumbed to exhaustion. She was sure it wasn't

127

only a truck that had hit her last night. It was a train, a plane, and Marks' brand-new shuttlecraft. Joy had wanted to get Cindy because she hadn't liked Sadie's color, but Sadie begged her not to, insisting she'd be fine. In reality, Sadie had never felt so sick in her entire life.

She'd finally let the tears fall because her being sick like this reminded her of the chemo treatments her mother had to endure. They hadn't worked, mainly because they weren't the latest and greatest for her type of cancer, but they were all her mother could afford. The free clinic wasn't the best place to go. Sadie had learned much later about their shady practices. The physicians would secure drugs from third-world countries, charging the government for the supplies as if they were legally obtained and pocketing the profits. It was a racket, and the patients were the unfortunate recipients of substandard care. It didn't matter to the clinic because the people they served were all throwaways, in their opinion. No one was worth saving.

Joy hadn't asked any questions. Instead, she'd just held Sadie, brushed away the tears, and told her she'd be there for as long as it took for the serum to work through her system. But Sadie wanted Joy to know the real reason she had cried. Because not only did Sadie want to know everything about Joy, she wanted Joy to learn all her secrets, too. Secrets she hadn't even told Carson because Carson only had the broad strokes after their many years of friendship.

Joy stirred, and her eyes popped open. Removing her arm, she fired off a round of questions. "Are you okay? Are you sick again? What time is it?"

"I'm good. Well, not exactly good, but the nausea has passed. Now I just feel achy and beyond exhausted. I didn't know a person could feel this weak. I'm not sure if I can sleep anymore, but the prospect of doing anything beyond sitting seems impossible."

Joy grabbed her fancy watch from the nightstand, glancing at the device. "Oh, wow! It's four o'clock. Do you think you could eat something?"

Sadie tried to pull her body into a sitting position. Joy grabbed one of her pillows and placed it behind Sadie, helping her reposition herself. Sadie nodded. "Yeah, I think so. At least my stomach is telling me it would like something to fill the empty cavern. Hopefully, my intestines are still there to process the food," Sadie joked.

"Where does the saying puke one's guts out come from?" Joy pondered.

"Not sure about that, but there are species that literally puke out their guts, like sharks, frogs, stingrays, sea cucumbers, and sea stars. It's because they don't have a lower esophageal sphincter like us to keep their stomach inside the body. Think of it like turning the pocket in your pants out. I guess they can wipe whatever toxin or bones off and put their stomach back."

Joy chuckled. "Okay, random information. How in the world do you know that? I thought I was a nerd to the nth degree."

"Hey, now. There is nothing wrong with enjoying the science channel."

"So, do you have a craving for anything special?"

"Don't laugh, but when I was little, my mom would make me a grilled cheese sandwich and tomato soup once I was well enough to eat after being sick." Sadie let a smile form on her lips. It was a splendid memory.

"That's a classic," Joy answered as she jumped from the bed. "I'll check with Cindy to make sure that would be okay. If we don't have the supplies handy in the compound, I'll get the grocery to send an express drone. Can I please have Cindy come check you out? You still look a little rough around the edges."

Sadie almost didn't ask Joy because this was not how she envisioned getting naked with Joy, but she desperately needed a shower. "Goddess, I hate feeling like an invalid, but do you think you can help me take a shower? I'm afraid I might pass out if I try to do it myself."

Joy's face turned bright red. "Oh, uh, yeah, of course," she sputtered. "I promise not to gawk at you. I'll just be there for support."

Sadie chuckled. "It's okay, Joy. I don't think you're some kind of lech. It isn't exactly how I wanted you to see me naked for the first time, but I trust you."

Joy smiled and blushed again. "Good to know. Shower or food first?"

"Definitely shower," Sadie answered.

"Let me check real quick about the soup and stuff for the grilled cheese sandwich and put in an order if we need supplies." Joy nearly ran out of the room as if her ass was on fire. Sadie hadn't meant to cause Joy discomfort, but damn, she was adorable when flustered.

CHAPTER TWELVE

It wasn't easy to find information on Alvin Marks, and Toni definitely hadn't discovered all the places he hid his wealth. But she had learned a great deal about the companies on the surface of that large iceberg that was his vast kingdom. Marks couldn't help himself. He was a braggart and a narcissist, which led him to boast about his more visible enterprises. Lately, he'd been promoting his Space Explorers corporation, which reminded Toni of an adolescent boy's wet dream. The craze started nearly twenty-five years ago, with two very similar billionaires competing for who would be the first to make space travel possible for the rich and famous. With their penis-shaped ships, the race was on.

Toni was in the midst of digging into those companies, including his propaganda network, and the social media giant he'd founded after many of the others went belly-up. Toni mused there was always the next best thing for the fad-enamored people to follow. Chasing each thread was frustrating but productive. She was finally getting somewhere.

Char entered the lab, and Toni glanced up to greet her wife. "Hey. What's up? Are the kids awake yet?"

Char smiled. "You better not let either of them hear you refer to them as kids. And yes, Joy tried to make a grilled cheese sandwich and tomato soup for Sadie. It didn't go so well. Our daughter is talented in many ways, but cooking is not one of them."

"Yeah, well, neither am I. Sadie must be feeling better."

"Marginally. Cindy hasn't stopped hovering. As a precaution, she hooked her up with another IV. Sadie was well enough to ask about plans for Marks. She's eager to get started. Have you found anything we can use?" Char asked.

"It's like a massive set of Christmas lights. You think you've almost untangled them and are ready to hang them on the tree, just to find several more require unknotting. It's worse than a Gordian knot." Toni perked up. "Good news, though. I did learn that he's been invited to a summit at the White House next month. It might be the perfect chance to get bots into him and grab the necessary biometrics. We'll need his DNA, retina, handprints, and facial. The guy's super paranoid. He uses all of them to gain access to his accounts in the Cayman Islands, where the majority of his personal fortune resides. At least I've discovered that much."

"How is learning he's been invited to a summit good news?" Char took a seat in the comfortable chair she'd finally been smart enough to bring into Toni's lab.

"Because I'm pretty sure I got invited as well. I never pay attention to the invites sent to me for the various conventions, speaking engagements, and such. Since I've carefully developed my recluse persona over the years, Dani doesn't bother bringing them to me anymore. Doubtful they would invite Marks and not me as the CEO of Solar Flair. I'll call Dani today and instruct her to graciously accept the invite," Toni assured.

Before deciding to share this one tech with the world, Toni had created the company Solar Flair with the help of her wife. All of the major players in the company were part of The Organization and kept a tight lid on every secret, including how the solar cells worked. Dani, Char's sister, knew since she had helped her develop the cells. So it was logical for Dani to become her right-hand person in the company. All correspondence went through her, and she'd accepted becoming the face of the company, allowing Toni to stay in the background, solidifying her reputation as a recluse. Of course, Joy knew how the cells operated, too, since she'd worked alongside Toni and Dani, but Joy would never divulge their secrets to anyone outside The Organization.

"Oh, no. No way are you going into the lion's den alone. I want a team on this, and getting people into the White House is no easy feat."

Toni pouted. "While Marks is a media whore, he always makes appearances on his turf. He's harder to get to than President Dawson. We need to strike while the iron is hot. I can do this, Char."

"Nope. Better find another way to have an entire team support you." Char stood and began pacing the room. "Don't you remember the threats you got when you founded Solar Flair? The other manufacturers weren't too pleased with the competition. Especially after Grace highlighted your company as the only socially responsible manufacturer not using materials from the mines for your solar cells. I'd put money on Marks being behind it all. In less than twelve months, you rose to the top of the market and nearly bankrupted Solio."

"All right. I suppose my reputation for eccentricity and paranoia will allow me to insist on having an entourage accompany me." Toni grinned. "Soph and Val can be my two bodyguards."

"I'm coming, too. Of course, the genius can't be expected to go anywhere without her lovely wife," Char teased.

Toni hadn't noticed Joy and Sadie entering the lab while she discussed strategy with her wife until Joy declared, "Whatever you two are planning, it better include us."

†

After eating a grilled cheese sandwich and miraculously keeping it down, Sadie felt a whole lot better. Cindy had rechecked her and recommended she take it easy for another twenty-four hours. Still, Sadie insisted on getting up and discovering if Toni and Char had developed any solid plans to deal with Marks. After overhearing the terse conversation between Joy's moms, the pieces all clicked into place. Holy shit! Toni was *the* Toni McFarland, the legendary creator of the tiny solar cell.

No one knew exactly how the tech worked. Many engineers and scientists had tried, without success, to figure out the mechanics, hoping to recreate her breakthrough discovery. Still, Toni never gave interviews or felt the need to explain anything. The general public didn't care because

Solar Flair cars were ten times more efficient than any solar-powered vehicle on the market. The woman Sadie had met did not at all compute with the reputation behind the person.

Sadie couldn't recall ever seeing a clear picture of a mature Toni. Sure, like everyone else, she'd read the single article about the child prodigy, complete with adorable photos of Toni as a child. The reporter had dug out old high school pictures and interviewed individuals claiming to be former friends. Even Toni's family remained oddly tight-lipped about someone rumored to be one of the wealthiest people in the world, but after that one article, there was radio silence. Nothing. Nada. It was as if the famously reclusive woman had single-handedly shut down the hype and press about her. There were no explanations other than supposition about the woman she'd become. The press gave up trying to track her down and refocused their efforts on Marks, who seemed to bask in the limelight. Despite his waning solar car business, he used his social media platform to refocus the spotlight on his accomplishments. Reading the glowing articles about him made Sadie sick to her stomach.

"You're up!" Toni exclaimed. "How are you feeling, Sadie? You look a little better."

"You're Toni McFarland?" Sadie interrupted.

"Um, yeah. But you can't share how charming I am with anyone. It would ruin my reputation," Toni teased.

"I would think that whatever lion's den you planned on galloping into would demolish the façade," Joy tartly noted. "The White House? Why are you going there at the same time Marks will be there? And why is that dangerous?"

"There's a tech summit coming up at the White House. Marks doesn't make a lot of in-person public appearances without an army of security, but he wouldn't miss this one.

It's too tempting because it will be a golden opportunity to brag. He'll undoubtedly assume I won't be attending, leaving him to bask in the spotlight. But this time, I plan on accepting the invitation. It will be the perfect occasion to obtain all the biometric data we need to drain his accounts," Toni explained.

"How are you going to get a retina scan, handprint, blood, and whatever else he's put in place as protection?" Joy asked. "That's a lot, Mama T, even with Val, Sophie, and Mama C helping. Please let us in on the mission," she pleaded.

"Voice recognition is also a common tool," Sadie added.

"Once we inject him with my bots, we'll have plenty of samples of his voice patterns. That will also help us discover all his accounts. I only need to uncover a handful because after we drain two or three, he'll undoubtedly try to move money, and we'll know exactly where he plans to relocate the rest of his fortune with my bots recording his every move." Toni leaned back in her chair and grinned.

"Can you get us into the summit?" Sadie asked.

Toni grabbed a pen on her desk and began chewing the end. Char gently took the pen from her and shook her head. Toni frowned. "I don't know. Getting Val, Sophie, and Char inside might be a stretch. This is the White House we're talking about. They aren't going to want a bunch of extraneous people there, adding to their security challenges."

"I worked on those solar cells with you, and I'm your daughter," Joy insisted. "You can make it a condition of attendance that I'm invited, along with a guest of my choosing. I'm positive that the prospect of you attending will be too great of a temptation to pass up any conditions you set."

"I don't like it," Char stated. "We've worked hard to keep you out of the limelight. That's the reason you have my last name, not hers."

"Then why are you taking a chance? If you accompany Mama T, you'll be outing yourself as her wife. Won't that lead the vultures to me?" Joy inquired.

"I never should have started my company," Toni grumbled. "Who knew it would become such a success?"

"Seriously, Mom? And you're supposed to be a genius. How could it not become a sensation?" Joy shook her head.

"Uh, she's not wrong about that," Sadie noted. "Even with all the technological advances in the past hundred years, your solar cell probably rates in the top three. No wonder you're one of the richest people in the world."

"So, how do we overcome this impasse?" Char asked.

"I'll think of something. Since you've so elegantly pointed out that having Char accompany me as my wife isn't such a grand idea, none of you will be joining me as family." Toni reached for the pen, and Char stopped her again.

"Hon, I know it's a nervous habit of yours, but I don't think it's healthy for you to ingest so much ink you begin peeing blue, even organic edible ink."

Joy started to laugh, then put her hand over her mouth. "Good thing I didn't pick up that habit."

Sadie smiled, then shrugged. "Wasn't blue lipstick all the rage a few years back? Maybe your mom started that fad."

"Nope, remember she has meticulously developed a recluse persona. Only members of The Organization know about her nervous habit. I guess they'll have to let you in now," Joy joked.

"Funny. Why don't all of you leave my lab and let me work out the details without everyone hovering over me?" Toni spat.

"Don't get testy, hon. It's a lovely evening, Joy. I suggest you show Sadie our gardens?" Char massaged Toni's shoulders. "I'll stay, and we can brainstorm ideas to get us all inside."

†

Marks rubbed his hands with glee. President Ronald Dawson had called to personally let him know Toni McFarland had accepted the invite to the summit. Marks noted a fair amount of surprise in Dawson's voice.

"It worked. I didn't think she'd bite. You should be cautious, my friend. She's never accepted an invitation before. Why now, all of a sudden?" Dawson asked. "Make sure that whatever you plan on doing doesn't come back on me."

"I got you elected and can easily have you replaced. Don't test our friendship, Ronald. If only you had found a way to shut down Solar Flair with some kind of regulation, I wouldn't have to take drastic measures. Let me also remind you of the NSA's incompetence. With all their resources, they still haven't found a shred of usable information on the saboteurs. Don't forget to invite the Russians. It can be seen as an olive branch, and then I'll take care of leading the public to believe it was them."

"And risk pissing them off? Are you out of your fucking mind? They're our partners in this total fiasco that is quickly turning sour before our very eyes," Dawson moaned.

"Which is why we need to shut her down. No matter what conspiracy theories I plant, someone is countering the information and subsequently winning the media war. It's all connected. I'm sure of it. I no longer have the ultimate control over SoBites. We haven't managed to catch the hackers or stop their Bites."

"Exactly! You no longer have control, so why should I continue to help you at the risk of getting caught in the net?" Dawson asked, his voice taking on that hysterical edge that grated on Marks.

"Because without me, you have zero chance of securing a second term and getting the 22nd Amendment repealed to serve a third term."

"I'm not even sure I want that anymore," Dawson grumbled.

"You lead the most powerful country in the world. Why would you want to give that up?" Marks asked. He was genuinely curious. In the back of his mind, he had always wondered about his chances at success if he ever tossed his hat in the ring. Before the recent attacks on his social media site and the decline of Solio, he'd given it serious consideration.

"Because I don't actually lead. I'm simply a puppet for people like you. You pull the strings, and I react."

Ronald Dawson sounded both tired and defeated, and that did not bode well for Marks. Perhaps he had chosen poorly. If President Dawson couldn't withstand the heat, Marks would need to find someone else. After he eliminated the irritants to his plans, maybe it was time for him to become president.

"If anything goes sideways, I will take you down with me. Just remember that. Your future depends on mine staying free of controversy," Dawson warned.

CHAPTER THIRTEEN

Joy kept glancing at Sadie, who seemed to hover between awe and a state of shock. Cindy had finally given Sadie the green light to return home, and they were on their way to Sadie's house. Finally, Sadie broke the awkward silence.

"How come you never said anything about who your mom is?" Sadie asked. "I drive one of her cars, for shit's sake. Is your car a new prototype not released yet? Why make up some touching story of how you and your mom bonded on the weekends, building a completely recycled car?"

Joy kept her eyes focused on the road, not wanting to show her hurt and annoyance at Sadie's assumptions about her and her mother. "It's not a new prototype, and I didn't fabricate that story. After we built the car, I was the one to encourage Mom to share the solar cell tech with the world. I was in my 'save the planet' stage. After everything you've

141

seen and heard, I would think you're intelligent enough to figure out why I didn't tell you everything. We'd had one date," Joy added as a punctuation to her answer.

"Okay. That's fair. I wasn't exactly upfront with you, either," Sadie responded. "I'm sorry. It's just so unbelievable that your mom is Toni McFarland. When I first learned about her company, Solar Flair, I scoured the internet, looking for more information. I was skeptical at first and thought it was a gimmick. Mining for materials used in the so-called clean energy revolution had been the norm until your mother's tech came on the scene. It seemed impossible to imagine. When it all appeared to check out, she became my idol."

"Mom's my idol, too," Joy quietly added.

"You're really lucky, you know. Not only are your parents still alive, but they're probably the most impressive women I've ever met. Both of them. Do you think they'll figure out a way for us to attend that summit?"

Joy smiled as she briefly caught Sadie's eye. "They will. Although, it might mean we have to don a disguise. My Aunt Kim is a different kind of genius."

"Why would we need to wear disguises?" Sadie asked.

"I doubt my moms want anyone to know who we are. Keeping a low profile has kept us all safe over the years. Mama T never changed her name, but Mama C has an alter ego when she's in public. It would make sense for Mama C to attend the summit as Heather Stiles, the lead attorney for Solar Flair. That's her alter ego," Joy explained.

"Wow! Is she really an attorney?" Joy asked.

"Yeah, she is. A brilliant one, too. Corporate law is her specialty. It was a way for her to get close to some very unsavory characters. Unfortunately, there are a lot of those in the corporate world." Joy pulled into Sadie's driveway and put the car in park.

"Do you want to come in?" Sadie asked.

"You're not tired of me yet?" Joy teased.

"Not at all. Besides, it will delay the ribbing I'll surely get from Carson. I might also need an objective observer if your mom's statement is accurate and Carson still has feelings for me."

Joy unclipped her seatbelt. "Okay. I'd love to come in, but I won't stay long. You still look a little pale to me. Are you planning on going to work tomorrow?"

"Yeah. It might actually work to my advantage to show up looking a little worse for the wear because I'm going to ask for a leave of absence. Do you think your mom can create false documents on my health, proving my need to take a medical leave? Carson suggested that Marks is in bed with the US Government because in all the time I've been there, I haven't found any damning evidence on that slimy bastard. The NSA has been more focused on finding out about The Organization."

Joy frowned. "Yeah, we know."

"Don't worry, though. The NSA doesn't have much more than a vague knowledge you exist except that you're predominantly badass women and a suspicion that your group is behind the attacks on the mines. Getting Marks takes top priority. If they turn down my leave request, I'll just quit. I get the sense that I don't need to be at the NSA anymore to obtain the information I need on Marks. You and Toni seem more than qualified to break into the NSA anytime you want." Sadie carefully emerged from the car and wobbled a little before Joy was right there by her side.

"You are still sick. Maybe I should stay the night?" Joy suggested.

"I'm okay. I was just a little dizzy for a second. While I wouldn't mind that one bit, Carson will be relentless in her teasing."

Joy wrapped her arm around Sadie's waist and walked with her to the door. "I can take a little teasing. Can you?" Joy grinned.

Sadie pulled out her keys and started to unlock the door. "Carson must be home." Opening the door, she called, "Hey, Carson. Hurry and put your clothes back on; I'm home."

Carson and Randi looked cozy on the couch as Carson lazily glanced in their direction. "Haha. If we were actually having sex, it wouldn't be in the living room. All my toys are in the bedroom," Carson quipped. "We were just chilling." After Joy and Sadie came closer, Carson jumped from the couch. "What the fuck happened to you? You look like shit, Sades."

The concerned look on Carson's face signaled how much she cared for Sadie. Joy thought her mom might be spot-on about Carson's feelings. But would that be a problem? Joy didn't know the answer to that.

Sadie waved her hand in the air and avoided eye contact with Carson. "I'm fine. A twenty-four-hour bug. I'll be good as new in the morning."

"I can stay with her tonight in case she needs anything," Joy offered.

Carson narrowed her eyes. "There's something you're not telling me. What gives, Sades? You've never lied to me before."

Fuck the consequences. Joy was not about to let Sadie shoulder the burden. She knew what it felt like to lie to someone she cared about. Even if Carson still loved Sadie, Joy believed she would never do anything to put The Organization at risk if she learned the truth.

Joy glanced at Sadie and nodded. "It's okay to tell her."

"You sure?" Sadie asked.

Randi interjected, "Um, your moms aren't going to be happy."

"What the fuck is going on? Can all of you stop with the riddles? It's like I've been invited to play a game, and everyone knows the rules but me," Carson huffed and turned her attention to Randi. "How the hell are you involved in all of this?"

Sadie swayed a little. "I think I need to sit. Carson, can you get me a glass of water? Then we'll all gather in the living room, and I'll fill you in on a few missing details I failed to share with you when I called."

†

Sadie sipped her glass of water, waiting for Carson to return to the couch. She ventured one last look at Joy, who merely nodded before Sadie launched into a thorough explanation of the previous twenty-four hours of her life. Joy added a few details to the story, particularly about her moms and The Organization. Sadie specifically omitted the part about Toni wanting to put bots in Carson, and Toni and Char's theory that Carson was still in love with her. Miraculously, Carson remained quiet, absorbing all the details until Sadie stopped talking.

Carson turned to Randi and stated, "So, you're a part of this organization? Did they send you to spy on me, or do I also have these foreign bodies in me?"

Randi held her hands up. "Not for lack of trying, but no, my moms won't let me join until I finish school. They're even more overprotective than Char and Toni. Although, I can see how you might not believe that with the drastic measures they took to protect Joy. But, uh, they did call and ask me to be extra perceptive."

"Extra perceptive? What the fuck does that mean? Do I have these bots in me or not?" Carson's voice took on a hard edge.

"You don't. I argued that it wasn't necessary. They gave me a week to convince them of your, uh…" Sadie didn't know precisely how to put into words Toni and Char's concerns.

"My what?" Carson met each person's eyes with her singular focus, practically willing them to spill whatever they were hiding from her.

Finally, Joy, with her quiet voice, filled in the blanks. "After seeing how you interact with Sadie, they worried you might still be in love with Sadie, making you a potential risk to the knowledge of our existence."

Carson sat back and nodded. "I see. So, if that's such a concern, why did you decide to tell me everything?"

Sadie noted Carson didn't deny that she still had those feelings, which did not bode well for their rash decision to come clean. "Because, Carson, I know you. There is no way you would put anyone I care about at risk. And I can totally see you joining The Organization. There's a reason you were on their radar. If I believed in a higher power, I'd think she molded you specifically for this purpose. I never thought the FBI suited you. Strict rules aren't exactly your cup of tea."

Carson glanced at Randi again. "Seems to me that you are part of this organization if they've tasked you with evaluating me. You'll do well. I had no idea your interest was strictly professional curiosity about my suitability as an agent."

"Whoa. Not true at all," Randi defended. "Toni and Char did not call me to spy on you. Alina filled me in on everything, but that was after we started hanging out. So get it out of your pride-infested head that the only reason I'm here is to check out your loyalties. I would never do that. Honestly, I haven't even settled on joining The Organization because I'm not cut out for subterfuge. Action, adrenaline rushes, kicking-ass, sure, but nerdy stuff or disguises aren't my thing."

"If you want to blame someone, turn your attention to me. I'm the one who suggested that Randi do an objective assessment since you were spending time with her and showed some interest," Sadie interjected.

Carson laughed. "Pride-infested. Okay, I guess you nailed that. Sounds like this organization is exactly what I'm looking for. I'm in as long as you swear on our friendship that I will not have to go through what you did to expel those bots. You can tell them I'd love to work with Sophie. That woman is a total badass. Can you guys get me included in the White House Summit assignment?" Carson grinned.

"Fuck. Everyone around me is having fun and getting action. I hate having to live vicariously through all of you. It's so unfair," Randi grumbled.

"You have what? Less than a year to finish school? Easy peasy. It will go by quickly," Carson mollified before shooting Sadie a smile. "Oh, and for the record, of course, I still love you, Sadie. You were my first love who became my best friend. But I'm also smart enough to recognize that we don't work as lovers. In this instance, opposites might attract but don't meet the test of time. You and Joy will, though. Anyone with eyes can see that. Above all, as your best friend, I want you to be happy. Besides, I have my eye on someone new that's more compatible on multiple levels," she added as her eyes shifted to Randi.

Randi grinned. "Good to know. If only my moms were as cool as Joy's. Speaking of the moms, who is going to tell them that Carson is in?"

"Draw straws?" Joy joked.

Randi shook her head. "No way. Either you or Sadie should. I bet they still feel guilty about putting those bots in Sadie. You can use that to your advantage. I'll back you up with my assessment that Carson's solid, and it was a good decision to jump the gun."

"Fine. I'll tell them," Joy offered. "But I think I should help Sadie settle into her bedroom before I call them." She shifted her worried eyes to Sadie.

"You should stay with her tonight," Carson suggested. She held up her hands. "I promise, no teasing. You aren't planning on going to work tomorrow, are you?"

"I was. Looking like shit will help me sell the need for a leave of absence to address my health issues."

"When I talk with Mama T tonight, I'll let her know you need supporting evidence, and she can whip that up for you." Joy grabbed her chin. "Look, I was thinking that just because you haven't been able to find anything about Marks at the NSA doesn't mean it doesn't exist. It's a vast organization. It would be nearly impossible to control every lever. Maybe you should tell them you managed to recruit me for that position they offered. Two people working from the inside are better than one."

"But the whole point of taking a leave is to focus on the mission to decimate Marks' fortune," Sadie argued.

"You can't honestly believe that he's the only problem? Granted, taking him out will be a major blow, but at the very least, the US Government is complicit in all his dirty dealings. From the start, you had the right idea—to work from the inside. As my moms always say, you must first find the snake's head before you can cut it off. In this case, there are multiple heads, and cutting off one won't get us to our ultimate goal."

"I hate to burst your little bubble, but I'm a bit of a Greek mythology nerd, and I believe the story about the Hydra is applicable here. When you cut off one head, two grow back. Hercules was able to defeat the Hydra with the help of his companion, Iolaus, who cauterized the necks so the Hydra couldn't grow back any heads," Randi interjected.

"So what is the modern equivalent of cauterizing the neck?" Joy asked.

Randi shrugged. "Beats me."

"Wasn't the lesson more about teamwork?" Sadie suggested. "Maybe we don't have to worry about a symbolic cauterizing of the neck."

Joy sighed. "Doubtful. The Organization has been fighting for over thirty years, and every time they took care of one asshole, another rose in the ranks and filled the void. I don't think it's possible to cauterize greed or power. In humanity's long history, no one has ever managed to do that."

"So why do y'all continue to stick your necks out if it's a useless fight?" Carson asked.

"I didn't say it was useless," Joy answered. "What if no one was there to stop Hitler? Obviously, over the years, The Organization has done a lot of good. I just meant that we have to be realistic and feel okay about cutting off as many heads as possible, even knowing new ones will take their place in the future."

Carson grinned. "Works for me."

"Me, too," Sadie answered.

"Besides, I'm all about the adrenaline rush. I'd hate to think that after we nail Marks, my life will turn boring," Carson quipped.

"Nothing worse than a boring life. One more year, and I can join the fight." Randi held up her fist for Carson to bump.

Joy stood and offered her hand. "Time to get you tucked into bed. After you're settled, I'll call the moms with an update and then, um, join you. Is that okay?" A flush started on Joy's neck and made its way to her face.

Sadie thought Joy's blush was adorable. She smiled and took Joy's hand. "Very okay."

†

Joy had settled Sadie and stepped into the living room to make her call. Not wanting to disturb Carson and Randi, who had their heads bent together, murmuring who knows what, Joy moved to the back patio and pressed the button on her phone. A gray tabby blinked their green eyes, watching warily from a perch on the patio. The feline's tail flicked from side to side, indicating irritation with a strange woman presumably invading what Joy suspected was their territory. Joy smiled. She wondered if the cat was Sadie's or Carson's. Her attention turned to her mother who had answered her call.

"Hey, baby. Everything okay? Sadie didn't take a turn for the worse, did she?" Char asked.

"No, she's okay. Still kind of weak, but she insists on going to work tomorrow because she's going to ask for a short leave of absence, freeing her to devote all her time to this upcoming mission. Is Mama T available?"

Toni's face entered the screen. "Right here, hon. What do you need?"

"Can you create some fake documentation on Sadie's need for a leave of absence?" Joy asked. "Something that would require her to be out for the next month."

"No problem. I can have that sent directly to the NSA as if it came from her physician," Toni answered.

Char narrowed her eyes. "There's something else you wanted to tell us, and you think we aren't going to like it. You have that guilty, pinched look."

"Um, yeah. I need to update you on a couple other items." Joy rushed to tell them everything in a few short sentences. "I'll just rip off the bandage. Carson knows everything. She's in. Sadie is going to tell the NSA that I plan on accepting their job offer."

"I see." Char turned her head to look at Toni. "Are you sure you didn't splice your DNA with my egg? Not only did our daughter get your brains, she got your impulsivity as well." Char shook her head.

Toni shrugged. "What's wrong with going on intuition? If Joy sensed Carson is solid, who are we to second guess her assessment?"

"Thanks, Mama T. Mama C, I know you wanted us to take our time and evaluate Carson, but we didn't have a viable option. Carson is scary perceptive. She knew something was off. So I made an executive decision, and I stand by it," Joy insisted.

Char pinched the bridge of her nose. "All right. I'm trusting your judgment, and I hope it does not come back to bite us all. I assume when you stated Carson was in, you meant she wants to join the mission to get Marks' biometric data."

Joy nodded. "Yup. She's eager to work with Sophie, too. Um, Carson already pegged Sophie, which I believe goes to her suitability for The Organization."

"Impressive. Okay, let's back up to the part where you've decided to take the job with the NSA. Can you share your rationale on that?"

"Besides the fact that they're a little too interested in us, I think working from the inside might help us uncover other individuals associated with Marks. We've always thought the US Government has its fingers in the pie. I plan on getting that proof. With both of us employed at the NSA, we're bound to discover something," Joy explained. "I'll agree to a start date after we take care of Marks."

Char shared a look with Toni, who grinned. "We're very proud of you, Joy."

Joy wanted to dance with glee. The conversation had gone so much better than expected. Her parents were finally seeing her as a capable adult. "Thanks, Moms Squared. I'm staying with Sadie tonight just to make sure she's okay. She was still weak when I tucked her in earlier."

"Good idea. We like her. She's good for you," Char added.

Joy smiled. "I think so, too. By the way, I don't think you have to worry about Carson and her feelings for Sadie. She does still love her but recognizes they aren't a match made in heaven. I believe her interest in Randi is growing. I definitely see a spark between the two of them."

"Randi could do worse than Carson, and vice versa. Hopefully, that won't cause problems. Seeing everyone around her involved in The Organization and going on missions is bound to drive Randi up the wall. We had better prepare ourselves for a call from Em and Jimena. Thanks a lot for that," Toni joked.

Joy held her hands in the air. "Hey, I don't control love. Far from it."

CHAPTER FOURTEEN

While Toni and Char weren't exactly pleased by the news that Sadie, Joy, and Randi had confessed everything to Carson, Toni convinced Char that if they couldn't trust their daughter, who was as bright and perceptive as any seasoned agent, they couldn't trust anyone. Char had also dragged Toni out of the lab, stating she needed a break. They had time before the summit to set their plans in motion. Char had a way of incentivizing everything. After all their years together, the magic had not departed. Like any couple, they'd had their rough moments, with The Organization's missions creating unique challenges. But they'd worked through every single one, and Toni could honestly say she both loved and lusted after her wife as much, if not more, than the day she realized she could never let this woman go. After a particularly satisfying night of sex, Toni grumbled loudly when her videophone alerted her to a call early the following day.

Grabbing her phone, her face scrunched in confusion when she saw that former President Sandra Murphy was calling. "Sandra?" she groggily answered.

Char sat up in bed and shot Toni a questioning look.

"Hang on, Sandra. Let me put you on speaker. I'd rather not activate video mode because, uh, we're…"

Sandra's tinkle of laughter eased some of Toni's concern. "Sorry, I guess it's a little early. Look, the reason I'm calling is that I caught the chatter about you agreeing to join the summit. What are you up to now, Toni?"

Toni glanced at her wife, who smiled and nodded. After so many years together, they could practically read each other's thoughts. Char had quickly put together the pieces, seeing an opportunity that had just fallen into their laps.

"I take it you'll be there as well?" Toni responded.

"Washington politics. President Dawson believes he'll gain favor with a certain faction by inviting me. You know that I still care a great deal about clean energy and where the major players source their raw materials. If I can have any influence on future policy, I'm not going to pass that up. My foundation can only do so much education regarding information to the masses to put pressure on the politicians. But to say I was more than a little surprised to learn you were attending as well is an understatement. Isn't that an enormous risk?"

"We're going after Alvin Marks," Char declared.

"And we need your help to get a few people invited. I can insist that Char accompanies me as Heather Stiles, Solar Flair's attorney, to protect my interests, but we also need Sophie, Val, Joy, Sadie, and Carson to attend. This may be our only chance to gather everything we need to take him down."

"Who are Sadie and Carson?" Sandra asked.

"Sadie currently works for the NSA in their cyber security. She's someone Joy recently started dating. Bright young thing and a new recruit. Carson is a rookie FBI agent. She's Sadie's roommate and also a new member. Before we learned about her connection to Sadie, Sophie had her eyes on Carson. Oh, and to make the spiderweb even more intricate, we think Randi is dating Carson now. Long story."

"Randi? As in, Em and Jimena's daughter? Oh, shit. Do they have a clue about any of this?" Sandra asked.

"Nope. And we aren't going to upset that apple cart. Randi is in the know about certain things, but not everything. And we aren't letting her anywhere near this," Toni insisted. "So anyway, the rest of the crib notes are that Sadie is extremely motivated for reasons that aren't important to share. I think I can argue for two bodyguards besides my attorney, which leaves Carson, Joy, and Sadie. I'll tell them I must have my top two engineers, Sadie and Joy, accompany me as they have more details about the technology. They'll be in disguise. That leaves Carson. Can you get her added to your security detail?"

"Sure, I'll work it out. Send me all the pertinent details. Toni, you need to be careful. Alvin Marks is dangerous. He has some powerful allies, which is the only reason he hasn't been directly tied to the attempts on Grace's life and the attacks on your company. I think the man is part bloodhound, too. Marks can sniff out a threat better than anyone I've ever encountered. He's always given me the creeps."

Toni could almost hear Sandra shudder on the other end of the phone. "Yeah, we know the risks. But the rewards far surpass those hazards."

"We have a month to put together a plan. We'll spare you the details. Plausible deniability," Char teased.

"I'm no longer the president," Sandra noted. "I don't think I need that anymore."

"You're still a prominent figure in Washington politics and amongst the circle of movers and shakers. We don't want to lose that advantage for future missions that we may need your special assistance for," Char stated. "Like it or not, Sandra, we've long counted you as an ally and unofficial member of The Organization."

Sandra laughed. "Wait until I tell Wynter that. You know she's always wanted to be considered an official agent in The Organization."

"Who said anything about Wynter?" Toni joked.

"Oh, now Toni, you know she'll be crushed to hear you say that." Sandra chuckled.

"We'll be in touch," Char said. "After this is all over, any chance you can handpick certain secret service agents to accompany you and visit with us at the compound? It's been ages since we've seen you."

"We'd love that. I'll make it happen," Sandra replied.

After Toni ended the call, Char asked, "Are we ready to set up a meeting and bring all the players together to share our plan?"

"As ready as we'll ever be. Kim is going to love this. She told me she had so much fun in Mexico and wondered why we rarely use her talents." Toni grinned.

"Goddess, I love that woman." Char brushed her hand across Toni's cheek.

157

Annette Mori

"Me, too. The Organization hit the jackpot when y'all recruited us all those years ago," Toni crowed.

"Yes, we did, my love, yes we did. In more ways than one." Char leaned in to kiss her wife.

†

Sadie had fully recovered from the expulsion process and was downright giddy at the prospect of planning their assault on Marks. Joy had swung by to pick up Sadie after completing the massive amount of paperwork the NSA required in their onboarding process. Although Joy wasn't scheduled to officially start for several weeks, she wanted to get all the background checks and other red tape out of the way.

They both knew Sadie had completely recovered from the effects of the serum used to expel the bots, but Sadie wasn't about to refuse Joy's company. Neither had ventured into sexual intimacy territory, but it was certainly nice to have Joy beside her every night. Surprisingly, Joy had no issues cuddling with Sadie. Beta had even accepted her presence, worming his way onto her pillow every night, which Joy eagerly embraced, confessing she'd always wanted a cat.

The ever-present shyness vanished as they crawled under the covers each night, and Joy wrapped her arms around Sadie in an adorably protective gesture. The ruse was both a blessing and a curse. If Sadie were completely honest, she'd have to admit that she craved more from Joy. She was ready to take things to the next level. Six days of feeling Joy through the thin material of her sleep clothes was driving

158

Sadie to complete distraction. All she could envision was letting her fingers and tongue map every inch of Joy's body. She'd have to broach the topic soon—for both their sakes because she could tell Joy had the same pent-up energy.

Joy rolled to the sprawling compound and put the car in park. "You nervous?"

Sadie shook her head. "No, more like excited to finally get things moving. Any chance you can share what to expect?"

"The team planning to attend the summit will gather in the main conference room. First, Mama C, as our leader, will lay out the plan. Then, anyone on the core team can offer suggestions or poke holes in what she presents to the group," Joy explained.

"Anyone?"

Joy glanced in the rearview mirror, and Sadie turned her head to see what had distracted Joy. Carson and Randi pulled up in Randi's new Solar Flair sports car. Never one for rules, Carson had allowed Randi to con her into dragging her to the meeting with them, even though she wasn't supposed to be part of the mission. She argued it was easier to ask for forgiveness than permission. Randi wholeheartedly agreed and convinced Joy to go along with it. If anyone had sway over Char and Toni, it was Joy.

Joy sucked in a large breath. "Yeah, anyone, even you, if that is what you were asking."

"So maybe they'll go for our plan to let Randi be involved without putting her directly in the path of danger," Sadie answered.

"It's not really Mama C and Mama T we have to convince."

Sadie stared at Joy in confusion. "So, who do we need to win over?"

"Her moms," Joy declared without a smile. "And honestly, Jimena is a tiny force. Way scarier than both my moms combined. She's got that fiery Latina thing going. But we won't have to convince Aunt Jimena and Aunt Em; that'll be Mama C's job. She'd never let us approach Aunt Jimena without laying the first stone."

Carson knocked on the passenger window, and Sadie jumped. "What the hell, Carson."

"You two coming, or are you negotiating the next time you plan on having sex?" Carson grinned.

Sadie flipped Carson off, hit the button to unbuckle her seatbelt, and pushed open the door, causing Carson to stumble back. Randi stood to the side, laughing. "Better check that cocky attitude of yours, Carson. These women can run circles around you without even trying."

Carson smirked. "We'll see about that. I put Sophie on her ass. I think I can hold my own."

"You haven't met Aunt Val yet," Joy mumbled. "I'd suggest that we—"

Randi interrupted, "Yup, Aunt Val is not someone you want to challenge. There isn't a person alive, man or woman, who can best her."

"Stop talking," Joy finished.

"Tchh. If she's as old as Sophie, I seriously doubt that." Carson sneered.

An imposing woman that Sadie had never met before with sandy blonde hair and piercing gray eyes, opened the door and scowled. "What the fuck are you all waiting for? An engraved invitation to enter?" Her demeanor instantly changed when her eyes shifted to Joy. Her lips turned up in a half smile. She jerked her head at Sadie. "This your new girlfriend, Joy?"

Joy smiled. "Uh, we haven't uh…"

Sadie took over. Sure, they hadn't completely defined their relationship, but she was confident they both felt the same way. "Yes, I'm Sadie Harris." She stuck out her hand in greeting. "And you are?"

"Aunt Val, the one that's going to kick that one's ass for showing disrespect." Val pointed to Carson. "After my lesson with you, Carson, I hope you will never forget that I'm not Sophie."

Carson gulped. "How did you?"

Val smirked. "The nerd's got this compound wired. You'd be surprised what you can discover with technology. Over the years, I've learned to give Toni the respect she's earned." Val cupped her hand over her mouth and whispered, "But don't ever tell her I said that. So, Carson, don't underestimate your elders."

Her eyebrow rose when her eyes landed on Randi, and she shook her head. "Hey Randi, your moms know you're here?"

"Not exactly," Randi mumbled.

"Hopefully, Carson hasn't injected you with her special brand of arrogance." Val smiled.

"Uh, no, I'm the one who pushed the issue with her. She just agreed to support me," Randi admitted.

Val gave the two young women an appraising look and smiled. "Mm, I see. I suppose there's a bit more I need to catch up on." Val slung her arm around Joy and led her into the main house. "Come on, mini-nerd, the rest of the team is waiting." She turned her head to catch Randi's eye. "You too, Randi. I'll do whatever I can to help you out."

"Thanks, Aunt Val," Randi answered with a wide grin and fist pump after Val turned around.

Sadie shared a look with Carson and grinned as the rest of the junior team followed Joy and Randi. She'd never seen anyone put Carson in her place.

†

Char shot Toni a warning look, but Toni couldn't help it. She burst out laughing as she held the tablet in her hand, watching the interaction between Val and the kids. She still thought of them as kids, even though they were all grown women.

"Sorry, but that was classic Val," Toni said.

"Keep laughing, and I'll make you call Jimena and Em," Char threatened

Toni clamped her mouth shut as the troupe shuffled into the large conference room.

"Sit," Char directed. "Randi, I will give you the courtesy of explaining why you're here first. This better be good."

Randi slinked into a chair and began her argument. "I know the moms and I have a deal, but I thought this might be the best way to ease into the inevitable. I have less than a year to finish college, and then they promised I could join. What's the harm in sitting in on a strategy session for a mission that isn't going to include bombs, guns, and darts? From what I understand about this mission, it's low risk. No fighting. I know it might be pushing it a little, but we kind of thought I could be helpful as tech support. Everyone inside the summit will be concentrating on getting Marks' biometrics, right?"

"That's the broad strokes, yes," Char agreed.

"Wouldn't it be helpful to have someone on the outside listening in on conversations when you aren't in close proximity to Marks? I could monitor those and give you on-the-spot intel. If shit is about to go sideways, I could let you know. I know Aunt Toni has a way of placing listening bugs on anyone she wants to."

Toni grinned and nodded her head until Char sent her a warning look. But what the hell, Toni was never one to hold her opinions inside. "It's not the worst idea in the world, Char. Sandra warned us about Marks, and I tend to agree with her assessment."

Char glared at Toni. "Then we'll pull Val or Sophie, and they can monitor those conversations. Two bodyguards might be overkill, anyway."

"Please, Aunt Char. Just talk to my moms. It's so unfair that everyone but me gets to be involved," Randi pleaded.

"Not true," Char answered. "Pepper, Alina, Grace, and Maria are not joining this mission."

Randi crossed her arms and groaned. "How is it possible that my moms are scarier to you than Aunt Val?"

Val put her hand over her mouth to stifle a laugh. "Good question, Char."

Char narrowed her gaze at Val. "They're not scarier than you, especially when you're safeguarding Pepper. Nothing more terrifying than a mama bear protecting her cubs." Char smiled. "Okay, I'll make you a deal. You get to convince your moms, that isn't my job. If they give you the okay, you will accompany either Val or Sophie, who will be lead in the support vehicle. Your choice. You don't take a breath unless one of them authorizes it."

Randi grinned. "I'll take Aunt Val."

"Don't try to con me, either, Randi. I'll be checking with Em and Jimena."

Randi dropped her head. "Yes, ma'am."

"Oh, for fuck's sake. Don't ever call me ma'am again," Char gently chastised.

"Okay, Aunt Char." Randi lifted her head and grinned.

"Now, onto the plan…"

CHAPTER FIFTEEN

Although wigs had come a long way, it wasn't like wearing a beanie. Sadie resisted the urge to rearrange the mop of curly brown hair. The contacts weren't a big thing because Sadie had worn contacts since the age of sixteen. However, she did worry the built-in cameras might irritate her eyes. She blinked at herself as she looked in the mirror. Kim had done an outstanding job of transforming both her and Joy. She'd definitely be tempted to get a nose job if she'd been born with the one Kim fashioned for her. It wasn't that Sadie was vain or anything, but the sizable Roman nose did not fit with her petite, heart-shaped face, although Kim had remolded her face as well. Sadie had to admit that her new nose, in combination with the now square jawline, made sense. She was almost handsome.

Joy stepped next to her, her eyes transfixed to the mirror. Nothing remained of the gorgeous young woman Sadie had come to know more and more every day. An earnest young man stared back at them, complete with thick black glasses and thinning blond hair. Joy's eyes were an unremarkable dark blue, not her normal stunning green. Sadie's new eye color had transformed to an equally ordinary brown, several shades darker than her rare shade of amber. Unfortunately, if Joy got close enough to Marks to capture a clear enough picture of his iris, she would need to remove her thick glasses. They couldn't take the chance of having any glare or reflection to alter what they needed to access his bank accounts. Joy had practiced removing and cleaning her glasses, appearing as if this was a usual nervous habit.

"You ready?" Joy asked.

"Yes," Sadie answered with a measure of conviction she wasn't sure she had in her.

Toni and Char entered the room, and Sadie thought she'd never seen a more stunning couple. Neither had to don disguises because they were both going as themselves. The challenge for them was to interact as colleagues versus a married couple that Sadie could clearly see were still madly in love with one another.

Although Carson had grumbled, Char and Toni had finally convinced her that wearing a disguise gave her more options in the future with her chosen occupation. She could still pursue a career in the FBI while working for The Organization. Other agents had done that. Sadie held her hand over her mouth to stifle a laugh. While she'd gone to the masculine extreme, Carson's disguise was the exact opposite. When Carson had argued against the long, flowing blonde hair that she'd had to put up in a neat bun, Kim had chastised her for being sexist. Not all secret service agents were square-jawed former military elite. Carson had muttered that at least she got to carry a gun and didn't have to wear a dress. The suit, however, was not something she'd ever buy. She'd never be caught dead shopping in the women's section of a virtual store.

Sadie whistled at Carson. "Looking good, Carson. Nice suit." She smirked. "I never knew you had curves." Sadie laughed.

"Well, you're definitely no longer my type, in that..." Carson waved her hand up and down Sadie's body and around her face, "get-up."

"Good," Joy mumbled too low for anyone to hear but Sadie.

Sadie smiled to herself. She'd never seen that side of Joy before. Possessive, with a side of jealousy. She brushed her hand down Joy's arm and said, "No matter what you look like, I'll always want to date you. It's that big brain of yours that I'm attracted to. Your gorgeous red hair and stunning green eyes are just the cherries on the top."

"Sadie and Joy, you're with us. Carson, the SUV is in the driveway waiting for you. They'll give you comms that we'll be connected to as well," Char instructed. "Remember, we have numerous contingencies to get what we need. Take advantage of every one as the opportunities present themselves."

†

Joy had never seen so many secret service agents before. Sandra had brought her contingent, including Carson, who remained impassive as she walked into the large conference room and stood to the side with the other agents. Joy

167

recognized Hank and Steve and repressed her urge to smile at them and run over for a hug. When Marks entered with two men who looked like they just stepped out of a fantasy game with big, ugly giants, she saw her chance. He was whispering to his goons as she tripped and fell onto Carson, pushing her hard enough for Carson to stumble. Marks glanced up, noticed Carson, and laid a steadying hand on her arm. Joy could tell Carson was seething. She hated playing the damsel in distress, especially since she assumed that being a badass secret service agent would have kept her from adopting that persona, despite knowing that Marks had a weakness for attractive women. Joy grinned to herself after transferring two listening devices to the goons. Carson took care of attaching one to Marks as she forced a smile, thanking him for his steadying hand. Joy quickly murmured her apologies. No question, Marks was in deep with the Russians. She'd seen enough Russian mobsters to peg Marks' bodyguards as Russian-born, and when she heard them speak, it solidified her assessment.

Carson nodded to Marks and regained her rigid posture. One handprint down, as long as no one else touched Carson's jacket in the same spot. If they were lucky, Carson had also managed to take several digital photos of his face and close-ups of his irises. Joy caught Char's eye, seeing the approving look before she turned away.

The invited guests milled about, engaging in small talk as everyone waited for the president to arrive. Toni allowed Marks to approach her but kept her distance, staring at the offered hand before making a show of reluctantly accepting it. While her mother could charm the pants off any man or woman, she had a part to play. As an eccentric recluse, she wouldn't readily accept a handshake from anyone.

Since the trickiest part of the mission was obtaining a small amount of blood, everyone needed to do their part. They'd weaved in a considerable amount of redundancy. Joy couldn't tell if the tiny device Toni invented to collect blood from a pinprick that a target would barely feel worked until Marks narrowed his eyes and looked at his hand. Joy prayed the device had performed as it was supposed to, collecting a small sample without leaving a trace behind. Toni had been obsessed with vampire books where, after the bite, their vampire serum miraculously closed the wound. She didn't exactly want her device, which acted like a vampire bite, to give any pleasure like in those books, but not feeling the sting would be a bonus. In the end, she'd had to be satisfied with an almost imperceptible prick that might feel like a mosquito bite or nothing at all, depending on the person, and the gel used to close whatever tiny hole was left from the collection device.

As luck would have it, Marks took a seat at the large conference table next to Char. He smiled at her while narrowing his eyes at Toni. Things seemed to go too smoothly. It couldn't be this easy. With a sleight of hand, Char had already dumped the bots into Marks' glass of water, and Joy was sure she'd captured several pictures of his iris since she was so close to him.

Comms sputtered in Joy's ear. And that's when she knew that when it seems too good to be true, it usually is just that.

"Don't let Marks or his bodyguards anywhere near Toni. They've got some kind of poison and plan on taking her out. Joy and Sadie need to watch out as well. They aren't satisfied with getting Toni. They also want to take out her top engineers."

Sophie's eyes turned into granite as she swiveled her head, trying to determine the best course of action. Toni smiled serenely, as if she didn't have a care in the world, while Joy's heart pounded in her chest. Val, Sophie, or Char would never let anything happen to Toni. She didn't know enough about Carson to determine if she'd stick her neck out for a woman she'd just met. However, when Carson narrowed her eyes, and a hard, determined look completely overtook her face, Joy felt certain she would.

Former President Sandra Murphy was not an agent, but she also had been around The Organization long enough to pick up on subtleties that others might not. The seat next to Toni was vacant, and Sandra quickly made her way to the empty place. At first, Joy didn't understand why she'd done that, as Joy and Sadie were about to settle into the chairs next to Toni, but later after the meeting had concluded, the fog lifted, and Joy could have kissed Sandra for that strategic move.

It happened so quickly that Joy wasn't sure what had actually occurred. Marks signaled for his bodyguards, and they approached quickly on a path that would take them close to Toni. With Char on the other side, Sandra flanked Toni, creating a partial bubble, leaving her front and back vulnerable to attack. Carson didn't hesitate to act, and Joy had difficulty deciphering what had transpired other than some kind of altercation with the two bodyguards. The other secret service agents quickly closed ranks, detaining the two guards, while the rest shuffled the president out of the room. Marks was complaining loudly about the treatment his bodyguards were getting. Still, two secret service agents assigned to the sitting president sided with Sandra's security detail, leading the Russians out of the room, with Marks trailing behind, threatening to bring legal action.

"What the hell just happened?" Sadie whispered to Joy.

"I don't know. Let's get the fuck out of here before someone makes another attempt." Joy murmured her response loud enough for Sadie and the rest of the team to hear but low enough that other summit participants wouldn't notice.

Joy's comm crackled in her ear.

"Marks made a call. He has a backup plan. No time to explain. Don't get into your car. Find the SUV instead," Val ordered. "I'll deal with it."

"Don't let Randi go with you," Char directed. "Soph, find Val and help her."

"I'm coming, too," Carson interrupted.

"No, Soph and Val can handle it. Get that jacket off and protect your sleeve. We need that handprint. Stick with Sandra. That's an order," Char commanded.

"I've got the location of the SUV, heading there now after making a short pit-stop. Sandra, our contingency plan is in play now. We'll need your help," Toni added. "Come on, girls, Sandra is going to show us to a location where we're going to make some last-minute alterations to our appearance."

In the chaos, Hank and Steve led the group to a location Joy didn't even know existed. Sandra grinned as they weaved their way through the White House to the secret passageway. Carson dutifully followed.

"Mom, the handshake. What if Marks already injected you?" Joy asked.

Toni shrugged. "He might have, but lucky for us, I planned for that possibility. Although, I don't believe my serum to counteract the poison is strong enough for a double or triple dose. If the bodyguards planned on giving me more love, I'd probably be toast in a few hours. I guess Marks is a redundancy kind of man, too."

"You're joking about this?" Joy asked with a fair amount of incredulity. "You knew this would happen," she huffed.

"We had our suspicions," Char noted. "The Russians are nothing if not consistent."

When they reached the room, Toni grabbed the large duffel and began handing out clothing, wigs, and other articles. She directed Sadie and Joy to remove their prosthetics and change into the clothes she held out for them. It was much simpler for Sadie and Joy to transform since they were removing items versus adding something to their appearance. Joy saw her mother grab a syringe with a needle and plunge it into her thigh.

Toni grinned. "Hope this serum isn't as nasty as the one I gave you, Sadie."

"It's untested? Shit, Mama T, why do you have to be so reckless?" Joy huffed.

"You got something in there for me to change into?" Carson interrupted, and Joy decided they didn't have time for a lengthy discussion over details both her mothers had kept from her.

"Nope, you stick with Sandra. You'll be riding with her as part of her secret service detail. There isn't a need for you to break character," Char explained. "Unfortunately, we can't take that chance. Marks is targeting us, and I'm sure he'll consider the collateral damage a bonus. Taking out Toni's attorney and lead engineers solves all his issues with Solar Flair. He wasn't interested in Sandra. To our knowledge," Char added.

"This way," Sandra directed.

"Randi, bring the SUV close to the Treasury Building," Char ordered.

"We'll find you," Toni added. "I have your tracking signal on my phone."

"On my way," Randi excitedly responded.

Joy was glad the new comms didn't require any activation, but if necessary, each agent could turn them off and on with a remote. Unless deactivated, the comms looped everyone into the conversation once a team member started speaking. Except for Carson, Sadie, and Randi, all the agents in The Organization knew to keep the chatter to a minimum, avoiding a chaotic stream of conversation.

Once they made it to the SUV, Char almost casually stated, while holding out her hand, "You don't need your comms anymore."

Joy narrowed her eyes and shook her head. "No way, Mama C, you aren't locking us out of whatever update Aunt Val or Aunt Sophie plan on providing."

As they all climbed into the RV, a grinning Randi blurted, "You are not going to believe what I just learned." She pushed one side of the headphones back as her neck craned around to make eye contact with Toni, who joined Sadie and Joy in the back seat.

†

Toni's eager eyes shined when Randi shared that she was dying to report something of import, but her comm crackled in her ear, and she couldn't absorb two updates at once. Holding up her finger and pointing to the invisible comm, Randi nodded in understanding and placed the headphone back on her ear. Putting the car in gear, she eased into the DC traffic.

"I had to call Ronda in for her expertise. The assholes planted a bomb in your car. I didn't want to take the chance that I might cut the wrong wires," Val informed. "We'll transport your car back to the compound once Ronda is satisfied she's disarmed all their gifts."

"Did they get away?" Toni asked.

"No, but we're still working on tying up loose ends. Two professionals with enhanced bomb-making and fighting skills. Honestly, I'm unsure how much information we can get from them. Best-case scenario, we tie them to the bombs and let the capitol police take over. Unless you prefer an alternate solution," Val let the suggestion hang in the air like a dark cloud.

"Take them out," Char stated with cold fury. "They targeted the wrong people. Sadie and Joy were in the car with us. Marks wants a war, he'll get one."

Toni glanced at her wife before hearing Val state, "It'll be my pleasure. Consider it done."

"Do you need us to send a clean-up team?" Toni asked.

"Nope, we got this," Val answered. "Fuck the old adage that playing with fire will get you burned; those that play with bombs, well—"

"The kids are still on the comms, Val," Char warned. "We'll meet you at the compound for a debrief."

"Got it," Val answered.

174

Toni turned and caught Sadie's wide-eyed expression as Joy took her hand. She couldn't worry about how Sadie reacted to the interchange. Randi had something to tell them, and Toni suspected it was huge.

"Sorry, Randi, what were you about to say?" Toni asked. When she didn't answer, Char tapped Randi on the shoulder and took the headphones from her ears, placing them on her head.

"I'll monitor the communication while you tell Toni what you learned," Char instructed.

Without taking her eyes off the road, Randi blurted, "President Dawson and Marks are in bed together. The two secret service agents are also loyal to Marks and President Dawson."

"I knew there was a reason to hate that slimy little toad-face," Toni answered.

"Duh, there are a lot of reasons to hate that prick," Joy added. "He's been trying to take us back to the dark ages when the rash of ruby-red states began passing all those draconian laws. It took years to unravel that mess. Sandra had to work really hard to swing the country back to some semblance of normalcy."

Toni laughed. "How the hell do you know that? You were the size of a peanut in Char's belly when that was happening and a toddler when Sandra got into office."

"History, Mama T. Sandra managed to turn things around, so they actually taught an accurate version to us," Joy stated.

Sadie finally entered the conversation. "I can't believe how casually you all discuss things? You're on a first-name basis with former President Sandra Murphy. She's like an idol of mine."

175

Joy shrugged. "The Organization is responsible for keeping Sandra alive. She's a close friend of our extensive chosen family. Her and Wynter. So, um, are you okay with the earlier conversation between Aunt Val and Mama C?"

"I think so," Sadie answered hesitantly. "I knew Marks was a bastard, but I didn't realize how far he was willing to take things. Can't you use the communication Randi intercepted to take him down, along with President Dawson?"

"Unfortunately, no," Toni answered. "The old ways of leaking something to the press no longer work because artificial intelligence has gotten so good that the press or justice department can't easily verify the evidence. And as we learned back in the dark ages, even holding a former president accountable is damn near impossible. A sitting president is another matter entirely."

"So, what are you planning on doing? We can't just let them both get away with attempted murder and everything else they're doing!" Sadie exclaimed.

"I know Carson got one handprint, but that might not be complete enough. Besides, don't we need both in case he uses an alternative hand?" Joy asked.

Toni grinned. "You underestimate your mother. She should have been a magician. Do you honestly believe she would let the chaos of the situation keep her from lifting prints from absolutely everything that man touched?"

"She got the bots into his water, right? Are they working yet?" Sadie asked.

"Don't worry. Everything is being recorded back at the lab, including all the conversations that Randi and Val monitored and both visual and audio from Marks that came online twenty minutes ago. My new long-lasting bots will give us data for the next two months. Every single evil plan. He won't know what hit him. I feel confident we'll learn something about President Dawson as well. They're both going down," Toni stated with supreme confidence.

Joy smiled. "I guess you're learning patience after all, Mama T. I can't believe you didn't have a tablet in that bag of extra clothing. You're actually going to wait to start listening in?"

Toni grinned. "It only took me nearly fifty years to learn a modicum of patience. I suppose Char has been a good influence on me."

CHAPTER SIXTEEN

Alvin Marks sat in a rich brown leather chair, seething. Every little plan, including all his contingencies, had gone to shit. First, he'd felt the tiny prick intended for Toni and feared the needle got turned around. They'd assured him Toni would barely register the tiny prick, but Marks supposed he was hyperaware, knowing he'd been given a golden opportunity. However, instead of Toni getting the full first dose of poison, it was quite possible he had inadvertently dosed himself along with Toni. At least the incompetent scientists who had developed the device had provided something to counteract the poison. He'd gulped down his water, hoping to flood his system before administering the serum that would probably make him sick.

"What the fuck happened?" Marks yelled.

"Don't you shout at me," President Dawson retorted. "I arranged your fucking summit. What did you expect would happen when your thugs tried to get anywhere near former President Murphy? You're lucky my two agents controlled the situation. Do you have any idea what would have happened if Sandra's security detail had detained your bodyguards? Toni McFarland has a successful solar vehicle that puts yours to shame. So what? You have other businesses. Your reckless insistence on vengeance is going to be our undoing. Let this one go."

"Don't you get it? It's not just my cars, but I'd bet my entire fortune she's also behind sabotaging my mines. Your administration has its dirty fingers all over the mining business. I doubt the American public would be too pleased to know their president was cavorting with our enemies. We're supposed to be in a cold war with Russia and China. A few well-placed Bites, and you're done for."

"Don't you threaten me, Alvin. I'm the one keeping your ass out of jail. You don't control the Justice Department. I do. Don't ever forget that. We've had a symbiotic relationship up until this point, but I can easily decide you're a harmful parasite that I need to expunge," Dawson warned.

"Maybe you're right. Clearly, I picked the wrong horse for this race. If you honestly believe I don't have other well-placed personnel in your administration, you're more naïve than I thought." Marks stood. "Consider yourself free from both my influence and support. Have a nice day, Ronald." Nodding to his two men, he strode from the room, making a silent vow to himself that he'd ensure every single one of his enemies got precisely what they deserved.

†

Toni grimaced and popped another two pills into her mouth, gulping down half her glass of water. She was too ill to even kick everyone out of her lab. Not only had Sadie and Joy followed Char and her into the lab, but Carson made a beeline to the sprawling estate right after she was dropped off at her house. Ronda, Sophie, and Val had arrived around the same time and let her into the large building where everyone always seemed to gather of late.

Too sick to tell them all to quit hovering, Toni hunched over her main computer and attempted to ignore the crowd that had gathered. Earlier, she'd contacted Katrina, who was on standby, to use the limited biometrics for the accounts requiring everything but an in-person visit and Marks' DNA. Then there were his day-to-day spending accounts, what everyone considered low-hanging fruit, that any hacker with the account numbers and Joy or Sadie's skills could handle. She established a separate folder for those accounts, complete with the digitized retina, hand print, and voice recognition files, not knowing which would be required, if any.

"How come I was a last-minute invite to the party?" Ronda asked with irritation.

Char shifted her concerned gaze to Ronda and answered calmly, "Because we needed to remain as unobtrusive as possible. This was a mission requiring a minimal footprint. Using explosives is anything but discreet. I hate to admit it, but we underestimated Marks and what he was willing to do. Clearly, he didn't concern himself with discretion."

Ronda crossed her arms over her chest. "Well, clearly, you needed my expertise," she grumbled.

"Yes, thank you for stepping up." Shifting her focus to her wife, Char noted, "Hon, you don't look so good. I'm getting Cindy. I'm glad you went with an injectable. It's faster acting."

"Yeah, I already poked myself twice with the serum, and you know how much I hate needles." Toni held up her hand. "Don't call me a baby." She managed a weak smile. "I'll be fine. No need to get Attila the Medic. You know what would make me feel a lot better?"

"What?" Char asked.

"Get everyone to clear out of my lab," Toni huffed.

Val glanced at Sophie, Carson, and Ronda, and jerked her head. "Char, we'll head to the conference room to debrief. We'll meet you there after you get Toni squared away."

"Thanks, take the girls with you," Char directed. "I'll be there shortly."

"I'd rather stay with Mama T until I know she's turned a corner," Joy stated.

Sadie remained quiet but didn't make a move to leave when Sophie, Val, Carson, and Ronda exited the large lab.

Her stomach lurched for the fifth time in less than five minutes, and Toni jumped from the chair, rushing to the bathroom.

After the first purge, Toni heard Joy ask, "Is Mama T going to be okay?"

"Stay here with your mom while I get Cindy," Char answered.

Toni attempted to return to the lab with a modicum of dignity but wobbled and eventually allowed Joy to lead her to the insanely comfortable recliner. Char had brought it to the lab for those days and nights she insisted on remaining by

181

her side while Toni obsessed over a new mission. Char had been one of the few individuals she tolerated in her lab. Her wife had learned over the years to be in the same room without creating that claustrophobic feeling. Of course, Dani and Joy were always welcome, too, but that was different. They were fellow inventors and deep into the same projects that Toni became entangled with.

Before Toni could insist that she needed to monitor Marks, Joy stated, "Sadie or I can oversee the different channels. If we called Aunt Dani, I'll bet she'd come right over, too."

Her stomach lurched again, and Toni started to lift her body from the chair, but Joy gently laid a hand on her as Sadie brought over the small garbage can from the bathroom.

"Thought this might be helpful," Sadie said as she handed the can to Joy, who helped Toni direct the next stream of vomit into the can.

Toni feared she must look like she was on the verge of death because Cindy didn't bother to lecture her. Instead, the only words out of her mouth before she'd efficiently started an IV and collected a blood sample were, "Oh, Toni."

Char stroked her sweat-filled forehead and pushed her damp hair to the side. "Can you give her anything more that might help?"

"Maybe. I'm going to analyze the blood first. I need to know exactly what poison we're dealing with. If the serum that Toni injected into her body to counteract the effects isn't right, we'll need to adjust the antidote to target the poison more effectively."

"I used a broad-spectrum serum, effective with over fifty different known varieties of poison. I specifically targeted the ones popular with the Russians," Toni explained.

Cindy nodded. "Let's hope that's the reason for how ill you are right now and not the poison. Broad-spectrum anything tends to be harsher on the body. The quicker I run this blood, the faster we'll have our answer. Come get me if she gets any worse." Toni watched Cindy stride out of the room like her pants were in flames.

Toni's heart raced, and sweat beaded on her forehead. It felt like the blood pumping in her heart was pushing so hard against the muscle that it would explode any minute, leaving a bloody mess all over her pristine lab. A pain she'd never experienced converged in her chest with a kind of pressure that Toni imagined might be present in a heart attack as she envisioned someone squeezing her heart until it popped. That was the last thought she had before losing consciousness.

†

Sadie watched as Toni's eyes rolled into the back of her head, and her body went limp. She felt utterly powerless to do anything as Joy started to fall apart.

With surprising calmness, Char directed, "Get Cindy. I'll start CPR. Tell her to bring the defibrillator and miracle drug for reversing the effects of a heart attack."

Joy ran out of the room, and Sadie knew that, at a minimum, she could take over when Char tired. It had been years, but she'd learned because her family hadn't been affluent enough to carry the expensive drug or have a home defibrillator. After a few minutes, Sadie could see the sweat form on Char's brow. Her rhythm was slowing.

"Let me take over." Sadie gently touched Char's arm. "I know what I'm doing. Your compressions are too slow now."

Char nodded, and Sadie eased into position to begin the necessary chest compressions. She'd barely been at it for thirty seconds when she heard Cindy's directive. "I've got her now."

Sadie stepped aside and watched Cindy plunge the needle into her chest. Then, quickly attaching the leads from the portable defibrillator, she announced, "Clear."

Sadie saw Toni's body lift slightly, then settle. Char's face pinched with worry, and Joy was overtly crying as she stood to the side.

"Clear," Cindy said a second time, pressing the button to shock her again.

Sadie heard the slight intake of breath as Toni's eyes fluttered open. She had never been so relieved in her life.

"I guess that was awfully rude of me to nap during this amazing soiree we've all been invited to," Toni quipped.

Cindy, who was all business now, ignored Toni's joke and stated, "I think I know what poison they used, but it will be another hour or so before I've confirmed. In the meantime, I'm pushing an antidote that won't harm Toni, but if my assumptions are correct, it should reverse the effects of the poison with fewer side effects than Toni's broad-spectrum serum. I'll add some additional anti-nausea to her IV as well."

"Thank you, Cindy." Char brushed away the tears that had escaped.

"I'm going to get the gurney now." Cindy's voice was low and not at all like the commanding presence Sadie was accustomed to. "We need to transfer her to the infirmary so I can keep watch. While I think we're out of the woods for now, I can't be sure until I've seen the results of the blood test. I should have done that the minute you roused me the first time. Goddess, I'm so sorry, Char. I knew the possible dangers if Toni's broad-spectrum serum didn't do the trick."

"Don't beat yourself up, Cindy." Char touched her arm. "You will always be the best chance any of us have at survival after we do stupid shit and take unnecessary chances. I know Toni better than anyone, and she doesn't exactly reduce the risks when offering herself up as a guinea pig. As the leader, I should have prepared for an additional contingency plan to counteract the poison. If anyone's at fault here, it's me."

"I'll get the gurney," Joy offered. "I think you should stay here, Cindy. Uh, you know, just in case you're needed again."

Cindy nodded.

"I'll help her," Sadie added.

Chapter Seventeen

Sadie had been a rock, standing beside Joy while they anxiously waited for Cindy to do her magic. She hadn't avoided falling apart as she watched her mother go limp, and life-saving measures had been necessary to bring her back to life. Toni's heart had actually stopped working. Joy had never considered the possibility of losing either of her parents before. Yes, they were in a dangerous business, but both seemed so young and in perfect health. They weren't like other people's parents, cruising into middle age with a few extra pounds and new medications to stave off their growing health concerns as they aged.

Joy had never been so frightened in all her life. When she'd roused Cindy and brought her to the lab, Sadie was actively administering CPR on her mother. She overheard

Cindy tell Char that the CPR both Char and Sadie performed before she arrived probably saved Toni's life.

Joy could tell that Char was torn between her duty as The Organization's leader and her love and concern for her wife. As the minutes ticked away and Cindy continued to monitor Toni closely, Ronda, Val, Carson, and Sophie finally found their way to the infirmary after waiting for over an hour in the conference room before Val shattered the silence.

Val seemed to take in the room and was the first to speak. "What's going on? How sick is Toni?"

Although Sophie and Carson remained quiet, waiting for someone to fill them in, Joy noted they seemed to read the room as accurately as Val. Even Ronda was uncharacteristically subdued, failing to interject a joke. Cindy had shared a quick look with her that Joy wasn't sure was a warning or an attempt to impart the gravity of the situation.

"We underestimated the impact of the poison and subsequent side effects of the broad-spectrum serum Toni developed to reverse the toxins. Her heart stopped for a short time," Char explained.

An uncomfortable lull permeated the room like a cheap perfume squirted too liberally in the air. A beep from the other room in the infirmary caused nearly everyone to jump.

"That'll be the blood test," Cindy announced. "I'll be back in a few minutes. Don't worry. If anything changes, I'll hear the warning bells."

Val's jaw tensed as she looked at Toni and the gray pallor of her skin. Everyone knew Toni wasn't out of the woods yet. It didn't take a medical professional to see what was right in front of all their eyes.

187

"If you don't give me the order to take Marks out, I'll go rogue and do it anyway," Val stated.

Char shook her head. "As much as every cell in my body aches for you to do just that, we stick with the plan. It'll be far more painful to Marks if we take every last cent of his fortune and demolish his reputation. I want that man to have to beg for food," she said with a quiet fury Joy had never heard from her mother. "We will ensure we've destroyed everything he cares about—power, money, and status. I want the names of every ally. Either we'll ruin them as well, or we'll make sure Marks is so untouchable that not one of them will come to his aid."

Sophie, the ever-practical agent, interjected, "Just tell us what you need, Char. Nothing is more important than this mission."

"Everything is being recorded, so I don't feel the urgency to act until Toni fully recovers," Char answered. "I suspect we'll have a treasure trove of information to begin our attack after Toni is completely out of the woods." Char stroked Toni's forehead. "I can't do a debrief right now, but I can tell you that President Dawson is a major player. We'll need to tread carefully as we design a way to neutralize him."

"Take all the time you need. In the meantime, consider us on-call," Sophie said.

A weak smile formed on Char's face. "You're always on-call."

"Yeah, but this time, none of us will leave the complex until we hear from you," Sophie assured.

"Toni shared with me that the long-lasting bots will remain in Marks' body for at least two months. That should be plenty of time to track down all his allies, especially once we drain his accounts one by one. I plan on spreading out the pain as he watches his fortune slip through his fingers." Char met everyone's eyes, communicating her resolve.

"I don't want to leave Mama T, but if you need me to take over in the lab, I will," Joy offered. "If I remember correctly, we don't have much time to grow the small blood sample. We'll probably need more than a few droplets to drain all his accounts."

Char frowned, and Toni's eyes fluttered open before she could respond. "She's right. I never got to finish what I was doing with the blood sample. How long has it been since you moved me to Cindy's jailhouse?"

"For once in your life, Toni, you need to follow every single one of Cindy's directives. She's in charge here. No more reckless testing on yourself," Char pleaded.

Toni started to get up, but Char gently pushed her onto the bed. "Jeez, from the looks on your faces, you'd think I died or something. People pass out all the time and aren't any worse for wear."

Cindy breezed into the room and looked slightly less concerned than before. "Please tell me you did not wake her?"

"Not intentionally," Char answered. "She overheard us discussing our plans."

"Well, you can all take your scheming asses out of my infirmary. I was right about the poison. What I've given Toni should counteract the effects. My primary concern is how Toni's broad-spectrum serum interacted with the poison and her body. I suspect that's what caused her heart attack. I'd like to tell you we're out of the woods, but I can't guarantee that. Let me monitor her over the next twenty-four hours, and

I should be able to give an update. No one is dying on my watch."

The beeping on one of the monitors increased as Toni croaked, "Heart attack?"

Cindy grabbed a vial and pushed something new into the IV. "Sorry, Toni, but I need you and your heart to remain calm. Everyone but Char should leave."

"Mama T, please don't stress. I'm going to take care of the blood sample. Everything else can wait," Joy stated.

Toni's eyes drooped, but she managed to say, "Thank you, baby," before her eyes closed and her jaw slackened.

"You'll let me know if anything changes with Mama T?" Joy asked.

Char nodded. "I promise."

Val slung her arm over Joy's shoulder and said, "Come on, mini-nerd, we'll follow you to the lab. It wouldn't be the same without a passel of agents bugging the lead nerdlet." Val gestured for the rest to follow them out of the infirmary. Ronda kissed Cindy's cheek and whispered, "I believe in you. Toni is the beating heart of The Organization. I know you'll make sure hers keeps pumping."

When they reached the lab, Joy found the tubes that Toni had started and rushed to complete the job. She knew they were on the edge of the time limit for the cells in the sample to degrade without beginning the process of replication. She sent positive thoughts to the universe, asking for whatever higher power to ensure it wasn't too late.

Unlike her mother, Joy had the ability to tune everyone out as she worked. She heard faint murmuring but powered on through the delicate process until she'd meticulously completed each step. Finally, Joy relaxed in her chair and closed her eyes. When she opened them a few seconds later, she surveyed the room and noticed the anxious eyes staring at her.

"Well?" Carson broke the silence. "Were you able to save the sample?"

"We'll know in about four hours," Joy answered.

"I hope you don't mind, but I felt restless, so I've been monitoring Marks while you worked on the blood sample," Sadie said. "Toni's bots are amazing. Although, Toni really should find a better password, I was into her computer within seconds."

Joy chuckled. "I'll tell her that, but I don't think she's too worried. The complex is like a fortress. She's never even bothered to put biometric controls on her main computer."

†

Sadie was relieved that Val, Carson, and Sophie had exited the lab an hour earlier. Sitting idle, watching Joy and Sadie monitor Marks and dig through Toni's computer for critical information, was far too dull for the action-oriented agents. Sadie thought she heard them discuss heading to the gym for a sparring competition.

This is nice. Maybe they'll give Joy a cubicle next to mine at the NSA. Sadie was concentrating intensely as she listened in on Alvin Marks, watching him pace and make several calls to various men. Some names she recognized, others were utterly foreign to her. She couldn't believe Marks had the balls to begin an active war with the sitting President of the United States, regardless of whether he'd been the one to orchestrate Dawson's ascent to that pinnacle of power. Marks was methodical in his approach. She had to give him

191

that. His unparalleled audacity matched his thoroughness in aligning all his pawns before action. A popular senator was already in the waiting, ready to step into President Dawson's shoes. It was almost unheard of for an alternate candidate to challenge a sitting president.

Still, the seemingly impossible had occurred nearly eight years ago when the country had, for the first time in American history, elected a third-party candidate. The country had finally had enough of the two-party system, and a more moderate candidate on the right caused an enormous upset after losing the primary to the sitting president and deciding to run as an independent. Unfortunately, he had zero political capital to pull off a second term after having the impudence to challenge the status quo. Both sides of the aisle actively opposed his policies, and he never achieved a single win to bring to the American people. His administration was an utter failure, lining him up for the dishonor of nearly upending the orange-haired clown in the historians' ranking as the worst American president.

Sadie looked over and saw a frown form on Joy's face. She broke the pleasant silence that had allowed her to commit her entire focus on monitoring Marks. "You okay? Did you learn something distressing?"

Joy sighed. "Not exactly. But trying to follow in my mother's footsteps is impossible. I don't know how she keeps track of these different information channels. I'm sure I'm letting her down because I'll never be as competent as her with all this stuff. And now, she's fighting for her life…" Joy's head dropped to her chest.

Sadie reached over and rubbed circles on Joy's back. "Didn't you tell me that Char's sister, Dani, often works alongside Toni? I'll be by your side to help. I might not be as good as Dani at all this yet, but I'll get there."

"I was looking over Mama T's notes on the serum to counteract poisons, and I'm having a hard time understanding them. She taught me all about technology, but since I was never interested in biology, we didn't focus on that," Joy shared the information, exasperation evident in her voice. "It's a good thing the process to grow the blood sample was relatively straightforward and easy to follow."

"Did she develop those serums all on her own?" Sadie asked.

"No," Joy admitted. "Aunt Cindy would sometimes work with her on healing remedies that gave us the upper hand in the field. Before Mama T invented the full-body armor suits that protect against any type of bullet, even the armor-piercing ones, they realized that the first few minutes after someone's been shot are critical. Combining their expertise, Mama T and Aunt Cindy developed this gel with amazing healing properties."

"Wow! So, we'll spend some time with Cindy and learn about this part of the tech role if you're slated to take over after your mother retires. Clearly, she isn't ready to hand over the reins just yet. I've only just met your mom, and she seems like she won't slide into idle very easily. She likes the action. Consider this a temporary assignment until she returns. You don't have to absorb everything in two hours."

Joy turned her head to look at Sadie; tears glistened in her eyes. "You said we'll spend some time with Cindy."

Sadie crinkled her nose. "Yeah, what's wrong with that?"

"Not a thing." Joy smiled. "I like that you've offered to be by my side."

Sadie felt her face flush. "Always, at least I hope so." Changing the subject, Sadie pivoted to bring Joy up to date on Marks.

"I know this is all recorded, but Marks is planning to make a move on President Dawson. Their relationship soured after the cluster at the White House today. He's lining up his loyal soldiers to put a new person in power. Not that I care about the welfare of President Dawson since he seems to be right up there on the dickometer, but Marks is eyeing the upcoming election and planning on supporting Senator Roch as a third-party candidate. I always thought the spelling of his name should be R-O-A-C-H because that guy is a cockroach," Sadie quipped.

Joy laughed. "He is, isn't he?"

"Unfortunately, with Marks' connections, if Senator Roch wins, it won't be a repeat of what happened eight years ago. There was a revolt against President Warrens because he didn't realize how alliances work in DC politics. Marks has those coalitions in spades. I've only been monitoring him for a few hours, and already I understand how deep his ties go."

"Who else is he in bed with?" Joy asked.

"Unfortunately, our supervisor's boss at the NSA," Sadie answered. "The guy even has allies in the Department of Justice. Although, I don't believe the Attorney General is in his pocket. Apparently, President Dawson still controls him, and that pisses Marks off. He's actually worried about that, which is why he's been nonstop on the phone, shoring up his support."

"Well, as soon as we start to redistribute his wealth, I don't think he'll be able to retain that support. Please tell me we've gotten lucky, and he's tried to access some of his funds. Everything will fall like dominos once we start draining his accounts. He'll panic and start checking every single one. Do you mind taking a break from monitoring Marks? I'd like to poke around in my mom's computer. Knowing her as I do, I'll bet anything that she started the process of unraveling Marks' vast fortune."

Sadie rolled her chair aside, and Joy moved her chair in front of the main computer. Rapidly typing on the wireless keyboard, Joy mumbled to herself, "I know the files are here somewhere; where the hell did you put them, Mama T?"

Sadie chuckled as she watched Joy work. A tiny crinkle in the middle of her forehead was barely visible.

"Gotcha," Joy exclaimed. "Wow! This probably isn't everything, but he really spread out his fortune. I think there are a few places we could slip in and grab the money before he has a chance to know what hit him. Bingo. Here's a folder titled Low Hanging Kiwis." Joy chuckled. "That's my mom's favorite fruit. Each financial institution has its own unique security protocols. Not all of them require biometric data or an in-person visit." She grinned. "Want to play Robin Hood with me?"

"Shouldn't we wait for your moms?" Sadie asked.

"Nope. We can do this. It isn't that hard with a few accounts. Piece of cake with master hackers like us. Besides, I really need something to take my mind off Mama T." Joy's face lost its former excitement.

"Maybe it would be okay if you popped in for just a few minutes to see how she's doing," Sadie suggested.

"Will you come with me?" Joy sounded tentative.

"Of course. Let's go. I'm not afraid of Cindy," Sadie taunted.

That made Joy laugh, which was precisely what Sadie hoped would happen. "Good, because besides Aunt Val, Aunt Cindy is the scariest one of all of the seasoned agents, and sometimes she scares the shit out of me. Although, she has a much softer touch with us."

CHAPTER EIGHTEEN

It was disconcerting to Joy to see her mother looking so ill. It didn't appear as though much about Toni had changed. She noticed that her Aunt Dani had joined Char and Toni in the infirmary. By the worried expressions on both their faces, Joy suspected Toni's health was not improving.

"Hey, Aunt Dani. Cindy hasn't kicked you out yet?" Joy asked.

Dani turned toward Joy, and a thin smile slowly appeared on her face. "I'm not as obnoxious as Val or Sophie. I haven't officially met Carson, but I heard she's made from the same cloth." Her eyes shifted to Sadie. "You must be Sadie. I've heard a lot about you. I'm always happy to meet another tech expert. There aren't enough of us in The Organization."

"I'm not sure if I'm in your league, but I'm happy to add whatever skills I possess to the pot," Sadie answered.

"Where's Aunt Candy?" Joy asked.

"She heard there was a sparring competition in the rec center, and after stopping by to check on Toni, she left to join them. Cindy also strongly advised her to, and I quote, 'get the hell out of my infirmary,' so she left without protest. It was pushing it for me to stay. Have you learned anything important yet?"

Cindy shook her head. "Nope, if you're going to have a business meeting in my infirmary, I'm going to have to ask you to leave. Toni periodically wakes and wants to be in the thick of things again."

"Sorry, Cindy." Dani hung her head.

Toni's eyes fluttered open. "What's going on? Anything I need to know about."

"Oh, for fuck's sake. That's why I didn't want any of you people hanging around," Cindy chastised.

Char stroked Toni's arm. "Please don't worry about anything but healing. Your body needs every ounce of strength to fight the effects of the blend of toxic chemicals in the poison and your reckless untested serum."

"It wasn't completely untested," Toni weakly argued.

Dani rolled her eyes. "I love you like another sister, Toni, but remember, I work side by side with you in the lab, so don't tell tall tales. I'd rather not be the one to rat you out to my sister." Dani glanced over at Char.

Char offered a smile to her sister. "No need to rat Toni out. I know exactly what goes on in that lab of hers. I'm instituting new rules once Toni recovers. No more using agents as guinea pigs with new tech. We must find a safer way to test everything, including bio-agents."

"It was the combination, not my serum," Toni insisted. "Live subjects will always be needed."

"I'll be your test subject. I'm younger and can tolerate more. No offense, Mama T, but you're not exactly in your twenties anymore," Joy noted.

Char's jaw tightened. "I'd rather neither of you put yourselves in a position where Cindy has to monitor your health."

A beep interrupted the conversation, and Cindy quickly strode to one of her blood analyzers. After viewing the data, she announced, "The numbers are going in the right direction. I feel relatively confident that Toni is on the mend. The worst is over."

"Thank you, Cindy. I don't know what we would do without you." In a rare demonstration of emotion, Char brushed away a tear. Joy had rarely seen her unflappable mother break down. She walked over and hugged her, then grabbed an astonished Cindy and hugged her as well.

Dani grinned. "Hey, what about me? Don't I rate?"

Joy chuckled and walked into Dani's outstretched arms.

"You girls should head home now that the danger has passed. Isn't tomorrow your first day at the NSA?" Char asked.

"Yeah, but we can't just leave. There's a ton to monitor, and we should start draining the accounts we know about—the ones that don't require his blood or a DNA sample," Joy answered.

"That's why I'm here," Dani interjected. "I'll take over the monitoring. We can wait on the accounts. I doubt his money is going anywhere in the next several days."

"Work the NSA angle," Toni croaked. "If they have anything on The Organization, you two need to make it go away or lead them in a different direction."

"That's it. We're done here." Cindy took a syringe from the drawer, drew some medication from a vial, and pushed it into the IV. "It's time for you to go nighty-night again. The rest of you can march your asses right out that door." Cindy pointed to the back door of the infirmary.

"I'm staying." Char pinned Cindy with a look that defied any argument.

Cindy nodded.

"You'll call if anything changes?" Joy asked.

"Yes. Don't worry," Char answered.

Joy leaned over and pecked her Mama T on the forehead. Sadie stayed by her side and followed Joy out of the lab, with Dani trailing both of them.

†

Sadie didn't know why they were returning to the lab, but she didn't ask questions. If she had to extend her fake leave, she would, even if it put her job at risk.

"Joy, hon, I can honestly take over. Do what your moms said and focus on the NSA," Dani gently suggested.

"I just want to copy a few files from Mom's computer," Joy explained. "I'll encrypt them. Don't worry. I really want to start the process while Mom is recovering. Poking the hornet's nest will result in a reaction you can monitor. Maybe that will provide even more information and let us know where and how he's keeping the majority of his

200

fortune. The man is a trillionaire. No way he has all his money in the US banking system."

"Okay, but don't try to deplete the accounts with more complicated security. The easier pickings will probably only be a sliver of Marks' vast resources, but my experience with these rich white dudes is that any loss is a major catastrophe for them," Dani shared.

"Got it, thanks." Joy shoved in a tiny storage chip she retrieved from a drawer and began moving files. "Almost done. Ten more minutes."

Sadie smiled at Joy. "Works for me. Are you interested in grabbing a pizza on the way home?"

"Yeah, that sounds good. Can you call ahead so it's ready for pickup? Do you want to ask Carson if she needs a ride back to your place, and she can join us for pizza?"

"Sure, I'll call Randi, too. What about your other roommates? Do you think they'll want to join us?" Sadie asked.

"Maybe. Probably. Alina is like a human garbage pail. She's always ready to eat," Joy answered.

"Then I better get three larges. I think I remember what y'all ordered the night I finally got you to go out with me," Sadie teased.

"Sounds like a plan. Do you know how to find Carson?"

"The rec room, right? I think I know where that building is located," Sadie answered.

"I'll show you," Dani offered.

"Just don't be telling her young Joy stories on the way."

Dani shot Joy an evil grin. "Now, where's the fun in that? Part of entering middle age is that we get to embarrass our nieces. Since Candy and I couldn't have kids, it's only fair. That's the rule. I might even have some pics to show."

Sadie giggled. "Ooh, can't wait. I bet Joy was adorable."

"Can you at least avoid my middle school years? No one looks adorable in middle school," Joy pleaded.

†

Joy finished transferring the files to her microchip and stuffed it in her pocket. The process had taken a smidgeon more than ten minutes since she traveled down a rabbit hole in her mother's computer, finding all kinds of fascinating information on Marks. She'd also read about Sadie's family and their ties to the mines. What Sadie might not know was how much the mining company had been aware of the dangers and had paid off several high-ranking government officials to look the other way. Reports on the hazards were conveniently lost or squashed. Litigants would have discovered the smoking gun if not for Marks' connections. Hell, it wasn't just a smoking gun he'd managed to bury, it was an entire armory of assault weapons. Joy debated about whether she should share the reports with Sadie. She had a right to know everything, but maybe it would open old wounds.

Joy walked along the path to the large gym on the compound. Someone had planted annuals, and Joy noticed the clusters of sweet-smelling heliotrope with their deep purple flowers. Bending to the bundle of color, she breathed in their scent and smiled when she thought she could almost taste the vanilla. Growing up, this was one of her mother's favorite flowers to plant. It always reminded Joy of vanilla ice cream, which happened to be her favorite. Aunt Val often teased Joy when she insisted simple flavors were best—plain

202

vanilla versus her aunt's all-time favorite, chocolate chip cookie dough. She'd kid her about having uncomplicated tastes but a complex brain.

After Joy opened the door, she saw Carson sprawled on the mat with a scowl on her face. "That was a cheap shot," she grumbled.

Val casually stood over her and smirked. "There are no rules in the field. Do you think the assholes you might have to fight will stick with decorum? Better learn street fighting in addition to the pussy ass moves Soph teaches." She held up her hands. "Hey, don't get me wrong, Sophie's training is useful. It teaches discipline. There's a place for both."

Sophie glared at Val. "Pussy ass moves? Care to take over training for the field agents?"

"Oh, hell no. I'm not a people person," Val answered.

Joy laughed, undoubtedly announcing her arrival. "Um, I don't think Sophie's much better at interpersonal skills."

Val shrugged. "Probably not, but at least she has the patience for it. I'd want to pound the shit out of the snot-nosed kids we've been recruiting lately. Present company excluded, of course," she added with a grin. She held out her hand for Carson and helped her to her feet. "Want to go again? This time, remember, no rules."

"I better not. I already feel humiliated that a person more than twice my age kicked my ass," Carson answered.

In what Joy knew was a rare declaration from Sophie, she noted, "Hey, don't feel bad, kid. Val kicks all our asses. She's the best fighter I've ever seen, man or woman. Also, don't let her fool you about the patience thing. She has that in spades. Like a tarantula, she waits for the perfect moment to strike. It's literally saved her life on numerous occasions."

"You guys want to join us for pizza?" Carson asked.

Val shook her head. "Gina is patiently waiting for me. I told her I wouldn't be long."

"Sophie?"

"Nah, Kim is waiting, too."

Joy grinned. "Aunt Soph and Aunt Val might be total badass fighters, but their wives are the ones who rule."

"Ha, that's what we let everyone think," Val argued.

"Oh, really?" Gina stepped into the exercise facility and arched her eyebrow. "No ice cream for you tonight," she threatened.

Val jogged over to her wife and pecked her on the lips. "Hey, baby. I was just kidding."

Gina glanced at Carson, then shifted her eyes to Sadie. "New recruits?"

Carson was the first to react by sticking out her hand and offering it to Gina. "Carson, ma'am. A pleasure to meet you." Carson added her other hand, clasping Gina's hand in both of hers.

"Well, aren't you the little charmer," Gina noted.

Val narrowed her eyes at Carson. "That's my wife you're drooling over," she said in warning.

Carson blushed, and Sadie shook her head and waved. "Hi, I'm this one's roommate." She pointed at Carson. "Sadie," she added.

"And Joy's new girlfriend," Val clarified.

Gina's smile grew. "Good for you, Joy, she's lovely."

"She's a talented hacker, too," Joy added with pride.

This time, Sadie's face flushed red. "We should probably head out soon. The pizzas should be ready by the time we arrive at Pete's."

"Good, I'm starving," Carson answered.

CHAPTER NINETEEN

Money burning a hole inside her pocket wasn't a phrase Joy could relate to. On the other hand, the microchip snugly stored in her zipper pocket practically seared a tattoo onto her skin. She wanted to start draining a few of Marks' accounts. It's all she could think of, but Joy was trying hard to be a normal person—someone who didn't ignore the woman she was completely gaga over. It was a dilemma she needed to resolve on her own without constantly seeking advice from her two best friends.

Sadie sipped on her beer and glanced at Joy, a frown forming on her face. "Hey, you okay?"

Joy moved her hand from where she'd recently been absently stroking the tiny chip, making sure it was still there. She wondered if the next awkward thing she might do would be to adopt her mother's nervous habit of chewing on pens. She looked up, forcing a weak smile. So far, Sadie hadn't run away. Maybe she could just be honest. Better than trying to be something she wasn't, and at this point, Joy was obsessed with getting a head start on Marks.

"I'm sorry. The chip in my pocket with the important files is all I can think about right now. I don't have my laptop with me, and it's literally driving me nuts, not to begin transforming Marks into the poorest man in the world, versus the richest."

Sadie chuckled. "You want to go back to your place, don't you?" she guessed.

Joy nodded with what she was sure was a sheepish expression on her face.

Sadie clapped her hands and stood. "All right, let's go? I'm hoping you won't mind a little company. Can I bring some clothes and stay the night? Beta will just have to get over being without me for a night. He's a spoiled brat and an attention hog. Carson and Randi can take care of him for me."

"He can come to our place," Joy suggested.

"Naw, he rules the roost here and might be a terror if we carry him to somewhere new. Although he's never marked his territory before, there's always a first time."

"Okay," Joy answered. The bliss Joy felt at that moment was unlike any euphoria she'd ever experienced before in her life. She hadn't off-put Sadie. Instead, Sadie wanted to spend the night with her, like any typical lesbian couple. Could she actually have found someone who understood her and accepted every part of her, even the ones that would undoubtedly affect their relationship? Like her mother, Joy could get overly obsessed to the point of blocking out everyone.

"Yes, of course. Tomorrow, we can commute to work together. I'd love it if you stayed."

"I'll grab my laptop, too. We can do this thing together. I don't know about you, but maybe we'll be able to keep ourselves in check if we combine forces. I tend to get uber-focused on something, and before I know it, it's three in the morning. Those days at work after one of those nights are incredibly painful." Sadie chuckled nervously.

"We should probably institute a bedtime," Joy teased.

"I know that was meant as a joke, but it's not a horrible idea. No matter where we're at with Project Poverty, we stop at midnight. Nothing past the witching hour. Deal?" Sadie stood and held out her hand.

Joy grabbed Sadie's hand and vigorously shook it. "Deal, but maybe we should seal those deals with a kiss in the future," Joy boldly declared.

"Cheeky. I love it." Sadie closed the short distance and pecked Joy on the lips.

"Ew," Randi and Carson said simultaneously.

"I don't know about you, Randi, but this sickly sweet gooeyness between those two is turning my stomach."

Sadie grabbed a throw pillow from the couch and tossed it at Carson. "Not everyone operates under the 'wham, bam, thank you ma'am' credo."

Carson smirked. "Nothing wrong with a good—"

"Do not finish that sentence," Sadie warned, then grabbed the empty pizza boxes in front of Carson.

Joy collected the empty bottles and cans and followed Sadie to her back deck. Seeing only one bin, she tossed her cans and bottles into the same receptacle where Sadie had chucked both pizza boxes. Sadie had packed up the leftover pizza for Alina who had let them know they'd already had

207

dinner, but she was sure she could eat whatever they hadn't finished.

Joy accepted Sadie's outstretched hand as she led her into the house and her bedroom, where Sadie tossed a few items of clothing into her bag and grabbed the laptop from the desk. Shoving the computer and the charging cord into a padded bag, she nodded at Joy, presumably indicating she was ready to go.

Joy held out her hands. "I can carry your bag or the laptop."

†

The minute Joy and Sadie opened the door to the home Joy shared with Alina, Randi, and Maria, Alina asked, "How's Aunt Toni doing?"

Sadie set the leftover pizza on the kitchen counter. The worry line between Joy's brows deepened, and Sadie thought Joy might come apart again, but she held it together enough to answer, "She was doing better a few hours ago, and Mama C hasn't called, so I assume she hasn't taken a turn for the worse." Joy plucked her phone from her pocket and dialed, mumbling, "I'm a shitty daughter."

Sadie put her hand on Joy's back and leaned in to whisper in her ear, "No, you're not. I suspect Toni will be thrilled to learn we've gotten a head start on Project Poverty."

Joy smiled and said, "I forgot to tell you I love that name. Mama C will get a kick out of it, too." Joy returned her focus to her phone and answered, "It's me, Mom. I was just checking in since you haven't called...okay, yeah, I know I

Love Hacks

asked you to call if anything changed, but I didn't just mean a setback. I also want to hear about any improvements. Surely there's been some change in her recovery, even if it's minuscule. Frequent updates will settle my nerves."

"Put Aunt Char on speaker, so we all can hear," Alina requested.

Joy pushed a button, and Char's voice blasted through the speaker, "….been a lot of changes. Toni is still sleeping. Her color looks a little better. Cindy assures me there are slight improvements in her condition. She's running a new blood sample now. I'll call you back as soon as she has those results."

"Give her a hug for all of us," Alina yelled loud enough for Char to hear.

"I've been praying for her," Maria added.

"I'm on speaker?" Char asked.

"Yeah, is that okay? You know how Alina is. She wasn't part of the mission, but that doesn't stop her from wanting to know everything. Besides, they love Mama T," Joy answered.

"It's fine, honey. Thank you, Alina and Maria. I'll tell Toni you asked about her. Joy, please don't stay up all night working on whatever you put on that microchip, and be extra careful that Marks can't track whatever you plan on doing."

"Aunt Dani ratted me out, huh?" Joy teased.

"Of course she did," Char answered.

"Don't worry. We only plan to grab the low-hanging fruit. Sadie and I made a pact that we won't work past midnight. We have a new name for the mission. We're calling it Project Poverty. After we're done with Marks, he won't have enough for a cup of coffee."

"Interesting names for all these missions. First Elephant Bites and now Project Poverty. I suppose it has a nice ring to it. Toni's going to love that. Hey, honey, I'll call you later; it looks like Toni's awake again. Not sure for how long, though."

"Bye, Mama C."

"Bye, honey."

Joy stood looking around, her brow furrowed. "I hadn't really thought this through too well. Normally, I don't bother to go into my room because it seems claustrophobic. The living room allows me to spread out and get comfortable with my extended hacking sessions. Mama T's lab had a lot more room to work."

"We can make ourselves scarce and head to our room," Alina offered. "It's not like we need to stream our shows on the big screen. But I will take that leftover pizza that Sadie set on the counter." Alina grinned.

Joy crinkled her nose. "Do you mind setting up out here?"

Sadie shook her head. "Works for me. I rarely use my desk back home, either."

The relief seemed to flow over Joy's face, and Sadie thought that even after all the time they'd spent together, Joy still acted unsure of herself occasionally. She'd come a long way, and Sadie felt privileged to see the side of Joy she let shine through with her close friends.

"Um, do you want to put your bag in my room?"

"Yeah, that sounds good. I know where it is." Sadie winked. "Be right back." Sadie set her laptop on the coffee table and shouldered her overnight bag. She didn't linger in Joy's bedroom, but when she returned, Joy was already balancing her computer on her lap and furiously pounding the keyboard.

She looked up briefly and smiled. "I hope it's okay that I started. There are maybe five accounts here that don't require DNA, but just in case voice recognition was required to tap into the funds, I downloaded a sample from Mama T's computer."

"What about handprint access?" Sadie asked.

Joy grinned. "I'm kind of known for my ability to multi-task. It's amazing how many of Mama T's traits I have, considering I don't share her DNA. While you were monitoring Marks, I worked on converting the prints to a digital format at the same time I was looking at the formulas for the serums. Although the biological stuff is like reading Greek, digitizing biometrics like fingerprints and facial, iris, or voice recognition is right up my alley." Joy ejected the microchip and handed it to Sadie. "You can load those files onto your laptop, and we'll split up the accounts. Do you know how to do this?"

"Um, I think I have the basics down; just another hacking job, right?"

"Sort of. But we need to ensure the transactions can't be traced back to us. And there's a special art to putting the money in a secure location that is nearly impossible to discover using whatever hacking or tech resources they possess. The locations where we'll send the money are in the chip. Assume they have someone on their payroll that is almost as good as Mama T."

Sadie ran her hand through her hair. She didn't want to mess this up, but she also didn't want to seem incompetent. "How about I look over your shoulder while you drain the first account?"

211

Joy grinned. "So, I have something to teach the great Dragonfire?" she teased.

"Maybe," Sadie hedged. She shot Joy her sultriest look. "You may have special hacking skills to share, but I'm looking forward to teaching you a whole new set of skills."

Joy blushed. "Um, does it bother you that I'm inexperienced, and we, uh, haven't done anything yet?"

Sadie lifted the computer from Joy's lap, set it on the coffee table next to her laptop, and took Joy's hand, turning to face her. "Joy, I'm in no rush to get inside your panties. We can go as slow as you want. When you're ready, let me know. Trust me, it will all come naturally to you. Making love with a woman is very different from making love with a man. Women understand other women's bodies."

"Okay." Joy shifted uncomfortably on the couch.

"Honestly, it really is okay. Our first time together will be perfect. I don't have one single doubt about that. Even if it takes a year or more for us to get to that place, it'll be worth the wait."

"A year?" Joy squeaked. "I'm not sure I can hold on for that long."

"Whew. Good to know because even though I'm committed to waiting as long as it takes for you to feel comfortable taking that next step, sleeping beside you has been a challenge. I'm not afraid to admit that."

Joy giggled. "Yeah, I think I kind of knew that."

Sadie laughed. "Ah, I get it… you're hoping to tease me to death. Is that your attempt to get back at me for giving you a run for your money when you tried to hack into my dark web group and the NSA?"

"Now I've got sex on my brain. We better get cracking, or we won't get this done before midnight, and I'd hate to break our pact." Joy grabbed her laptop and began typing. "Watch and learn. I will be your Yoda tonight."

Sadie belly-laughed at Joy's last comment. "Oh my Goddess, a Star Wars reference? You *are* a nerd."

"Hey, that franchise might be old, but it's classic. At least once a year, I force my friends to watch a Star Wars marathon with me."

"I prefer the old Star Trek franchise. Granted, some were better than others, but a lot more to choose from," Sadie countered.

"I could be talked into a Star Trek marathon, but that might last longer than an entire weekend. We'd have to be choosey about which series and which episodes to watch." Shifting gears, Joy began explaining the process. "Usually, I open all the relevant files first. I like to have handy each digitized file. Different accounts require unique security protocols. But, before that, I found a brand new code that Mama T developed. It's frickin' brilliant. We can use that code to keep the tech specialists Marks uses from tracking us. If they try to find the accounts or the location of the hack, it'll put a nasty virus into their computers."

"Good thing it's a new code. I would have been miserable if you'd used that code on me. Although, I do have a few safeguards that might have prevented the disaster. I'd rather not test them because I've seen your mother's brilliance firsthand. Should I load all those files first?"

"Yeah. And grab that code, too," Joy answered. "I'll show you where to put it."

Sadie rubbed her hands together. "This is going to be so much fun. Best date ever!"

"And you call me a nerd?" Joy laughed.

CHAPTER TWENTY

Sadie put her hand over her mouth but didn't manage to hide her yawn. Joy tried to give her an extra ten minutes while she made the coffee, but Sadie had awoken the minute Joy slipped from the bed. Joy was used to staying up half the night and practically guzzling an entire pot of coffee to function the next day. She wondered if this was abnormal for Sadie.

"Sorry, I should have had a second cup," Sadie announced at the tail end of her yawn. "But it seemed like you were hoarding the pot," she teased.

"Should I have made a second pot?" Joy silently berated herself for being so self-absorbed she failed to notice that Sadie might have wanted more coffee.

"I'm kidding, Joy. You look like a whipped puppy right now. I don't usually have more than one cup a day. They actually have decent coffee at the NSA. If I need a second cup, I can grab one when we get to work."

"I guess we shouldn't trust the pact in the future. Neither of us had the willpower to stop."

"True, but think of how many accounts we hijacked last night? Hey, how come you aren't yawning this morning?" Sadie asked.

"I'm used to this. Mama T and I often worked through the night. It's amazing what several strong cups of coffee will do to trick my body into believing I got enough sleep."

Sadie flipped on her blinker and made the turn into the massive parking lot at the NSA. "You nervous about your first day?"

Joy nodded. "A little. I don't do well meeting a lot of people. I've never worked outside The Organization. It's a bit overwhelming to me. I delayed pursuing a normal job because I've never been good with people. You already know I have a kind of social anxiety disorder. School was hard enough for me, but it's important to have an alternate identity. I know that. It helps keep The Organization hidden. The NSA makes sense, but that doesn't mean I'm not scared shitless."

Sadie put her car in park, undid her seatbelt, and turned to Joy, laying a comforting hand on her thigh. "Since I was the one who recruited you, which, for the record, was quite a boon, I asked that I be the one to show you around. I'm your orientation buddy. After you finish with HR, I'll stick to you like glue. I also asked them to station you next to me. We aren't more than five feet from one another. You'll be able to do this job with your eyes closed."

Joy took a big breath. "Okay. Let's do this." She followed Sadie into the massive building.

Sadie stopped at the security desk, showed her ID, and then placed her hand on the scanner. "Hey, Joey. How's it going? This is Joy Stiles. It's her first day. Can you give us a temporary badge, and I'll take her to HR?"

"Sure thing, Sadie. I have her on the list today; I just need to see an ID."

Joy fumbled in her sling pack, pulled out her driver's license, and handed it over to him. Joey looked carefully at the picture on her ID, then at Joy.

Nodding, Joey handed Joy her license and instructed, "Place your left hand over the scanner and keep it there for ten seconds while the machine records your print."

Joy followed his instructions and heard three beeps. Joey typed something into his computer, then held out the temporary badge. "Okay, you're good to go."

After a whirlwind of introductions and relatively painless onboarding with the human resource department, Sadie collected Joy and led her to her new desk. Joy felt calmer now that she was in front of her computer, and Sadie was the one who would train her. It didn't take her long to learn how to navigate the system, including inserting Sadie's code that allowed her to poke around the NSA network without anyone knowing. Joy thought it was ingenious how her code displayed a fake monitor for onlookers that might pass by their cubicles. If anyone at the NSA caught either of them entering places they weren't authorized to go, it would mean more than simply being canned. They could see significant jail time for spying. The NSA did not have a sense of humor regarding unauthorized access to top-secret documents.

Joy had almost immediately located the files about The Crusaders. What a ridiculous name. She was deep into sending those files to the main computer at the compound through a secure back door when her phone rang. She wasn't sure if she was allowed to answer personal calls while on the job, so she looked over at Sadie.

Sadie smiled. "Go ahead. You can answer your phone. We're given a lot of leeway as long as we do our job."

"Hello."

"Joy, you and Sadie need to get home right now and destroy both laptops," Dani said.

"What? Why? What's going on? We already used Mama T's code that injects a worm. I can't just leave. It's my first day. Besides, Sadie's laptop is in her car, not at my place."

Sadie looked over, her face screwing up in confusion. Joy quickly scribbled a note. *Laptops are compromised.*

Sadie's face paled.

"The code wasn't finished. Damn, I don't want to get Toni involved. Char is going to kill me. She gave me the evil eye when I went to the infirmary to update her. We'll try to handle this remotely. Can Sadie at least give us access to her laptop?" Dani said.

"I think Mama T already wrote a code for that. I don't know if it works when her laptop is off, though."

"Have Sadie take a break and get her to turn on her laptop," Dani directed.

"Won't that just make it easy for Marks to track?"

"Not if we send them on a wild goose chase," Dani answered. "Toni just walked into the lab." Relief was evident in Dani's voice.

"Okay. We'll get on it. Is Mama T well enough to do this?" Joy asked.

"I think so," Dani answered. "At least for the time being. Char might kill her for leaving the infirmary. I'll call Alina and hope she's home. Will she be able to turn on your laptop?"

"Turn on, yes, keep on, no," Joy answered in exasperation. "This is bad, isn't it?"

"Yeah, honey, it is. I wish you would have asked me about the code before grabbing it and using it last night," Toni answered.

"Sorry, Mama T. We just wanted to help."

"I know. It'll all be okay," Toni soothed.

"Screw it. I never really wanted to work at the NSA, anyway. I'm leaving right now. Either they'll accept the family emergency story, or they won't."

"Val is on her way to the house. She'll meet you there. She has a chip with the diversion code," Toni said.

Joy ended the call, and before she even had a chance to stand, Sadie said, "Let's go. I drove us here. It makes sense that you need me to take you home."

Sadie made a beeline to a middle-aged man and engaged in a hurried conversation before he glanced at Joy and nodded. Joy and Sadie rushed to Sadie's car, and Joy was thankful that Sadie was an accomplished driver. Weaving in and out of traffic, it was a miracle they weren't stopped for exceeding the speed limit, bordering on reckless driving. Joy barely managed to juggle Sadie's computer on her lap to turn it on for Toni to take control.

†

"How the fuck did you let this happen?" Marks screamed. "I pay you good money to protect my assets. You're supposed to be the best in the business."

The scrawny, balding man with pale pock-marked skin, hunched over his computer. "I disabled the worm. Just a few more lines of code to unravel, and we'll track down the hackers. I recognize some of the code. It's the same person who ran that dark web group. I've gotten the identities of everyone but the person attached to the computer who drained your accounts. He or she is good. Most likely the same hacker who first developed that group."

"Names?" Marks demanded.

The man printed a page and handed it to Marks.

"Everyone is replaceable. You better hope you learn the name of the person who did this," Marks threatened. "The little bastards stole fifty billion of my hard-earned dollars."

The man rolled his eyes, and Marks was tempted to put a bullet in his head, but getting a replacement would not be easy, so for now, he let the man live.

"Shit, they're using diversion software. I can't be sure of the origin of the signal. It's probably completely random, but one of those locations is the NSA. It could be relevant, though, because we've been tracking micro-breaches at the NSA. Just this morning, someone accessed the Crusdr files. If I were a betting man, I would say that at least one of your hackers works at the NSA, or maybe they're part of The Crusaders. You should press your contacts there and get them to set up a sting operation. I've gone as far as I can go. There are over a thousand locations to check, multiplying by the second. Before too long, every address in the city will be listed. This diversion code is unlike anything I've ever seen before."

"Can't you stop it?"

"No. I can't break their code." The pasty-faced man lifted his hands from his keyboard and sat back. "Sorry, there's nothing more to do. You should move the rest of your money into accounts that require several layers of bio access, including DNA entry."

"They already are in those secure locations. Unless they can impersonate me and produce a blood sample via a finger prick, they won't be able to drain those accounts. None of these remaining accounts allow easy access. This means I'll have to personally travel to the Cayman Islands and move money into something more liquid for use with my daily expenses. I'm a busy man. Do you have any idea how much of an inconvenience this is?" Marks shouted. "When I get back, you better have more information. In the meantime, I'll have my men track down the other members of that dark web group interested in The Crusaders. I expect you to follow up on that and give me the name of the person who started the group."

†

Sadie watched as Val lifted her phone to her ear. "Yeah, okay. Got it. Text me the list. That many? Shit, how many agents do we have who can cover these nerds? You sure you don't just want me to take out Marks? Problem solved. Just give the order. All right. I'll hold off for now, but if either Joy or Sadie are at risk, all bets are off. I'll take Mr. Feldman." Val slipped her phone into her pocket.

"Are we okay now?" Joy asked.

Val nodded. "For now. Unfortunately, your dark web buddies are at risk. Would any of them be able to finger you as the group administrator?"

Sadie shook her head. "I don't think so. I was pretty careful about my identity. Wouldn't they have found me by now if they'd discovered who I was?"

"Toni is worried, and I trust her judgment," Val answered. "Apparently, Marks has a tech guy who's pretty good. Clearly, you two weren't careful enough, or we wouldn't be having this last-minute fire drill." Val frowned. "I gotta go. It's protect-a-nerd day. They'll all be getting brand-new state-of-the-art laptops. You need to shut down your dark web group."

Sadie's fingers flew across the keyboard. After about thirty seconds, she announced, "Done. I developed a kill program after I established the new group just in case I needed it."

"Good. Dani is monitoring Marks, so at least we know his plans. The only good thing to arise out of this cluster fuck is our ability to follow Marks to the Cayman Islands. Kim already developed a latex mask of Marks. We'll be able to send Steve who is his approximate size to close those accounts. That should send him into panic mode. Besides the small hiccup, you guys did well. At least it got the ball rolling in an exhilarating way." Val grinned. "I was getting bored lately. My favorite pastime is scaring the shit out of nerds."

"Aunt Val, don't do that, please?" Joy pleaded.

"Oh, all right. But I will need to engage in a few of my interrogation tactics to ensure Mr. Feldman doesn't know who you are, Sadie. I'll try to be gentle, but," she shrugged, "finesse isn't my strong suit."

"Will Marks do physical harm to them?" Sadie asked.

Val nodded. "Probably."

"Can you help them disappear?" Joy asked.

"Toni's working on that. They'll all have new identities, and we'll use the money you stole to set them up in a new location. They'll have a better chance than if the government put them into witness protection, but they don't stand a chance if we don't get to them first. Really, enough chit-chat. I have to go now," Val insisted.

"Thanks, Aunt Val."

Val slipped out the front door and roared out of the driveway. Sadie heard a siren and raised one eyebrow at Joy.

Joy answered Sadie's questioning eyebrow, "Comes in handy when our agents need to get to a location fast without collecting a tail. I even have one."

"Can I get a fake siren and lights, too?" Sadie asked with excitement.

"They're actually not fake. Illegal, yes, but not fake," Joy clarified.

"Even better."

†

Marks paced his office, waiting for an update on the list of names he'd given to his men. The blasted hackers were all over the United States, but surely at least one of them would have the information he needed. He hoped it was Daniel Feldman because he was right there in the DC area. Patience wasn't Marks' forte. It wasn't that he didn't trust his men to excise the information from this rogue group. He simply got a perverse pleasure watching them work, and even more gratification when he saw the light in his enemies' eyes slowly fade. He supposed, in some people's minds, that would make him some kind of deranged psychopath. Marks truly believed he could literally get away with murder if he was the wealthiest man in the world.

Glancing at the address for Daniel Feldman, Marks waved away his men and climbed into his luxury sports car. He seethed every time he was reminded of the fact that his top-of-the-line solar vehicle wasn't nearly as lavish or comfortable as his competitor at roughly half the cost. Fucking McFarland. He hoped she was suffering or, if he was lucky, dead. He wasn't even sure a partial dose would have any significant impact on her health.

"Four three one Cherry Lane, Georgetown," Marks directed.

"Finding the fastest route for four three one Cherry Lane, Georgetown," the robotic female voice said.

Marks followed his navigation system until he reached the address. He brazenly pulled into the driveway and parked behind the official-looking vehicle, thankful for the relative cover of Feldman's tidy landscaping. The upscale neighborhood did not surprise Marks. He assumed Feldman obtained his money through nefarious means, which Marks did not begrudge the young man, as long as he wasn't the target of those scams. Maybe he was, and that would provide Marks with ample justification for what he was about to do. Not that he needed an explanation. Extracting information was dirty work sometimes, but business was business. Nothing personal.

The front door was open as Marks strolled inside. It was quiet. Too quiet. He should have detected something. His men were already here. Torture wasn't silent. As he stepped farther into the large home, his eyes shifted to something he'd never seen before. Both of his men sat on the floor with their hands and feet secured with zip ties. Neither appeared conscious.

"What the fuck is going on?" he bellowed. Kicking their feet, he yelled. "Do I have to handle every fucking thing, personally?" Turning around, he stood face-to-face with a woman with the coldest gray eyes he'd ever seen. That was the only thing he registered before the world went black.

†

It could have been minutes or hours, Marks wasn't sure about the timeline, but it didn't matter because when his eyes blinked open, his hands were cuffed to a hospital bed. Tugging on the cuffs, he heard the metal clank against the rails on the bed. "What is the meaning of this?" he screamed.

An attractive woman in a tailored navy suit stood casually beside the bed. "Welcome back, Mr. Marks. We have a few questions for you. We already transported your associates to the station for questioning. My name is Special Agent Amanda Forrester."

"Am I under arrest?"

"Not yet. The cuffs are a cautionary measure for now. What is your interest in Daniel Feldman?"

"I guarantee that losing your job will be the least of your worries if you do not remove these cuffs in the next ten seconds. I won't be answering questions without my attorney present. And, trust me, after he's finished with you, you'll regret ever detaining me."

The woman smirked. "Call your attorney, Mr. Marks. You're going to need him. Innocent men don't make threats. Cornered men do."

†

Toni still felt like someone had twisted her insides like a rag needing the water squeezed out. Char wasn't happy with her but recognized the dire situation they were currently trying hard to contain. She agreed to let Toni do her magic, but once she averted the crisis, Char expected Toni to promptly return to the infirmary and follow Cindy's care plan to the letter.

"How much longer?" Char asked.

"Two hours, max," Toni answered.

"Two hours! I thought you temporarily neutralized Marks, and at least two of his men have indicated an openness to accepting a deal in exchange for their testimony."

"We owe it to those kids to give them new identities. Marks would have targeted none of them if it wasn't for us. His men beat one so badly before Hank could get there, it's still touch and go for him," Toni explained.

"Bloody nerds should have kept their noses out of our business," Val grumbled. "They brought this on themselves, trying to find out who we are."

"They're only kids, Val." Toni stopped typing and glared at Val. "Just when I believe you've developed some humanity, you prove me wrong. For fuck's sake, they're the

226

same ages as Pepper and Joy. I'm not leaving them vulnerable. Besides, at least two of them have mad skills like Sadie. Maybe we can turn this into an advantage for us. Too early to tell, but I believe both may be perfect additions to The Organization. We're a little light on tech support."

Val sighed. "Fine. You're right. I'm just irritated that Marks got so close. You have no idea the willpower it took for me to simply neutralize him versus opt for a more permanent solution."

Although Dani was monitoring Marks, while Toni attended to the other tasks that only she could resolve, she noticed something on the monitor that caught her eye. Grabbing the second set of headphones, she slipped them on and held up her finger.

Shit, Val is going to go apoplectic with the latest development. Toni watched, feeling completely impotent to do anything but observe how everything unfolded to the detriment of their efforts. Marks made a flurry of calls to his passel of attorneys. The agent had removed his cuffs, and it looked like they were releasing him. The brief conversation with his attorney, who had entered his hospital room, provided all the information Toni needed to know to bring Val and Char up to date.

"What? You have that pained look like you're constipated. Either you need to get your ass back to the infirmary, or you have bad news for us," Char noted.

Toni pulled one side of the headphone from her right ear. "His men have clammed up. Marks sent his attorneys to represent everyone who is currently in custody. All they have is the security footage from Feldman's house that I had to alter so Val's ninja routine isn't in living color. It was a rush job, so it's possible a clever police tech will discover my hasty attempt to cover her tracks. That'll only strengthen Marks' insistence on his innocence. He'll claim his enemies are trying to set him up, and his proof will be the missing footage."

"That isn't like you to leave any evidence behind to find," Char noted.

"I'm not 100 percent recovered yet, and there were so many things to attend to at once," Toni admitted. "They also have the printed list that a search warrant found in Marks' car." Toni ripped off the headphones and tossed them on the desk, letting irritation get the best of her. She glanced at Dani, making sure she was still watching and listening.

"I got this, Toni. You concentrate on everything else. If I have something to report, I'll let everyone know." Dani returned her attention to the large monitor.

"His attorney plans to spin the story, making Marks out to be the hero and blaming this on us. Well, on the unknown group they've named, The Crusaders. As far as we can tell, they still have no clue who we are. The spin is that he discovered the dark web group and feared the terrorists might target the hackers trying to uncover their identity. So he sent men to protect the kids, intending to recruit them for his team of tech staff that are looking into the extremists sabotaging his mines."

"How confident are you we've averted a catastrophe?" Val asked.

"Ninety-nine percent," Toni answered. "After digging into the kids who are a part of Sadie's dark web group, I haven't found anything to connect us or anything that reveals who Sadie is. That's the good news. The bad news, and the reason for that one percent, is that Marks' tech guy keyed into the breaches at the NSA. If they go looking there, they might find something that could lead to Joy or Sadie."

"I want round-the-clock protection on both of them," Char directed. "Val, can you take the lead on that?"

"Just let me take out Marks," Val requested.

"No. I want this to be supremely painful to him, and that means leaving him with zero financial resources. Death is too easy. We continue with Project Poverty. Maybe his getting out is good news. Now we can send our body double to the Cayman Islands. I have a feeling a good chunk of his fortune is there, waiting for us to snatch it from right under his nose."

"Is Steve ready?" Val asked.

"He is. Soph is going to meet him there with everything he needs to close Marks' accounts. Timing will be important to ensure the movement to untraceable accounts occurs without complication," Char answered. "Can you do this, Dani?"

Dani shook her head. "I wish I could, but this part is not within my area of expertise. Can Joy handle this?"

"She can," Toni answered with pride. "As soon as I give her the revised code that wasn't quite finished, she'll be set. We don't want a repeat of what happened earlier when they drained his more liquid accounts. I can't wait to bankrupt Marks. Except for the mines, his vanity companies are all being propped up using his personal wealth. And from what I understand, the mines aren't doing well either, with the success of our nonstop missions sabotaging the largest ones. Katrina agreed to help with the medium security accounts spread out in various places outside the Cayman Islands. The vast majority of his wealth is located there, but the other accounts aren't exactly pocket change. I need to send those biometric files to Katrina to get her going."

"You have two hours, and then it's back to bed," Char ordered. "I know you want to watch as Joy finishes what you started, but I need you fully recovered. Something tells me Marks isn't finished with us. Not by a long shot. While he still has the resources to come after us, he's dangerous. We take his fortune away, and that peril disappears. Poof. Like magic. I'll call Joy."

"No need." Joy had a purposeful stride as she entered the lab, with Sadie closely following. "We had a suspicion you might need help."

†

Joy had created the mess. The least she could do was hightail it to the compound to help her mother unravel it. Sadie was more than happy to accompany Joy. Joy was glad her mother still trusted her. It didn't take away the shame that she was responsible for the current chaos, but at least they weren't locking her out.

"I'm so sorry," Joy blurted. "I had no idea the code was incomplete. When I saw the code and recognized it in your computer, I thought we could get a head start."

"It's okay, honey." Toni smiled at her daughter. "Katrina has the files she needs already. So, I'm just going to finish up on these identities, and then I promised your mother I would return to the infirmary. Can you and Sadie stick around until Marks makes his move? Once Steve moves the money to the temporary account, I need you to run the code for the rapid transfer process."

"I can help with the new identities," Sadie offered.

"Me, too," Joy added. "It'll be a while before Steve does his thing, right?"

"Yes!" Dani shouted as she pulled her headphone from her ears. "Oh, yeah, he's rattled all right. He's on his way to the Cayman Islands and called the person who handles his accounts. They set up a meeting for first thing tomorrow morning. I've got the account numbers. His private plane will arrive in less than four hours."

"Perfect. We have time to execute a simple plan. Val, take Ronda with you. I need you to get to the Cayman Islands and help Sophie divert Marks while Steve meets with the banker and moves his money. Marks is going to be late for his meeting because rich people don't care about inconveniencing those they view as beneath them." Char grinned. "Soph can scope out how to hijack his driver. I presume he uses one when visiting the Islands. You and Ronda are going to create a massive traffic jam tomorrow morning. Dani, if he calls to arrange for a driver, we need that information."

"I'm on it," Dani responded, placing the headphones back over her ears.

Joy didn't like how pale Toni looked as her face took on the gray pallor she had seen before Toni had her heart attack. Beads of sweat were forming on her brow.

"Mama T, please let us finish up on the identities. Sadie and I are master hackers. It'll be a piece of cake for us. You already took care of everything else."

"You sure?" Toni wobbled as she stood, and Char was immediately at her side.

"Get Cindy, please," Char directed. Her voice was calm, but Joy knew her mother, and Mama T had rattled her again.

"I'm okay," Toni said just before Joy watched her Mama T pass out for the second time in less than twenty-four hours.

CHAPTER TWENTY-ONE

Sadie felt helpless with the flurry of activity around Toni. She wanted to be a rock for Joy but didn't know precisely what Joy needed at that moment. It had to be hard watching her mother's health take a dive for a second time. The only good news was that Toni had merely passed out. Her fragile system did not have enough juice to keep her going while she continued to fight the toxins. Cindy had assured everyone that Toni did not have a second heart attack. Still, she warned Char that if Toni didn't get the rest she needed, this would continue to happen, only delaying her ultimate recovery.

When Toni's eyes fluttered open, she smiled weakly at Char. "I'm okay, love."

"No, you're not. Joy and Sadie will take over. I don't care if Marks sends an army our way. You are not leaving the infirmary until Cindy says you're one hundred percent recovered," Char declared.

"I know we messed up before, but we got this, Mama T," Joy pleaded.

Toni nodded. "Honey, if you only knew how many times I missed something in a code that put others in danger. It happens. None of us are infallible. No one is. The key is to learn from our mistakes. I trust you both. Besides finishing on those new identities and running the rapid transfer process, I need you to enter fresh territory that's right up your alley."

"Anything," Joy answered.

"You're going to hack into the guy's computer that started this whole crisis. And this time, you're going to infect his computer, leaving that nasty worm," Toni said. "Ask Dani for his name."

"Won't he just buy a new computer and continue his work?" Sadie asked.

"Yup, that's just stage one of my karmic justice plan. On his next computer, we'll leave evidence that he was the one to hack into the NSA, poking around looking for information in that Crusdr file you found, among other highly illegal things, including stealing from Marks. We'll plant evidence that he diverted money from one of Marks' smaller accounts," Toni noted.

"That'll be a death sentence for him. We can't do that," Joy exclaimed.

"We won't do the second part until Marks has no resources left to act," Toni explained. "Before the authorities try to retrieve the money for Marks, we'll move it again. But this time, there won't be a trace of the money because we'll use the rapid transfer process."

"Enough plotting and planning for now. You two have work to do, and Toni needs her rest," Char ordered.

"I wholeheartedly concur," Cindy added as she pushed something into the new IV she'd inserted into Toni. "This should knock her out again."

†

His primary tech's face appeared on his video phone as Marks relaxed in a chair, sipping the scotch he'd ordered from room service. "This better be good news."

The tech's crooked teeth appeared in what Marks assumed was a victorious smile. "It is. I think I've found the hacker. It all fits."

"What all fits?" Marks asked.

"I pulled on a thread and did some digging. After narrowing down possible hackers with enough skill to drain your accounts and poke around in the NSA's highly secure files, I found an employee at the NSA who also happens to have a tie to your mine in Idaho. Turns out her parents worked at the mine, and both are deceased now. One from a mine accident and the other from cancer. That particular cancer is more prevalent in the area close to the mine. I don't think it's a stretch to presume this young woman has an ax to grind with you."

"Name?" Marks barked.

"Sadie Harris."

"Send me the address in an encrypted message. I already have the police on my ass. I don't need them to find anything else to tie me to this mess." Marks sat back in the leather chair and sipped his scotch. Things were finally going his way. He'd take care of this thorn and, to be on the safe side, move the rest of his money. Marks knew it wasn't a coincidence that every single person on that list his tech had supplied was now in the wind. They had to be working with that terrorist group. He wanted to at least get to this woman before they thwarted his plans to take her out. Now that he knew they were protecting the hackers, he'd forewarn the assassin. The guy was expensive but efficient. Maybe his tech guy wasn't so inept after all.

Marks heard the clicking of keys in the background as the pasty-faced tech looked down. "What the fuck?" he exclaimed.

Marks felt a sense of irritation that the man wasn't even looking at him anymore. His full concentration was on his computer. Then the screen on his videophone went blank. He lost his connection to the tech. After numerous attempts to get him back, Marks stood and paced the room.

When his phone rang, he punched the button to answer. "This better be good."

"Somehow, they installed a worm in my computer. I'll need new equipment as soon as possible if you want me to continue to work on this."

"Get whatever you need. When can you send that address?" Marks asked.

"Not until I get a new computer and what I need doesn't exactly come cheap or easy. It's not like I can order one online that's powerful enough to do the job. It's a special order item."

"Never mind, I'll get the information another way. She works for the NSA, right? I'll call my contact and get the address from him." Marks ended the call, seething at this latest wrinkle. He was so close.

Love Hacks

†

"Shit. Not good," Dani blurted.

Joy heard Dani but was too elated to react after installing the worm. "I think it's done," she announced. "Wish I could see his face right now."

Char strolled into the lab. "Whose face?"

"Um, Char, we've got new problems," Dani interjected. "I did see his face, right before he went dark, but not before he pegged Sadie as one of the hackers. He hasn't sent Marks your address yet, but when Marks gets it, I don't think he's planning on paying her a friendly visit."

"Carson's a sitting duck. We have to go back to my place, right now," Sadie exclaimed, the panic evident in her voice.

"Whoa. Hold on. First, from what I've heard, Carson is not some wilting violet. She's put Sophie on her ass before. They're after you, not her. Plus, Marks does not have your address yet. And he's still in the Cayman Islands."

"He's planning on contacting someone in the NSA. Not sure who that is just yet," Dani added. "Wait, he's making a new call. Give me a minute to listen."

Char nodded. "I presume the NSA has your home address?"

Sadie nodded. Joy saw her wide-eyed expression. "It's not just Carson; Randi is at our place right now. Um, they're sleeping together," Sadie said.

Char grabbed her phone and pressed the button. "Fuck, it's going directly to voice mail."

"Shit, she's my emergency contact, too," Sadie interjected.

237

"I'll handle this. You two stay here, and under no circumstances are you to return to your house," Char directed before nearly running out of the room.

"Screw that," Joy announced. "Dani, I'm putting on comms. Please let me know if you learn anything else that'll help us. Sadie, grab those pens lying on the desk. The silver ones. My mom hasn't been out in the field in many years. She's not like Val. She does yoga more than street fighting. Let's go."

Sadie held out her hand. "I need a set of comms, too."

Dani snatched two pairs of contacts from the table strewn with various gadgets and drone parts. "Pop these in to give you an advantage in the dark."

"Thanks, Aunt Dani." Joy grabbed the contacts and handed one case to Joy.

†

Marks didn't like losing, and whoever this shady organization was, they were always a step ahead. He couldn't figure out how they managed to do that. He felt confident that his phones were tamper-resistant and untraceable. It had to be his tech support. Somehow, they'd managed to infect the man's computer and undoubtedly put two and two together to protect the hackers. He sent an encrypted message to the assassin with the name and address of his target, then placed a call to the man. He wanted to provide additional incentive to wrap everything quickly. Marks lacked the patience to wait for the assassin to accomplish the task within his own timeframe. He didn't care if the man thought he was an arrogant prick who often pushed back on any suggestions of how and when the assassin performed his duties.

"I'll double your fee if you get this done tonight. Triple if you can learn more about the terrorists safeguarding the other hackers. Names, base of operations, anything. I already know how the bastards get their funding. I can't be sure, but it could be tricky. They might have someone protecting this young woman. Whoever they are, they're efficient and accomplished. Keep your antenna up."

"Are you telling me how to do my job?" the man barked.

"No, simply providing fair warning that you may run into traffic."

"Deposit half into my account, and I'll let you know when the job is done. I'll expect the second half within ten minutes of my call."

Before Marks responded, his assassin had ended the call. Shit, he would have to tap into the remaining deeply hidden account that allowed movement of funds after hours. There were other accounts to worry about, but he decided to have those monies moved to the Cayman Islands since they had cornered the market for untraceable premium security products. His other accounts in the US did not require a DNA sample or in-person visit, which made him nervous. They also were not liquid enough for daily transactions. At least the hackers hadn't touched those accounts, yet. Of course *yet* was the operative word. He wouldn't have any liquid funds remaining until he could get to his accounts in the Cayman Islands and establish new accounts with the same amount of liquidity for his day-to-day business.

Typing his password and other security information into the tiny keyboard on his phone, he moved one-hundred-sixty million into the assassin's designated account. That left a measly two thousand dollars. That wouldn't be sufficient funds to last a single day. Marks grumbled to himself. "Fucking terrorists. I'm going to make them pay for the inconvenience they've caused me."

†

Sadie screeched into her driveway and put her car in park. Before Joy untangled her seatbelt, Sadie had already jumped from the car and rushed inside. A disheveled Carson blinked at Sadie. Randi emerged from the back bedroom, pushing her hand through her hair and tying the drawstring on her sweats.

"I thought I told you to stay put," Char said as her jaw tightened.

Joy rushed into the room. "Mom, you haven't been in the field in years. I have."

"As tech support, Joy, not protective detail." Char took a deep breath, and Sadie saw her trying to calm her emotions.

Carson crossed her arms over her chest and glared at Char. "I'm not exactly without skill. I can take care of myself and Randi."

"Who says I need your protection?" Randi huffed.

"Fine, we're both capable of handling this situation on our own," Carson noted.

Dani's voice crackled in Sadie's ear. "Marks hired an elite assassin. Based on the fee, I think I know who this guy is. The Ghost has operated under the nose of every major authority in the world. He's never been caught, with every kill flawless. Please give Char this information. He'll strike

240

tonight because Marks provided a pretty large incentive to meet that timeline."

"Dani said to tell you that Marks hired the Ghost," Sadie relayed.

Char pinched the bridge of her nose. "Fuck. I wish Val wasn't in the Cayman Islands. Okay, lights off. Now! At least we have the element of surprise, and I plan on taking advantage of that."

Sadie pulled the contact case from her pocket and plucked the contacts from her eyes. She handed the open case to Carson. "Here, you can probably use these more than me. I don't have fighting skills like the rest of you."

Carson nodded and carefully put the contacts in her eyes. "Wow! These are amazing."

Char looked at Joy. "Are you wearing a pair?"

Joy nodded. "Yeah, but I'm not giving them to you."

"We do not have time to argue, Joy." Char lifted her hand palm up.

Joy shook her head and turned her attention to Carson. She pulled a pen from her pocket. "Sorry, Carson, I don't have a lot of time to show you how to use the dart pens, but it's simple. Point and click." Joy demonstrated by aiming her pen at a bunch of bananas on the kitchen counter. A tiny dart landed in one of the bananas, then dissolved into a fine powder approximately twenty seconds later. "To use the telephoto lens in the contacts, blink three times rapidly. Two quick blinks to return to normal focus. They'll auto-adjust based on the amount of light in a room for optimal clarity regardless of how dark it gets."

"Got it," Carson acknowledged. "I can't wait to go on more assignments. This shit is next level."

A barely audible beep emitted two quick bursts of sound from Carson's watch, which she never removed. Placing her finger on her lips, she whispered, "I think we have company."

Char motioned to everyone and mouthed, *spread out.*

CHAPTER TWENTY-TWO

It was true that Joy had never actually engaged with the enemy before. They always relegated her to stay in the vehicle and run tech support, which she was very good at. No one was better at flying the drone. A sense of calm flowed over Joy as she took Sadie's hand, intending to lead her to the kitchen where all the sharp, pointy objects were, but Sadie had other ideas.

Joy didn't know where Sadie was taking them as she felt along the wall in the pitch black. Since Sadie had given her contacts to Carson, she couldn't see as clearly as Joy. She leaned in and whispered in her ear. "Where are you going?"

"Bedroom. I have a gun there."

Joy wanted to know why Sadie, a hacker and tech specialist, would own a gun, but now was not the time to explore that stunning fact. Since Joy could see clearly in the

243

dark, she took the lead, pulling Sadie along until they reached her desired destination.

"Nightstand," Sadie murmured.

After quietly closing the door behind them, Joy quickly crossed the room and carefully opened the top drawer of the nightstand. She cringed when she heard the barely audible groan of the wood. The gun lay innocently next to a small vibrator. Joy smiled, making a note to herself to ask about the toy after everything settled. She had so many questions. While Joy was still technically a virgin because she didn't believe pleasuring yourself counted, she'd undoubtedly read enough and listened as Alina talked openly about her sex life to know all the different sex toys available to healthy, active lesbians.

Plucking the gun from the drawer, she handed it to Sadie and noticed the red flush on her face. Apparently, Sadie knew exactly what was in her nightstand drawer, besides the gun.

Joy's voice sounded excessively loud when she asked, "Do you know how to use a gun?"

Sadie shrugged. "Not really. Carson got it for me. In close range, I figure I can't miss."

"In the dark? Gimme that thing. I have firearms training," Joy whispered.

The two women settled on the other side of the door, not in the direct line of sight, but close enough to disarm an intruder the minute he entered the room. The stillness of the night added to the complete absence of sound besides Sadie's almost labored breathing.

The waiting was getting to both of them, as evidenced by the change in Sadie's breathing pattern. It had been thirty minutes since whatever Carson had installed as a safeguard tripped earlier in the evening. What the hell was the man waiting for? It was unnerving.

✝

Dressed in all black, the man crept onto the property. He could clearly see the outlines of five potential targets, including the one who had gestured to be quiet. His device also picked up sound, any sound, so he knew something had tripped and caused an alert to his presence. While that was an added complication, it couldn't stop him. He was the absolute best in the business for a reason. The only question was whether he would try to neutralize them before taking them out. The triple fee was rather tempting. If he was able to extract the information Alvin Marks needed, the money could pay for that yacht he had his eye on.

Everyone expected assassins to enter properties like burglars through windows or doors, but he had a different approach. Depending on the house, either the attic or crawl space was a better option. Ideally, cutting into a ceiling was easier than the floor unless there was a trapdoor to access the crawl space.

His legendary patience was the other significant difference between him and other trained assassins. He'd let them wait until their anxiety reached a fever pitch. The longer they waited for his arrival, the more advantage he had. They might believe they had the upper hand, but the foolish targets would be wrong.

Two hours had passed since the trip wire, or whatever they'd used to announce his arrival. It was time. He'd go through the attic and hopefully find his way to the bathroom next to the room where two of his targets huddled to the side of the bedroom door. He saw the gun in the woman's hand but wasn't worried because their focus was clearly on the wrong door.

When the man was younger, he believed his inventions, like the tool that would quietly cut through any material as if it was a hot knife through butter, would make him rich and famous. But it never worked out for him. The substance he coated the tool with acted as a kind of acid. It wasn't a clean enough cut, leaving an unsightly jagged edge that wasn't appealing to builders or construction workers. So he found other ways to use his inventions and landed on a much more lucrative career using his tools.

†

It wasn't like she'd heard anything because the room remained deathly quiet. It was the smell that alerted Joy. The breeze had picked up in the two hours they waited patiently for the assassin to strike. Along with that almost pungent odor that reminded Joy of vinegar, she felt a slight breeze.

When she turned her head, she saw him and yelled a warning, "Sadie, watch out!"

But it was too late. The intruder had already injected her. She felt Sadie's body stiffen beside her. Her first thought was to check Sadie's pulse, but instinct took over as she raised the gun. Unfortunately, Joy wasn't quick enough, as the man knocked the gun from her hand. Joy reacted quickly, avoiding whatever he had in his hand. She landed a blow to his chin, causing his head to snap back.

Scrambling to a fighting position, she attempted to hold the man off, but he was too quick. Char, Randi, and Carson burst into the room, and Joy liked their odds. She focused on fighting alongside the others. When Randi crumpled to the floor, she noticed a small device in his hands and shouted to the others, "He has darts."

Joy watched as Carson landed a dart in his neck, but it didn't slow him down or stop him. After Char went down beside Randi, Joy saw her opportunity and kicked his hand, sending the device flying across the wood floor. She clearly saw the look of surprise on his face before his attention became laser-focused. The knife in his hand magically appeared, and Carson barely avoided a deadly jab.

Joy had forgotten about the comms when Dani's voice crackled in her ear. "You grabbed the wrong pens. He's online now. A tracking dart must have landed. I'm sending reinforcements."

"Hey asshole, this place is going to be crawling with police in less than five minutes," Joy shouted.

It didn't seem like he'd even heard Joy as the man traded blows with Carson and managed to slice her arm before she landed a solid kick to his groin. Joy looked around the room for the gun or something to hit him with.

While the two of them were still engaged in hand-to-hand combat, Joy finally spied the small device he'd held in his hand before she'd kicked it out. She started to scramble to reach it, but somehow he knew her intentions and landed a blow to her head, causing her to stumble to the ground, far away from the object.

Carson was holding her own, but Joy saw the blood dripping from her arm and wondered how long her adrenaline would last. At least she'd kicked the knife from his hand, leaving him without that advantage. Joy had never been so happy to hear the sirens blaring. Apparently, that was enough to cause the man to perform an acrobatic move, allowing him to bust the bedroom window and escape before the cavalry showed. Carson started to follow, but Joy shouted, "Stop, Carson, let him go! I need your help."

Carson hesitated for a second, then seemed to survey the room. She rushed to Sadie and put her fingers against her neck. Pushing out a breath, she murmured, "Thank the Goddess." Approaching Randi and Char, she repeated the check. "Everyone's alive."

"Dani, we need medical."

"Already on their way," Dani answered.

Joy didn't know of a time she felt so relieved, but the police would have uncomfortable questions if they didn't move Char. There would be every reason for Joy and Randi to be at Sadie and Carson's home because they were seeing each other, but no reason for her mother to be there late in the evening.

"Where can we hide Mom?" Joy asked.

Carson wrinkled her nose. "Why do we need to hide Char?"

"It's our people, Joy," Dani answered.

"Never mind. I thought Dani sent the police," Joy answered.

"Is that why you didn't want me to go after that dude? Fuck, now he's gone, and we'll be looking over our shoulders until he strikes again," Carson grumbled. "Screw that. I'm not leaving my home because some douchebag wants us dead, or worse."

Love Hacks

"I've got him on my monitor. Let's see how the fuckturd does when we send Val after him?" Dani sounded furious.

"It's okay; Dani is tracking him. You landed a tracking dart instead of a paralyzing one. We grabbed the wrong pens. Sorry," Joy apologized.

Candy burst into the bedroom, followed by two agents Joy knew, but hadn't spent much time with. Like Carson, they were relatively new to The Organization.

"It's okay, Aunt Candy. The place is secure. He's gone, and Dani is tracking him," Joy explained.

A young woman with a bag hurried inside and squatted before Char, checking her vitals and using the tiny device Cindy and Toni had developed to do quick field evaluations. She moved to Randi, then Sadie, and announced, "Vitals are good. It's likely a short-acting paralytic agent. We'll know more after we transport them to the compound." The young woman touched her ear and said, "Three to transport. None with life-threatening injuries. A foreign substance suspected with paralyzing effects."

"Can you please attend to Carson's arm?" Joy requested.

"I'm fine." Carson grabbed her arm. "Check out Joy first. She took a nasty blow to her head. He was using some kind of device, kind of like brass knuckles, only more modern. It felt like his fists were made of hard metal."

The young woman shook her head and muttered, "Correction, bringing in five. The other two might be walking and talking, but there are likely injuries requiring more than basic first aid. I recommend head and body scans."

"I got Char. You two help with Randi and Sadie," Candy murmured. "Let's get them to the compound, and then we can debrief in the lab. Do you two need any help?"

Carson scowled. "Pftt. No. I told you I'm fine. I'll take Randi's other side."

"I got Sadie. He didn't ring my bell hard enough to lose consciousness. Quit being a Cindy clone," Joy grumbled.

The young medic shook her head. "Field agents."

CHAPTER TWENTY-THREE

Toni heard a flurry of activity in the medical bay and forced her eyes open. When she saw Char being brought into the room, her heart rate increased, and the staccato beeping of the monitor caused Cindy to turn her attention toward Toni, who was ripping at the wires and attempting to get to her wife.

"Stop right there," Cindy ordered. "Char is fine. Nothing a brief nap, IV fluids, and some nonaddictive pain medicines won't cure. In fact, whatever he used is a short-acting but quickly dissipating paralytic agent. I don't believe he intended to render any of them unconscious for a long period of time."

"What the fuck happened while I was asleep?" Toni demanded to know.

Joy sat up, then answered, "Marks sent an assassin after Sadie." Someone had rolled the portable imaging machine next to her bed.

Toni hadn't seen her daughter lying in bed. Her panic intensified.

"If you don't lay your ass back down and relax, I'll put you out with a heavy dose of your own paralytic agent, and you'll deserve every bit of the pounding headache that will follow when you wake after an eight-hour slumber," Cindy warned. "We're going to take films as a precautionary measure only. Joy didn't lose consciousness, so I suspect it's just a nasty bruise. She'll be tender for a while but nothing major."

Toni relaxed in her bed. "Tell me you got the bastard."

Joy looked away. "Um, not exactly. But Dani's tracking him."

Carson stood propped against the wall with a frown on her face. Toni noticed a large bandage wrapped around her arm, with a serious amount of blood staining her shirt. "I almost had him. Fucking coward ran."

Candy stood off to the side, looking supremely uncomfortable.

"Candy, how could you let this happen?" Toni grumbled.

"Char didn't call," Candy answered.

"Don't blame Aunt Candy. Everything happened so fast, Mama T."

"What time is it? When do Val, Sophie, and Ronda return from the Cayman Islands?" Toni asked.

"Not for several hours," Candy answered. "Dani gave me the Cliff Notes. After Cindy checks out Joy, I'm supposed to take her back to the lab. We have time. It'll be at least six hours before Steve does his thing, and we need Joy to begin the transfer process."

Toni sat up again. "I can do it. Let Joy recover."

"What happened to Joy?" The combination of grogginess and panic in Sadie's voice melded together. She ripped out her IV and stumbled to Joy.

"I'm fine. Just a little bump on my head," Joy answered.

"Why don't we wait until I get the results of the scan? I'll be the one to decide which one of you I'll release for a very short time to do whatever is so fucking important that you'd sacrifice your health," Cindy ordered, leaving no room for argument.

Toni pouted. "Fine. But if there is anything, and I mean anything, abnormal in her scan, I'm going. Regardless, the minute Val returns, I want her to track down the assassin. Doubtful Char will disagree he's the perfect candidate for elimination. I'm also inclined to give the order to take out Marks. I'm tired of playing defense."

"Mama T, I don't think Char was holding off on Marks for the reason she's given to us. You know her best. What is the real hesitation?" Joy asked.

Toni sighed. "Char is tired of shutting down one psychopath only to have another emerge before the body is cold and buried. Marks has a deep bench. His contacts are influential and go all the way to the top. We wanted to uncover the names of every single player. At least those in the United States. We'll worry about the other countries later on. She assumed we could manage the risks because we would know his every move in real time. No delays. I don't think either of us knew the lengths he would go to or how quickly he would act."

Cindy turned her focus to Sadie and shook her head. "Sadie, I really wish you hadn't ripped out your IV. You're lucky there are so many stubborn agents to care for, dividing my attention, or I would have ordered you to stay put. How's your head?"

"No worse than the migraines I get from time to time. I bet you have a cocktail to help with that."

"It was in the IV," Cindy answered in exasperation. She shook her head again and prepared a syringe. "Come here and I'll provide you with a quick acting injectable."

Sadie grinned. "Thanks, Cindy."

Sadie offered her arm as Cindy efficiently administered the fast-acting serum to offset the effects of the paralytic agent. After Cindy finished injecting Sadie, the impressive young woman returned to Joy's bedside, keeping plenty of space for Cindy to operate the portable scanning machine.

Toni smiled when she saw Sadie stuck like glue on the other side of the bed, holding her daughter's hand and looking at Joy in a way that left no doubt about her feelings for Joy. Cindy pushed the button on the imaging machine. A soft blue light emanated from the compact device as it slowly moved over Joy's head. The slight buzz and clicking sound had Toni craning her neck to look at the 3-D images displayed on the large screen. Everything looked normal. Toni couldn't see even the slightest hairline fracture on the image as it turned, showing every angle of her skull.

"Okay, Joy, everything looks good so far, but can you please turn on your side?" Cindy instructed.

Joy followed Cindy's directions, and Toni continued to strain to view the new images. Still nothing.

"Two more views, Joy, and then we're done. Can you turn on your other side?"

Joy shifted on the bed and followed Cindy's instructions. The new images popped on the screen, and Toni felt increasingly relieved that she couldn't detect any major injury.

"I know he didn't hit you on the back of your head, but can you please lay on your stomach so I can get one more shot, just to be on the safe side?" Cindy kept staring at the large screen with the rotating scans displaying in four different quadrants on the monitor. "All right, Joy, your scans are all clean. No damage to that big brain of yours. The swelling is normal, and you'll have a large bruise to contend with, but nothing a simple ice pack and some aspirin won't cure."

"Thanks, Aunt Cindy. Can I go to the lab now?" Joy asked. "I want to check in with Dani."

Cindy narrowed her eyes. "Didn't I hear that it'll be at least six hours before you're needed?"

"Yeah, but she may have an update, and the transfer is tricky, so I need to be ready. That means a bit of prep," Joy countered.

"How much prep time?" Cindy asked.

"At least an hour," Joy answered.

"I can help. I'll bet with Dani and me assisting, we can cut that time in half," Sadie offered.

"Don't you both have work tomorrow?" Toni asked.

Joy shrugged. "It won't be the first or last time I've pulled an all-nighter."

"Me, too," Sadie added.

"We're young, Mama T. We can still do that." Joy grinned.

"So can I, you little smartass. You better not suggest we're past our prime in front of Char. She's a bit sensitive about that." Toni chuckled.

"What am I sensitive about?" Char groggily asked.

Toni smiled at her disheveled wife. It was rare when Char wasn't in perfect control of a situation. "Welcome back, sleeping beauty."

Randi stirred in the bed beside Char and slowly moved to a sitting position. She grabbed her head. "Why does it feel like a thousand tiny gnomes are hammering my head?"

Cindy turned her attention to Char and Randi. "Side effects of whatever paralytic agent he used. One of my special IV cocktails should get rid of your headaches quickly. After a good night's sleep, you should return to optimal health. And don't pull them out like that one did." Cindy pointed to Sadie who had the good sense to keep her mouth shut.

Toni smiled at how alike Joy was to her as Joy hopped off the bed and took advantage of Cindy's momentary distraction with her other patients. "So, can we go now?"

"Fine, but if nothing is happening, as I suspect will be the case at this hour, try to catch a few hours of sleep," Cindy suggested before working quickly to push more medicine into both IVs.

"You aren't going to tell my moms what happened tonight, are you?" Randi asked.

"We'll talk about this tomorrow. Randi, after Cindy releases you, please take Carson to one of the spare bedrooms in the complex. Neither of you can return to that compromised location until we resolve everything. In fact, I'd suggest you sell that house and purchase something new.

If you need funding for that, we can cover it," Char directed. "Or we can have another house built on the compound. We have plenty of acreage for that."

"I'm not moving," Carson insisted. "Let the bastard come for me. I like my odds, especially since Dani is tracking his every move right now."

"We got a tracking dart into him?" Char asked.

"Yeah, unfortunately, the dart I landed wasn't one to incapacitate him," Carson noted. "We grabbed the wrong pens."

"It's my fault. I pointed to the wrong pens and asked Sadie to grab them," Joy clarified.

"This discussion can wait until tomorrow when my head doesn't feel like it's about to explode, and I can think clearly. For now, either remain in the infirmary or please find a room and get some rest," Char requested. "No one leaves this compound until we have a solid plan."

"Does she mean we aren't going to work tomorrow?" Sadie mumbled.

Char sighed. "Am I the only one with a lick of sense? Of course you aren't going to work tomorrow."

Sadie shrugged. "Didn't really want to continue working there, anyway."

"If you're quitting, so am I. Probably not the best thing for my anemic resume," Joy joked.

"At least you have a built-in excuse. A family emergency could be so many things that would provide the perfect excuse to quit. They might even offer a leave of absence to get you to stay," Sadie noted.

Joy grinned and grabbed Sadie's hand. "Come on, we have a date with the lab."

†

Dani relaxed in her chair with her eyes closed. Joy almost didn't want to wake her because she looked so peaceful. Candy had followed Sadie and Joy into the lab. She'd indicated her need to check on her wife and ensure there weren't any hiccups after the assassin's failed attempt.

Apparently, they weren't quiet enough as they entered because Dani's eyes popped open, and a serene smile blossomed on her face. "Hi, honey. Is everyone doing okay? I know you called and said there weren't any life-threatening injuries, and I appreciate that, but I want to make sure there aren't any long-lasting effects."

"As long as you don't count a powerful thirst for revenge, I believe everyone is fine. Any more updates?" Candy asked.

"No, it's all quiet now. Although, Marks and the Ghost were spitting nails at each other. Neither is thrilled. I think I know where the Ghost has gone. He's holed up in a remote location. They're both sleeping. I've got the monitor set to alert me if either one wakes up."

"Sounds like they'll send Val to take care of the Ghost." Candy crossed the room and leaned in to kiss her wife. "If Char concurs with Toni's assessment, which I've no reason to believe she won't, once Val returns, it'll only be a matter of providing his location."

Dani nodded. "Good. This guy is the most prolific assassin in the world. He's never failed. At this point, he won't let his pride suffer. He'll finish the job even if Marks doesn't pay the balance. Failure would ruin his reputation."

Joy took a seat at one of the computer stations. "Sadie and I are going to prep for the transfer. I assume everything is still a go?"

"It is. The Cayman Islands are an hour behind, and the meeting is at seven," Dani answered.

"The bank is open that early? That's unusual," Sadie remarked.

"Not if one of your customers is the richest man in the world," Dani noted.

"I wonder why he didn't make the bank exec open earlier tonight?" Joy asked.

"I think it has something to do with the timing of transactions. No matter what, a person can't force the entire banking industry to adhere to electronic transfers anytime they want," Dani explained.

Joy began typing on her keyboard. "First step is we have to hack into the bank. Then we install the code into their system." She leaned over and whispered into Sadie's ear. "The first one inside gets to choose what sex toy we use the second time we make love," Joy teased.

Sadie laughed. "Okay, fine, yes, I have a vibrator in my nightstand. And, I have an entire stash of toys in my closet. But why the second time and not the first?" Sadie bantered.

"I want *au naturale* the first time. Just tongues and fingers."

"I can work with that."

†

Sadie and Joy worked side by side for forty-five minutes. Sadie laughed at Joy when she pouted about being ten seconds later than Sadie, who had hacked into the bank in record time. After installing the code, they were ready. Dani suggested they sleep for a little while. Steve was slated to check in ten minutes before entering the bank. He'd voluntarily agreed to inject the new sixth-generation bots into his body so The Organization could monitor everything while he impersonated Alvin Marks. The bot would enable Dani to give instructions in real time through a two-way audio bot. However, the video feed was one-way only. He didn't need or want the distraction of seeing Dani or any other tech in the lab.

After Sadie had nodded off, she felt the gentle touch to her shoulder and woke with a start.

"It's almost time," Joy said.

Positioning herself between Joy and Dani as she looked over their shoulders, her eyes were riveted to the monitor showing Steve march confidently into the bank. Sadie caught his reflection in the glass and gasped. If she didn't know any better, she would swear the man was Alvin Marks. He even sounded like him.

"Is Steve some kind of master impersonator? He sounds just like Marks," Sadie exclaimed.

Dani grinned. "A tweak to voice distortion technology. That's my own special invention. All I need is a few samples; the technology does the rest, changing Steve's voice patterns to those that match the ones I input into the device."

"That is fucking amazing, Dani." Sadie watched as Steve provided answers to the security questions, laid his hand on the scanner, then placed his eye into the device, confirming his retinas matched the ones attached to the account. Placing his index finger into the machine that would collect a drop of blood, a green light blinked twice, and the bank executive nodded. Sadie exhaled the breath she'd been holding. The blood Toni collected had worked. Sadie didn't know what special tech the agent impersonating Marks had used to transfer Marks' blood to the device versus his own. She would have to ask about that later.

"Thank you for your patience with our security measures. I'm sure you understand how important it is for us to ensure the safety of your funds, given the rare request to move all of them to new accounts. Might I suggest our state-of-the-art technology that will allow you to move a portion of your fortune into an account with greater liquidity that doesn't require a personal visit to the Cayman Islands? Perhaps you'll consider keeping all your money with us and not transferring an allotment into the bank already compromised?" The man shot Steve a pointed look.

Steve paused as if he was considering the executive's suggestion, then haughtily answered, "Very well. I'd like one hundred fifty billion transferred to that account. I presume you don't intend to charge me for your new fancy technology."

"Oh, no, Mr. Marks. We only wish to provide the highest level of customer service and security. We offer this device to all our clients with vast resources that require extra protection. Basically, it's a smaller, portable version of the biometric technology in this physical location. As soon as we've concluded the transactions, I'll assist you with calibrating the device and installing your biometrics."

"Are you ready, Joy?" Dani asked.

Joy grinned. "Yup."

Joy's fingers flew over the keyboard, and Sadie tried to keep up with what she was doing, but Joy was too fast. A

Annette Mori

series of numbers kept flashing across the screen, rapidly progressing until all Sadie could see were quick bursts of light. A list of twenty numbers appeared on the monitor, and Joy pressed a button, taking a screenshot before they disappeared ten seconds later.

"What did you just do?" Sadie asked.

"Not me, the program," Joy answered with pride. "It moves the money around too quickly for anyone to track. That money has literally traveled to not less than one million different locations. The last screen shows us the twenty accounts where the money now lives. The Organization owns the bank where we deposit all our funds. It's in a remote location free from any governmental interference. We've never been hacked. I'm not saying it's impossible, but anyone with the skills to hack our bank resides at this compound or has a personal connection to The Organization. Katrina pops up every now and again, but she'd never steal from The Organization. Besides, Katrina is helping us with Marks' medium security accounts. I don't think she views this job as a hardship because she'll be taking ten percent off the top as her fee. That's hundreds of millions of dollars."

"Okay, wow! That's amazing," Sadie answered.

"I think it's time for popcorn now." Dani switched her screen to Marks sitting in the back of his car, clearly fuming over the traffic jam.

Joy popped from her seat. "I'll make us some." Sadie had never seen Joy so giddy. She felt honored to have a front-row seat to this portion of the mission.

Dani leaned back in her chair, casually pressing a button on a small device. "Hey, Val, Dani here. Everything is going well. Steve is almost done. We need you, Ronda, and Soph to

262

get on the jet and return to the compound pronto. Um, unfortunately, Marks sent an assassin after Sadie. Everyone's fine," she quickly added. "No. Char has her reasons for not giving the order on Marks, but it's your lucky day because I believe she's going to ask you to eliminate the Ghost. Carson got a tracking dart in. Yup, I know exactly where the bastard's holed up. Great, see you soon."

✝

It was well after eight when the driver pulled to the front entrance of the bank. Nothing seemed to be going his way lately. After the call last night when the Ghost had informed him of the complications he'd encountered, Marks felt more than a little queasy about the traffic jam this morning. His panic only increased when the wiry bank executive approached and asked, "Did you need something else, Mr. Marks?"

"What the hell are you talking about? I called ahead to let you know I would be late."

"I'm sorry, I'm confused. You were right on time this morning," the man answered.

Marks could feel the sweat on his brow and suspected all color had drained from his face. He knew it would be pointless to confirm his suspicions, but he needed to know. Maybe if he were lucky, he'd be able to divert catastrophe. "Whomever you dealt with this morning was not me."

"Do you have a twin?"

"No, you dumbass. It was an imposter."

"Impossible. Our security protocols are flawless. I don't know what this means, but I don't appreciate whatever game you're playing. If you feel the need to—"

"I don't have time for this. You need to move those funds from wherever you transferred them to. Right now," Marks bellowed.

"Very well, but we'll need to go through the whole biometric security process again. Will that include your liquid funds as well? If so, I'll need the device provided to you this morning."

"I don't have the device, you imbecile. Never mind, let's concentrate on the bulk of my estate. You need to hurry this along."

"Right this way, Mr. Marks."

After going through all the security measures, Marks watched as a deep crease formed in the middle of the man's forehead, and sweat dripped down the side of his face. "That's impossible."

My companies, I still have my companies.

Several thoughts filtered through Marks' mind as he faced the reality of his predicament. He might be able to borrow from either SoBites or Solio, just to have day-to-day spending money. Both were on the verge of bankruptcy, so the board would bark. Neither board was happy with recent events. His efforts to support the extreme right agenda had gone too far, causing advertisers and consumers to push back. Everything that had previously turned to gold under his leadership was now turning to shit. Even his mines had significant financial woes with the constant sabotage, and his connections with other governments had recently taken a turn in the wrong direction. They no longer returned his calls, choosing to do business elsewhere.

The sudden realization that he was drowning in debt and might not survive caused his stomach to turn. He rushed to the bathroom, barely making it to the stall before vomiting the entire contents of his stomach. With as much dignity as he could muster, he strode out of the bathroom and into the bright sunshine.

Looking around for his driver and finding no one waiting for him, he shouted, "Where the fuck is my driver?"

A few men and women glanced in his direction but quickly looked away, scurrying from what Marks assumed looked like some crazed man in an expensive suit. He really had no options.

When he returned to his hotel room, he made a few more calls confirming that whoever masterminded this massive attack had drained every single account. Major or minor banks—it made no difference because the bastards had tapped them all and left him nothing. The final nail in his coffin was the voice message on his secure phone from the Ghost. He was coming after Marks. Not only did the lethal man believe Marks had set him up by sending him to a place where some kind of elite operative team waited for him, but the money was no longer in his account. No one stiffed the Ghost and lived to tell about it. They'd won. He had nothing more to live for. Money and power went hand in hand. If he no longer had the money, his ability to wiggle out of trouble ceased to exist. Marks knew he was dead man walking.

†

The loud noise startled everyone in the room. Joy had wanted to see Marks squirm, but she wasn't prepared to have a front-row seat to his suicide. She turned her head in horror. Joy's role in The Organization meant she wasn't up close and personal with violence or fighting, despite the requirement that every agent possess combat skills. Sure, she'd seen the aftermath of a fight, like when they'd shot Aunt Val during the siege on the mine in Mexico, but that was so much different from watching a man put a gun in his mouth. Joy felt personally responsible. She'd been the one to move most of his money.

The room began to close in around Joy, and she needed air. She was vaguely aware of someone following her as she burst from the lab, running into the tranquility of the compound's carefully tended gardens. Sitting on the stone bench in front of the massive mimosa tree, Joy held her head in her hands and let her tears fall, punctuating the enormity of the moment. She felt a hand on her shoulder.

"I killed him," she sobbed.

"Oh, Joy. No, you didn't," Sadie soothed. "That man does not deserve a single tear shed on his behalf. After everything he did to my family and yours, I'm glad he's dead. And I won't apologize for that. If you knew how many families he's ruined, both directly and indirectly. I'm only sorry he killed himself before we found all his co-conspirators."

Through bleary eyes, Joy saw her mother approach. "I heard what happened. You might have come out of my womb, but you're every bit your other mother's daughter. I'm glad you followed in her footsteps and learned the tech role. There's nothing wrong with wanting to stay far away from the horrors surrounding our fight with evil men, but make no mistake, Marks was pure malevolence. Sadie, I know this may be a lot to ask, but we need you to stay employed with the NSA. Can you call this morning and request a personal day to assist Joy with her family emergency?"

Sadie nodded. "Of course, but why?"

"We know of at least one connection at the NSA. There may be more. I suspect those Crusdr files are only the tip of the iceberg," Char answered. "After that, please take Joy to her room and stay with her? Emotions tend to run high when fatigue is involved."

"I should probably call my direct supervisor at the NSA, too. No sense in wasting this opportunity to learn more. I can't believe I made popcorn as if watching Marks kill himself was a sick form of entertainment. Who does that?"

Char laid her hand on Joy's shoulder. "Hon, you had no way of knowing Marks would make that decision. He gave no indication that he'd do anything but punch back. Remember what he did to your mother. And he sent an assassin after the woman you love."

Sadie's head snapped up, and Joy blinked her eyes. Her mother wasn't wrong. She did love Sadie, but there had been no opportunity to confess that fact to Sadie, who deserved to hear this from her and not her mother.

Sadie looked from Char to Joy, then asked, "Is that true?"

"Oh, I'm sorry. I thought you might have told Sadie that by now. I'll leave you two alone to talk. By the way, your mother has turned the corner and is champing at the bit to get into the thick of things, so you two have plenty of time to figure stuff out without worrying about anyone." Char winked, then gracefully exited the garden.

Joy kept blinking. She felt a panic attack coming and couldn't stop it. Gulping for air, the small circles Sadie was making on her back finally registered.

"Deep breaths, Joy. It's okay. I love you, too. It isn't the worst thing to hear it from your mother first. Maybe not the best, either," Sadie joked.

Did Joy hear that correctly? Did Sadie just tell her she loved her, too? Joy took a chance and looked Sadie in the eye. At that moment, she saw it written on Sadie's face. It was the same way her mothers looked at each other. She'd also noticed that same tender look from Alina and Pepper. Both had found the love of their lives with Maria and Grace. Joy never thought it would happen to her, though.

"You do?" Joy wasn't sure if that was a question or a statement.

Sadie nodded, responding as if it were a question. "Probably for more than a few hours, maybe even since the first time I saw you having a panic attack. We fit." She stood and held out her hand. "Come on, I've been given a directive. I need to make a quick call so we both can keep our jobs; then it's nap time."

Joy accepted Sadie's hand. "I swear I didn't tell Mama C I loved you before, uh, I had a chance to..."

Sadie smiled. "I know. Your mother is scary observant. And supremely accurate. I've no doubt she figured out that I'm in love with you, too."

Joy chuckled. "Probably." Joy felt a little lighter now, like despite what she witnessed, love rose to the surface instead of despair. Could it be that simple? Having someone you love help you through whatever guilt or pain the world dished out on a regular basis? The perfect balm to soothe a gaping hole.

"Yeah, I guess I assumed that."

Joy grinned. "She probably thinks we're already having sex, too."

Sadie lifted one eyebrow. "Are you trying to tell me you're ready now? Or do I need to wait for your mother to tell us it's time to get busy?"

Joy laughed. "Get busy? You couldn't think of a better euphemism for sex?"

"Nope. Too tired. But after my nap, well, all bets are off."

CHAPTER TWENTY-FOUR

It took a while, but Joy's breathing finally settled into a steady rhythm, indicating she'd fallen asleep. Sadie lay awake, a broad smile on her face. Joy loved her. Joy actually hadn't said the words, but that didn't matter to Sadie because she hadn't disputed what her mother said, basically confirming the truth of her words.

The exhilaration she felt knowing Joy reciprocated her feelings caused Sadie to remain awake until exhaustion finally took hold, and Sadie allowed her body to relax as her arms wrapped around Joy, creating a cocoon of love.

Several hours later, Sadie's eyes fluttered open when she felt Joy stir beside her. Goddess, the woman was a vision of beauty with her long red hair splayed across the pillow. Those enchanting green eyes popped open, and she said, "Hey."

Sadie turned her head and began teasing Joy. "You ready to knock boots, tap that, bump uglies, engage in bedroom rodeo, bow chicka wow wow, tip the velvet, do the no pants dance, take a trip to pound town—"

"Stop." Joy laughed so hard she began hiccuping. "Did you stay up all night thinking of those euphemisms?"

"Nope. I have more if you don't like those." Sadie turned on her side to face Joy. "You are so beautiful." She stroked Joy's cheek, wanting desperately to touch every part of Joy's body.

Joy blushed. "Um, I don't know about you, but I feel grungy right now. Plus, I hate that feeling in my mouth when I first wake."

"You want to shower and brush your teeth, don't you?"

"I do. Will you wait in bed for me?" Joy asked, blushing again.

"Oh, no, you aren't getting all squeaky clean with your minty-fresh breath without me," Sadie answered.

"Uh, you, uh, want to shower with me?"

"Well, yeah, but not if you're uncomfortable. I just meant I'd like to take a shower, too, with or without you. Whatever you're okay with."

"Is it always this hard?" Joy asked.

"Is what always this hard?"

"Um, planning the first time to…"

"I'll go easy on you and not subject you to more euphemisms, how about my personal favorite, make love," Sadie answered.

"Yeah, that."

Sadie chuckled. "Is that what we're doing?"

"We're not?" Joy crinkled her nose in that adorable way that Sadie had fallen in love with.

271

"Oh, yes, we certainly can plan it out if that's what you need," Sadie teased. "But Joy, you have to be ready. I can wait as long as you'd like."

"I'm ready. Well, I will be as soon as I've taken my shower." Joy smiled coyly.

Sadie grinned and nodded. "Separate showers, then. I think our first time should be in a bed, not up against a shower wall. Logistics can be tricky in the shower. I wouldn't want either of us to feel like we're being water-boarded."

Joy jumped from the bed. "Okay, I'll go first, or you can also use the other bathroom attached to the guest bedroom down the hall."

"I won't run into anyone?" Sadie asked.

"Nah, this wing of the complex is rarely used. There should be towels in the cabinet below the sink. New toothbrushes are in the drawer, and everything else you'll need is in the shower. I think there is even a clean robe hanging on the door."

†

After exiting the shower, Joy had the urge to check on her mothers. Although Char had assured her that Toni was doing fine, she needed to see that for herself. Joy refused to let the thought that maybe she was using this excuse as a diversionary tactic take root. Sure, knowing precisely what to do was scary. Who wouldn't be their first time? But it wasn't like she was sixteen. Joy was a bloody adult. It was way past time, and she couldn't imagine a better person to share this with.

Noting that Sadie hadn't returned from her shower, Joy quickly donned a pair of shorts and a T-shirt, traveling the corridor to the lab. If Toni was well on the mend, that's where she would be. She heard the hair dryer in the guest bath and hoped she had a few minutes before Sadie knew she'd gone.

Dani and Toni were laughing together when she entered the lab. It wasn't like she viewed either of them as callous individuals, but she supposed they'd both been in the business long enough to see horrific things. Life went on. At least The Organization had never lost an agent. They'd come close a few times. And no one could argue that a few of their agents suffered invisible injuries not necessarily recognizable.

Toni turned her head in Joy's direction. "Hi, honey. Where's Sadie?"

"Taking a shower. I need to head back soon lest Sadie thinks I abandoned her, but I wanted to make sure you were really okay." Joy shuffled her feet and looked down.

"Oh, that's sweet of you. Yeah, Dani and I were following up on a few leads. We've been reviewing all the footage of Marks in case we missed anything. He made several calls to various contacts. We're especially focused on the ones at the NSA, but others have piqued our interest."

"Maybe Sadie and I can help?" Joy suggested.

Toni narrowed her eyes. "What's really going on, Joy? Char told me she let the cat out of the bag and thought you two might not come up for air for a very long time." Toni grinned.

Joy sighed. "Ugh. I hate that I have no experience, and when I say zero experience, that isn't hyperbole. Sadie is the first woman I've even kissed. And, we, um, haven't taken it any further yet."

"I guess we never had the sex talk with you." Toni laughed. "For a while, we worried you might be asexual because you never showed interest in anything but lab work. Well, worried isn't exactly the right word. There's nothing wrong with being asexual." Toni stumbled over her words.

Joy laughed nervously. "I don't need the sex talk, Mom. I know how things work. I'm just worried I won't be any good at it."

"Oh, well, my only advice is to be honest about everything. Communication is key. Tell Sadie what feels good to you and ask her what she likes. It's really as simple as that."

Joy nodded. "I figured as much, but it still scares the shit out of me."

"What scares the shit out of you?" Sadie asked as she pushed open the door and entered the lab. She hadn't bothered to put on clean clothes and was standing in the lab dressed in the spare robe that hung on the guest bathroom door. It was the sexiest thing Joy had ever seen. She swallowed, hoping to moisten her mouth, which had suddenly gone dry.

"You weren't in the room, so I came looking for you. I figured you'd be here." Sadie offered a gentle smile. "You look good, Toni. How are you feeling?"

"Almost one hundred percent," Toni answered. "I told Joy that Dani and I were following up on a few leads. We'll loop you into that because we need your help, but not right now. Both of you deserve a break from all of this."

"Is Aunt Val back yet?"

"They're all back, but Val is on another mission. We're monitoring the situation. She insisted on going alone, and we agreed that might be best, but we have Sophie and Ronda on standby in case she needs reinforcements," Toni explained. "Now, go, enjoy the rest of the day. There's plenty of food in the kitchen. Feel free to take it back to your room." Toni grinned.

Sadie approached Joy and took her hand. "I could eat."

And with that simple statement and the look on Sadie's face, Joy knew she couldn't delay this any longer. She didn't want to, anyway. Sadie looked so beautiful. She'd blown dry her hair and found the spare mascara, which was the only thing Joy ever used. Joy ran her hand through her wet hair, wondering if she should have spent more time getting ready.

"Okay, let's raid the fridge and take our bounty back to my room." Joy smiled as she led Sadie out of the lab.

†

After they'd cut up some apples and cheese, and grabbed nuts, grapes, and other finger foods, they returned to Joy's bedroom and giggled while they set up a picnic on the bed. But Joy seemed nervous now, and Sadie was never one to dance around an issue. "Are you okay? You seem a little...off."

"Sorry, I'm a teeny bit nervous, I guess."

"I meant what I said earlier. I can wait however long it takes for you to feel comfortable," Sadie answered in earnest.

"I know. I think a little nervousness is to be expected, but that doesn't mean I'm not ready because I am. Mama T gave me some good advice. I sure hope you're okay with conversation during, uh..."

"A vocal lover, huh?" Sadie teased. "Yup, more than okay with that."

"I just meant that it's okay to direct me. Tell me what you like."

"I know what you meant. I was just teasing you. Sex can be a lot of things, fun, intense, pleasurable, a profound connection with another, and I hope we experience every one of those. Maybe not all at once, but the truth is that I've no doubt we'll be compatible, especially if we keep the communication open and frequent."

"That's what my mom said."

"Well, she is probably the most brilliant woman on the planet," Sadie remarked as she popped a piece of cheese and apple into her mouth.

"Hey, please tell me you don't have a crush on my mother," Joy joked. "That's just too weird."

Sadie shrugged. "Maybe more like heroine worship. But honestly, what card-carrying lesbian wouldn't have a tiny crush on both of your mothers? I'm only human, but I'm in love with you, not your mothers. Plus, I only want to make love with you."

Joy picked up the tray of food and set it on the nightstand. Sadie didn't miss how Joy's eyes smoldered with desire. Her intent was clear, but Sadie presumed Joy needed her to take the lead.

Lifting the edge of Joy's T-shirt, she pulled it over Joy's head, letting her hands caress Joy's sides. Joy shivered, then reached for the tie on Sadie's robe. Sadie allowed Joy to push the robe over her shoulders, leaving her naked and vulnerable before a partially dressed Joy. That needed to change pronto. Sadie gently pushed Joy onto her back and helped her remove her baggy shorts.

Starting with a kiss, Sadie moved her body on top of Joy's and felt a jolt of arousal now that they were skin on glorious skin. She broke the kiss and hovered over Joy's lips. "This okay?" Sadie asked.

"Very okay. Your skin is so soft. How do you like to be touched?" Joy countered.

"I'm very sensitive everywhere. There aren't any spots off-limits, but I'm small inside, so more than a couple of fingers are uncomfortable. What about you?"

"Um, I don't know about inside. I've only ever touched myself, and soft seems to work well."

"Do you think you might like it if I tasted you? It's something I've kind of been dreaming about," Sadie confessed.

Joy nodded. "Yeah, I think I might like that."

†

After three hours of exploring every inch of each other's bodies, Joy lay on her back, her breathing finally starting to return to normal as she exclaimed, "Wow! That was so much better than touching myself. I didn't even think it was possible to have that many orgasms."

Sadie smiled. "Now we know we are compatible in every possible way. I love you, Joy, and can't wait to continue exploring all the wondrous ways of making love."

"I love you, too. Goddess, I just realized I've never actually said the words. I'm so sorry." Joy frowned. "Relationships are like strange little alien beings to me. Are you sure you want to do this with such a neophyte?"

Sadie's heart was so complete right now. She knew Joy loved her without saying the words, but hearing Joy voice them out loud made her spirit soar. "There's no other I'd want to take this wondrous journey with."

"Is it normal to want to taste you again?" Joy asked.

Sadie chuckled. "Yeah, I think so. Although I'll admit you're the first woman I've wanted to spend this much time in bed with. Normally, I'm done after an hour and can't wait to return to my computer. Not that I've had all that much experience. Three previous lovers don't actually make me an expert. I guess this is what love feels like."

The two women would not emerge from the bedroom for several more hours, finding their way into the shower before venturing to the lab, which seemed like the central hub at the complex despite Sadie's perception that Toni hated when the agents crowded into what she considered her domain.

CHAPTER TWENTY-FIVE

The man sat in front of his massive screen and seethed. Now he'd never get his money. Granted, he hadn't completed the job, and that had been a first for him. The truth was that he could simply let this all go. He hadn't been paid, so there was no need to make a second attempt. It would be more challenging now. He didn't have the element of surprise, and his target was probably in the wind. But his pride would not let him walk away. He had a reputation to uphold, and if there was even the slightest possibility that it would get out he hadn't completed the job, that would not do. No, he'd take out the woman to preserve his pristine standing in the elite community of assassins.

The man hadn't heard a sound, nor had any wires tripped, but he sensed something. Another predator. Moving to his wall of security cameras, he squinted at the screens, seeing nothing. Then he noticed why he'd sensed something was off. The same moth fluttered in front of the camera in the exact same flight pattern. His cameras were on a loop. Fuck. Someone had breached what he thought to be impenetrable security.

Grabbing his gun and activating the device he attached to his hand that would send lethal darts into an opponent, he began a sweep through his mansion. The evidence of the breach lay innocently on the floor. Someone had managed to cut a small hole into his basement window. The locking mechanism was gone. There was an intruder in his house. Sensing another presence, he quickly pivoted. The woman was quicker than any person he'd ever encountered, as she easily kicked the gun out of his hand, but the deadly assassin didn't know about his poison darts. He grinned as he let one fly. But instead of it landing into her neck, the dart bounced off her bodysuit, and that's when he knew he'd finally met his match.

He hadn't even managed to activate the metal coating on his hands, giving him the upper hand to a close fighting situation before feeling the prick of a needle. The last thing the man saw was the woman's cold gray eyes.

†

Joy couldn't stop the perpetual smile on her face. She heard a soft knock on the door and pulled the covers to her neck. "Do you think if we ignore whomever it is, they'll go away?" she whispered.

"Hey, Joy, sorry to disturb you guys, but Char sent me to come get you. Val is back, and we're all meeting in the conference room," Dani said through the door.

Joy glanced at the clock and realized the late hour. "Give us five minutes, okay?" Joy announced.

"Sure thing. I'll let Char know you're on your way," Dani said, before Joy heard her retreating steps.

"Are they going to tease us?" Sadie asked.

Joy didn't know the answer because she'd never been in this situation. "I don't know, maybe? Although I doubt Mama C will let them while we're discussing future plans. They save the conference room for serious business. We usually keep banter to a minimum. We're probably safe until after the meeting, then perhaps all bets are off."

"I don't care. Totally worth the ribbing we'll get. I wouldn't put it past Carson to be the first to make a comment. I know how to handle her, though," Sadie informed.

"Will she be upset? I believe she still has feelings for you."

"I don't think so. She's my best friend. Whatever feelings still linger, she genuinely wants to see me happy, and I'm in delirious bliss right now. I don't think I could conceal that even if I tried. And I don't want to hide it, anyway," Sadie insisted. "We better get dressed and join them before they send Carson next," she teased.

When they entered the room, Carson grinned and quipped, "Nice of you to tear yourselves apart from one another and join us."

Joy didn't know Carson all that well, but she sensed the words were said without malice because Sadie smiled and playfully punched Carson on the shoulder.

"Sit," Char directed. "I'd prefer for this meeting to end at a reasonable time. Please restrain yourselves from teasing Joy and Sadie. While the important loose ends have all been snipped and cauterized, we have a lot of work ahead of us. Starting with acquiring a few additional businesses and bankrupting others."

"Bankrupting?" Sadie asked.

"Yes, we plan to force the mines to close, but salvage and transform Solio and SoBites into socially responsible companies," Char explained. "Since both are on the verge of bankruptcy, The Organization can absorb both for a song. We'll let his other companies either falter or survive on their own. With Marks out of the picture, I'm not exactly sure of President Dawson's future. We'll need to carefully monitor him and Senator Roch. Both have ties to Russia and China."

"A lot of people are employed in the mines. Isn't there a way to transform them as well?" Sadie asked. "Trust me, I hate that the mines even exist, but a lot of folks depend on that work."

"Good point, but we believe we can create new jobs by expanding our recycling centers wherever the mines exist. We'll also pump other resources into those communities," Char explained. "The two of you will continue to work at the NSA. I don't like how much effort has gone into discovering our identities. I'm also a little worried that the government might swoop in and take over the mines now that Marks is gone. They aren't going to just let them close without a fight."

"What about his connections with China and Russia?" Grace asked. "Even if we close the mines in the US, who'll stop those governments from getting their slimy mitts on the abandoned mines? I'd almost prefer our government taking control. Maybe we'll have a chance of implementing common-sense regulations to protect people."

"Good point. That will be something to watch," Char answered. "Sorry, but if I've learned nothing else in the thirty-plus years in this business, it's that when we squeeze one part, like a balloon, another bulge appears. Our work is never done, but we're closer to our end goal than we've ever been. The microchips we've handed out have detailed information on which teams we'd like each of you to be a part of. I believe we've matched your unique skills with the appropriate team, but if after you've thoroughly reviewed the materials, you believe we got it wrong, feel free to let me know that, and I'll juggle around the tasks to match your preferences."

"How come you never offered this before?" Ronda asked. "You've always said jump, and we've all said how high. You getting soft in your old age?" she teased.

Char turned her laser gaze to Ronda.

"Whoops. Now you've done it, Ronda." Toni shook her head. "Never use the 'old' word."

Joy saw her mother's jaw clench, but she responded with her signature calm. "There are new members I've not had ample time to thoroughly consider their skills. I believe I know exactly what the rest of you have to offer."

Val shrugged. "No issues here, Char."

Ronda held up her hands. "Sorry, I was mostly kidding. You know I'd follow you into the depths of hell."

Char smiled. "I know, Ronda. Okay, let's do this. We'll meet again tomorrow night after you've had a chance to review the materials."

As everyone exited the room, Sadie whispered, "I can't believe Ronda said that. I'd never want to be on your mother's bad side. Val scares the shit out of me, but your mom is someone I'd never think to challenge."

"Deep down, Mom's a teddy bear. Don't get me wrong, she's still a badass, but I think she's trying to generate the same kind of loyalty with our new recruits as she has with the senior agents. Giving them permission to speak up is a good tactic," Joy answered.

"Good to know."

"I'm confident she put us on the same team with a singular mission. I'm glad about that."

"Me, too. I can't seem to get enough of you. I don't worry about spending too much time together, even if our specialties are identical, unlike your moms."

"You don't think us being attached at the hip so soon is an issue?" Joy asked. Now that Sadie had pointed out the obvious, she began to worry.

"Nope. I wouldn't be a proper lesbian if I didn't think about how long I needed to wait before asking you to cohabitate with me. Although, Beta and I are a package deal, so take as long as you'd like to consider that. It's not like we can't continue alternating nights at our respective homes."

Joy could almost feel her heart expand in her chest. "You mean that?"

"Every single word," Sadie confirmed.

"I don't know why we've never gotten a cat. I've always loved cats, so I can't wait to literally become a walking, talking, lesbian stereotype. Plus, Beta is such a sweet boy. I think I've used living with Alina, Maria, and Randi as a crutch. Along with Pepper and Grace, they've been my only friends. My entire social life revolved around them. What little I had," Joy responded. "I think you know I'm not exactly a party girl. You might get bored living with me."

"Nope," Sadie insisted. "I've never experienced as much excitement as I've had in the last month."

"Well, in that case, want to go house hunting this coming weekend?"

"I can only think of one thing more appealing than that." Sadie waggled her brows.

Joy chuckled and shook her head. "I better hold on because I just jumped on the ride of my life, huh?"

"Yes, and I sincerely hope it never ends. Life with you will never be boring. I'm so glad you let me inside."

"Me, too. I love you," Joy declared.

"Love you, too," Sadie answered.

EPILOGUE

Carson watched her best friend plop on the couch they'd wrestled into Joy and Sadie's new home. Beta meowed loudly, and Sadie reached over to let him out of his carrier. He sniffed the carpet and began an exploration of the strange new location.

She tried her best to be happy for Sadie, but a twinge of jealousy floated to the surface at the most inopportune times. She attempted to separate her feelings to understand why she felt this way. Things were going relatively smoothly for her and Randi. If she let herself, she might even discover that it was possible for her to fall in love with someone else.

Spending time helping Sadie and Joy move into their new place brought some clarity to the situation. What she missed was just hanging out with Sadie. Even when they were dating other people, she'd always been able to come home and dissect everything happening in her life with her best friend, and now she couldn't.

Randi was going through her own jumble of emotions. Every day Carson traveled to the compound was a reminder that Carson was in and Randi remained an outsider. It only got worse after Carson was injured. That was a particularly painful reality considering Randi's close connection to all the agents in The Organization. She could observe but never touch. Every day that passed, Carson watched Randi draw more into herself. She worried that the depression wasn't going away. She'd even gone so far as to express her angst with Char, who seemed to listen intently and not wave it away as nothing to be concerned about. Char had promised to talk with Randi's parents.

Carson had landed on the team with Sophie, Val, and Ronda. It was exhilarating working with women whom Carson considered the three most skilled field operatives in The Organization. At least Char had paired Sadie and Joy with their team to provide tech support. She'd get to spend more time with Sadie, which pleased Carson but created issues with Randi.

The Organization knew ignoring the mines while concentrating on Solio and SoBites was a gamble. But they'd had little choice, considering how distracted they'd been resolving the other major issue that had come up after Val eliminated the Ghost. It was wishful thinking that the mines would no longer be a priority issue. Now there was a patchwork of ownership, with some controlled by the government and others supervised by nothing more than foreign thugs. Of course, on paper, the shell companies appeared to be American, but the reality was ownership lay in the hands of dangerous men from Russia and China. It was as if they came to an amicable agreement on who would take ownership of which mines. An unfortunate outcome of The Organization focusing on other businesses meant the mines were now staffed with undocumented immigrants, many of whom were nothing more than slaves, with the majority of workers as young or younger than the kids working in the Mexican mines. It hadn't mattered when The Organization exposed the whole underbelly of the industry several months earlier. The focus stayed on the politicians, leaving the mines to continue operating with impunity. That required a sharp turn in their focus.

Nostalgia directed their first mission after all the upheaval of the past several months. Caution had dictated a pause after another team had hit the mine in California. Things were messy for a short time after Senator Roch had gone on his rampage, but now they were back on track. One mine at a time, the teams would shut down the deplorable practices in the US, and then they could consider doing something about the rest of the world. Before the shit show with Roch, Sadie had desperately wanted to hit the mine in Idaho. Tomorrow, the team would leave for the state. However, Sadie hadn't wanted to wait until after the mission to move. Sadie and Joy had already been delayed by several months after their first house fell through. Sadie insisted they'd waited long enough. Joy had agreed, and not because she'd do anything for Sadie, but Carson sensed she was just as eager for them to have their own space. Carson tried not to take that personally. They were in love. So in love, it was almost sickening to watch.

"You nervous about tomorrow?" Sadie asked.

Carson settled on the loveseat she and Randi had carried in earlier. "Nah. Are we taking a break?" she asked. "Remind me why you didn't hire movers?"

Sadie grinned. "Team-building. Besides, we don't want strangers messing with our stuff. Joy and I have a lot of expensive tech to protect."

"You could have had them move the big items for you. Besides, couldn't you have just packed up your equipment and put it in boxes? Who would go through someone's packed items?" Carson asked.

The look of horror on both Joy and Sadie's faces was almost comical. "You can't be serious," Joy stated.

"I wish I could go with you guys." Randi's voice was wistful.

"You'll be done with school soon enough, and then you can talk with your moms. You made a deal with them. I doubt they'll go back on their word," Carson placated.

"They won't, but it's hard to see everyone trotting off to various missions while I sit at home reading some boring text on macroeconomics," Randi grumbled.

"Have you decided what you want to do yet?" Sadie asked.

"Not really. Of course, I can't wait to officially join The Organization, but Char insists I have an alter ego. I don't want that to be anything boring, so joining the police force is a consideration, but I'm kind of drawn to the military, too. Unfortunately, I'd have a harder time joining missions if I'm stationed somewhere remote. Plus, I'd have to complete my tours of duty first."

"Not the FBI?" Carson pouted.

"I don't think so. Even though it would be great to work with you and Amanda. With my luck, they'll shuffle me into some boring specialty like healthcare fraud and abuse. I wouldn't put it past my moms to influence the agency, so I'm not assigned to anything too dangerous."

"You think they would really do that?" Carson asked.

"In a heartbeat," Randi answered. The phone buzzed in Randi's pocket, and she held the screen in front of her. "Speak of the devils. Hey, Mom Squared." She paused, jumped from the loveseat, and punched her fist in the air. "Thank you. I love you both. Yes, I'll be careful. I promise to call with frequent updates." Randi ended her call and grinned like a madwoman.

"Well?" Carson asked.

"Guess who's going with you guys tomorrow?"

"Really?" Carson was happy her talk with Char actually worked.

"Yeah, apparently, Aunt Char called my parents and convinced them I'd be safe with your team." Randi shot Carson an appraising look. "I suppose it didn't hurt that the other less experienced team was so successful with the California mine. Besides sparring with you, Soph and Ronda have been working with me on the sly, so I'm not coming onto the team cold."

Carson stood and pulled Randi into a brief hug. "Welcome to the team. I, for one, am delighted."

Randi stepped back and smiled brightly at Carson, before leaning in and pressing her lips to Carson's. "Thank you. I know you said something to Char, and I don't really care what it was. I'm just grateful for your interference."

Joy and Sadie crowded around Carson and Randi, slapping Randi on the back. "This is going to be so much fun," Sadie declared.

"Yeah, it is," Carson answered. "Is it pizza and beer time?"

"See, I told you. Perfect timing. They're already taking a break," Alina said.

"Sorry, I was hoping we would get here sooner, but we ran into traffic. I'll bet Pepper and Grace got caught in it, too," Maria added.

"We did." Pepper strolled into the room with Grace by her side. "You guys taking a break already?"

"Yeah, I'm a little hungry," Joy answered.

"I'm starved," Alina exclaimed.

"What else is new?" Pepper teased. "Well, the gang's all here now, so let's order those pizzas. I just wish we didn't have to leave again to do another promotional tour for Grace's new documentary. We'll miss all the fun."

"Guess what?" Randi blurted.

"What?" Alina asked.

"I'm going on the mission tomorrow."

Alina held her fist for Randi to bump. "Epic. Now we have something to really celebrate besides the lovebirds moving in together."

"Let the celebration begin." Carson reached into the cooler filled with beer and hard ciders. She passed out everyone's preferred beverage, then popped the top of her can and raised it in the air. "To our newest recruit. Long live The Organization."

AUTHOR'S NOTE

Thank you for your support of my books. You are the reason I continue to write and am inspired to spin these tales. If you enjoyed this book, I hope you will consider leaving a review or rating the book on Amazon, Goodreads, or wherever you are comfortable. Look for the third book in the series, *Love Sins*, due out Fall of 2024. A sneak peek follows this note. Additionally, as a thank you to all of my subscribers on my mailing list I offer links to free short stories. Here is the link to subscribe: http://eepurl.com/cS7nr9 I promise not to bombard you with messages but will only send an email when I have a new book release or a new offering of a free short story.

Peace,
Annette

SNEAK PEAK

LOVE SINS

Prologue

Jessica Green pushed her thick black glasses up her nose while her body bent in an uncomfortable position as she examined the tiny new solar cell she hoped to show Dani first thing Monday morning. She respected the hell out of Dani, but if she were honest, she would have to admit her disappointment at never meeting the infamous Toni McFarland. She'd heard that Ms. McFarland made a rare appearance at a summit a few months back and hoped she'd finally visit her flagship manufacturing plant where Solar Flair housed their state-of-the-art research and development facility. But apparently, her idol's unusual foray into the world was a one-off. Maybe someday she would meet the woman.

Her phone buzzed on the table, and with a practiced move, she flipped the magnifiers on her glasses up and glanced at the videophone gyrating against the wood. Not recognizing the number, she returned the magnifiers to their previous position and refocused on her work.

"You've got mail," the automated voice announced.

Jess sighed and grabbed her tablet. First a phone call and now a video mail message. She'd have to tweak her spam filters and add a block to video mail like she'd done with phone calls. Although, bots didn't usually leave video mail messages. Occasionally, she'd get a call from her emotionally stunted father. He wasn't much for conversation or staying connected except to provide for her every need with his vast financial resources. It wasn't until after her mother and father divorced that he finally hit pay-dirt. Jess wasn't sure which invention had made him as rich as he'd always insisted would happen.

Her father was an enigma. A brilliant man who was unnecessarily paranoid. About what, Jess didn't know. His once-a-year obligatory call came from an unregistered phone and never on the same day. Somehow, his calls consistently penetrated her spam filter. Jess wondered why he didn't just save the task for her birthday or maybe Christmas, but no, he always picked a random day out of the year. She supposed she was being too harsh by labeling his attempt at connection a chore, but she suspected that was how he viewed it. Who knew? It certainly felt like a duty to Jess.

Jess tried to remember the patient man who used to let her hang with him in the garage as he tinkered away. Whenever she had asked a question, no matter how childish or ridiculous, he would stop what he was doing and answer her. Lately, Jess was sure nothing was left of the man she once knew. The last call was so awkward it lasted barely five minutes. Maybe he was giving up on face-to-face interaction and left a video mail message instead.

Accessing the message, she frowned when she saw the overweight middle-aged man with thinning hair appear on the screen—definitely not her handsome father, who could be the poster boy for fitness.

"Ms. Green. I tried to call earlier, but whatever software you installed blocked me from leaving a video message on your phone. I'm calling about your father's estate. He left very specific instructions for me. We had an arrangement that if he did not check in with me at least once every three to four months, I would need to begin preparation for liquidating his assets to place in a trust for you, Ms. Green. You are the sole heir to his estate. You can reach me at 206-354-7845, and we can discuss the arrangements in further detail. I have an envelope for you as well. Your father left you a letter."

Jess slumped in her chair for some minutes before calling the man and arranging a time to meet on Monday. She didn't want or need his money, but she wanted to know who her father had become. She was curious about what was in the letter. It wouldn't surprise her to learn he'd skipped town and found a remote island as a retreat from whatever boogeyman her father imagined was after him.

†

Jess sat across from her father's attorney and blinked twice. She had assumed her father had finally made his fortune from one of his inventions but had no idea how wealthy he was. Her mother rarely talked about her life before Bob, her mother's second husband.

At first, Jess kept her distance from Bob, desperately missing her father. After the divorce, contact with her biological father was minimal at best, and Bob slipped effortlessly into his role as her stepfather. While Bob provided all the love and emotional support she needed at that young age, her father evolved into nothing more than a sperm donor with money to burn. Not wishing to deny her daughter the opportunities afforded her with her father's money, her mother had reluctantly accepted the steady flow of checks provided for her schooling and any other needs she might have.

If Bob felt insecure about accepting the money to send Jess to the best private schools in the nation, he never let on. Neither he nor her mother ever kept a penny of the money sent for Jess. Not only had she been able to attend an elite college, including a world-renowned graduate school, without incurring a suffocating amount of debt, but also the excess funds remained in a trust account given to her when she'd turned twenty-five.

But now, the attorney was informing her of the extent of her father's estate. This was an obscene amount of money. More than Jess could ever spend in a lifetime. Despite being surrounded by privileged kids starting in high school, Jess had simple tastes in almost everything. She enjoyed her job at Solar Flair and wasn't about to give that up just because her wealth now placed her in the top one percent, if what the attorney informed her was correct.

Mr. Comey was talking again, and Jess looked up, attempting to focus on his words. "What? I'm sorry. This is just so…"

He pushed the letter toward her and handed her a set of keys. Her father had meticulously labeled each one, except for a tiny brass key. "This is the letter he instructed me to give you, along with a spare set of keys for his various properties. I have a list of those assets for you. His primary residence is not too far from this office. Do you have any questions?"

"I have a lot of questions, none of which you'd be able to answer."

"Perhaps the letter will provide the information you seek," Mr. Comey suggested.

"I do have one question. You stated my father gave specific instructions in the event he failed to check in with you?"

"Yes, that is correct."

"Has anyone done a welfare check?" Jess asked.

"You mean at his primary residence in DC?" the attorney clarified.

"Yes."

Mr. Comey cleared his throat. "I'm afraid the estate has an impenetrable security system. DNA access only. Your father was a cautious man and programmed your DNA into the system."

"More like a paranoid asshole," Jess mumbled. Jess pushed the set of keys toward Mr. Comey. "You know what, I'm not even sure I care whether a welfare check was done, and I don't want any of this."

"It is certainly your prerogative to do whatever you wish with the money, but it is yours, Ms. Green." He set the keys in front of her again. "Donate to your favorite charities if that makes you feel better. In the meantime, the liquidated funds will go directly into the trust account your mother established for you. I would recommend opening new accounts. Transferring the funds into that account is only a temporary measure. The bank cannot provide any guarantees on that amount of money. You'll need to spread out your wealth now. I can provide the names of reputable real estate agents if you wish to sell any or all of his houses."

"I'm sorry, Mr. Comey. It isn't fair to take my frustrations out on you. The truth is that you probably knew my father more than I did. He wasn't exactly the doting type."

"Honestly, Ms. Green, I didn't know your father well either. He was a private man, but the fact that he made arrangements to leave you his entire estate suggests he cares or cared for you. I can't say for sure if he is alive or not; I'm simply carrying out his instructions. Perhaps the letter will shed more light on everything."

Jess pushed back her chair, grabbed the letter and keys, and held out her hand. "Thank you, Mr. Comey."

The attorney shook her hand. "Please let me know if I can be of further assistance." He plucked a card from a holder on his desk. "Here's my card should you require any legal services in the future. I specialize in estate planning, but our firm has other attorneys I'm sure would be able to meet all your needs."

†

After calling her boss, Dani, to let her know she'd need the rest of the afternoon off, Jess laid the letter on her kitchen counter before opening a hard cider. She took a healthy swig from the bottle. Whatever was in the letter was sure to require liquid strength. Jess wasn't sure who had scrawled her name on the envelope as she lifted it from the counter to inspect every inch. Flipping it over, she looked for additional writing. Nothing. Deciding to take the plunge, she slipped her index finger under the corner, pushing it along the edge to open the letter and acquiring a paper cut for her efforts.

"Fuck." She sucked the small amount of blood oozing from the cut, but not before a red smudge appeared on the outside of the letter. Unfolding the paper, she noted the neat cursive writing. She briefly wondered why her father had elected to communicate old school in a hand-written letter. For a man obsessed with technology, this did not compute with Jess. Focusing on the words, she began to read.

Dear Jessica,

If you're reading this letter, that means I've finally been caught. I must admit I never anticipated this would happen. However, on the off chance someone was better than me, I had to account for the possibility. If I'm lucky, you'll never find out how I acquired the great wealth that is now yours. Although I did not set out to pursue this line of work, it suited me. Guilt is a luxury intended for those with a conscience and the mastery of emotions that I do not possess. Yet, that does not mean I did not care for you, Jessica. You may be the only thing in this life that mattered to me. I suppose I am trying to say that if I had any capacity for love, you would have been the recipient of that love. Try not to judge me too harshly. I simply played the cards dealt to me.

I've kept a close watch on your career, and it seems, in one small way, you've followed in my footsteps. You're a talented engineer. I'd like to believe your intelligence and creativity are two traits my gene pool provided to you. While my inventions may not have a practical application for what society considers honorable work, you are welcome to expand on them and find a principled purpose. The military may find them useful. Although I'm not at all convinced the government or our armed forces are ethical choices. I leave that to you to decide. I've kept detailed notes in my main workshop at my primary residence in DC. Your DNA will allow you access. Keep the keys hidden in a secure location until you need to use them. Remember the cabin? Those were better times.

I wish you a good life, Jessica.

The last three lines of the letter were a complete mystery. Why would Jess need to hide a set of ordinary keys? Tossing the note on the counter, she walked to her living room with her drink and settled on the couch. Jess had to admit she was curious about his workshop. Opening the file Mr. Comey had provided with the various addresses, she found the one for his DC residence. No time like the present.

"I suppose it's time to uncover what you've got tucked away in that workshop of yours."

†

Jess grabbed the set of keys Mr. Comey had given her and headed out the door. Once she slid into her car, she provided the address via a voice command and listened as the robotic voice directed her out of the most condensed part of the city. When Jess finally reached the site, she wondered if she was in the right spot. If there was a house behind the massive gate, she certainly couldn't see it. However, the row of cameras suggested whatever was behind that gate was well-protected.

Climbing from her car, Jess reached the impressive barrier at least twice as tall as her own height. An entry pad with a blue light glowed despite the brightness of the sun. Not knowing exactly how her DNA would open the gate, Jess pulled off her glove and placed her thumb in the center of the blue light. She felt a tiny prick and pulled her hand away, noting the minuscule bead of blood that had formed on her thumb and the blue light changing to green. Before Jess had a chance to react, she heard a kind of grinding sound, then a click before the gate's lock popped open. She pulled on the heavy metal until the opening was large enough for her car to drive through.

Cherry blossom trees lined the long driveway—beautiful sentries offering a kind of softening to what Jess assumed might be a little overwhelming to the casual observer. It wasn't until she'd traveled down the flawless asphalt a fair distance that she noticed the massive structure. As Jess approached what she assumed was the front door, an overwhelming feeling of dread flowed over her body. Although, that sentiment wasn't because she expected a second prick to her thumb after repeating what she'd done at the gate when she found the blue light. A green light flashed before she heard a beep and tried the door.

Jess pulled her hand away and sucked the blood from her thumb. "Sheesh, this must be what it felt like in the old days for people with diabetes to test their blood sugar levels.

Macabre, Dad. Your place could be the perfect haunted house," she grumbled.

The minute she walked inside, the odor of death smacked her in the face. It was at least thirty degrees warmer inside, so she unzipped her jacket. Gagging, she pulled her sweater over her nose and mouth. Jess tried to remember if her father had ever talked about a pet. She didn't want to come across some dead cat or dog that her asshole father had left to fend for themselves. That might break her heart. While she was definitely a dog person, she loathed seeing any dead animal on the road, and that was especially true of cats or dogs hit by a car and left to suffer before finally expiring.

Making a beeline to the windows in the front room, she made quick work of opening every single one to let the fresh air flow inside. The smell was still overwhelming as she began searching for the source. Maybe her father had left food out. Rotting meat or fish could be the culprit of that nauseating smell. Her next stop would be the kitchen—as soon as she could find it. The place was enormous, and she checked every room on the main floor. Jess had never seen such opulence. Not only were the rooms smartly decorated, but she assumed the artwork, carefully chosen, was worth millions.

She let her nose guide her to where the odor seemed most offensive. Finding a door, Jess knew she'd discovered the source of that awful smell as she cautiously descended into relative darkness until she reached the bottom, and the light shone through the windows in the daylight basement. She stopped in her tracks when she saw the body, or what was left of the body. Holding her hand over her mouth, she climbed the stairs, looking for a bathroom or a sink, anything. She didn't make it far enough as she vomited on top of what she assumed was a very expensive carpet. She could clean that up later. Quickly gathering her phone from her pocket, she dialed 911. The one trait she didn't inherit from her father was his paranoia. In Jess's opinion, not having to give your location when making an emergency call was helpful. She'd never turned off her GPS tracking, providing emergency personnel with an automatic address whenever anyone made a 911 call.

"Nine one one. What's your emergency?"

Jess couldn't stop her body from trembling, which came out in her voice. "My father, um, he's dead."

"Are you sure, ma'am? Did you check for a pulse? We can send an ambulance to your location."

"I'm sure."

Annette Mori

ABOUT THE AUTHOR

Annette is an award-winning author, published by Affinity Rainbow Publications, who lives in the beautiful Pacific Northwest with her wife and their four furry kids. With over thirty published novels, six Lesfic Bard Awards, and one Goldie Award for her fourth novel, *Locked Inside*, she finally feels like a real author. Annette is as much a reader as a writer and is always looking for the next sapphic novel to queue up. She came up with the One Fan at a Time tagline, because it rolled off the tongue much better than One Reader at a Time. After pondering who she was at her core, she feels it was all about connecting to each reader on a personal level. Annette would be the first to admit she doesn't do well with the masses. If someone picks up her book and it touches them, she believes she has achieved what she wants with her writing by reaching each reader. It is who she is at her core. Drop her a line. She loves to hear from readers.

Email: annettemori0859@gmail.com.

Sign up for her mailing list: http://eepurl.com/cS7nr9
Check out her blog: Everyday Occurrences:
https://annettemori0859.wordpress.com/
Visit the Affinity Rainbow Publications website for her
books and many other outstanding
authors:www.affinityebooks.com

OTHER AFFINITY BOOKS

Strength Within by Mia Barnes

Samantha Wilson is an award-winning freelance writer with a passion for being the voice of others. Despite vowing never to go back, she returns to Milwaukee, Wisconsin, for an assignment. Her return awakens memories that force her to confront her sad and lonely childhood, including the violent attack she'd rather forget. Moving away and making a quiet, successful solo life for herself, leaving the life she knew behind cannot keep Sammie from facing her past.

Fortunately, her best friend, Zoë, flies in from New Mexico to be by her side while she confronts the demons of her past. Sammie has a knack for helping others find their happy endings. Will she finally let Zoe help her become whole again and maybe discover her happy ending in the process?

Mom's Last Wish by Charlene Neil

After fifteen years away from home, Lucy Donald receives an email from her mother's personal assistant, Cameron Bishop, compelling her to return. Soon after Lucy's arrival, threatening letters start to appear, and Lucy realizes her life is in actual danger. She seeks comfort in the arms of the alluring Cameron Bishop, but can Cameron really be trusted?

Lucy's return home and the events that unfold lead to an intense and suspenseful atmosphere.
Left to uncover the mysteries by herself, she finds herself grappling with the dilemma of not knowing whom to trust.

The Next Generation by Annette Mori

Despite Toni's legendary brilliance, even she could not stop the march of time. After learning her daughter, Joy, and Joy's two best friends, Pepper and Alina, attempted to deceive the senior agents in The Organization with a bogus Spring Break cover story, she convinces her wife it's time to let the Next Generation take over.

The last thing Pepper Maggio expects after agreeing to lead a mission is literally running into the woman she's followed for years. Not only is Grace Turner beautiful, but she's a passionate crusader for the same innocents that The Organization vows to protect. Along with her two best friends, the three young women embark on an adventure to save the day. But the mission quickly gets out of hand as the human traffickers target not only Grace and her film crew, but also the young Mexican woman who managed to catch Alina's eye. Maria might be the bravest of the bunch as a survivor of one of the Mexican mines, but she's a sitting duck if they don't intervene. They might be the Next

307

Generation, but they'll need the full support of The Organization, including Pepper's lethal mother, Val, to get out of Mexico alive.

Turn the Page by Ali Spooner

Continue the journey with Whit and Eli in this final installment of the Cast Iron Farm series. The brilliance of their twins, Mack and Zack, rapidly develops, challenging Whit and Eli to keep up with their education. Their sensitivity to others and kindness are far beyond their youth and a testament to the family's efforts to help them grow into young adults. In addition to more adventures, a budding romance, and wedding bells ring for the Fortner family once more as a new generation begins life on Cast Iron Farm.

A Breath of Scandal by S Anne Gardner

Adele Visconti, Contessa de Caravagio, is passionate and wild and doesn't know the meaning of the word no. One day by chance she turns her head and in a very old cliché fashion she sees a face across the expanse of a Polo field and goes to meet it. Unknowingly this would change her life forever.

When Gillian meets Adele, she is in a committed relationship. The last thing she wanted was to be sucked into the maelstrom that is Adele. However, Adele was something that she could not fight against and her world was turned upside down from the moment they met.

Will their relationship survive against a tide of intrigue, manipulations, passion, family, and most importantly reconnecting the magic of their love for each other.

<u>The Sky People by Ali Spooner</u>

After a beautiful wedding, Eli and Whit return to plan the next phase of their relationship. Whit discovers the identity of her father, and he shares a future with her that will change life on Cast Iron Farm forever. Twins bless the Fortner family, and Eli shares a special secret with Mitch, who bonds with the children in a unique way. Ride along as the Fortners begin a new chapter of their story.

<u>Love Bonds by Annette Mori</u>

When Mila Thompson, a rookie police officer, discovers her mother is missing, she engages the assistance of San Diego's number one detective, who is more than a little reluctant to enter the fray, noting she works in homicide, not missing persons.

Bernie doesn't play well with others, which is why she doesn't have a partner at work or in her personal life. When Mila approaches her, she tries hard to refuse the request, but Mila will not accept no for an answer. For reasons she does not understand, Bernie doesn't want to say no to Mila, who can charm her way into anything, including smoothing the rough edges of Bernie's crusty heart.

Things get complicated when the women in The Organization have an unusual tie to Mila's mother. This sets up an action-packed adventure with twists and turns and a healthy dose of love. Find out the future of The Organization and whether an unlikely pair can find their way to love.

<u>Holy Water and Whiskey Scars</u> by Ali Spooner

Faith Wilson and Logan Bronson have family secrets to protect and a legacy to uphold to support their small rural Appalachian community. Their commitment to each other is

309

strong, and their desire to aid the struggling families however they can, lead them both down an exciting but dangerous path. Will their love continue to grow and be the glue that binds the community together, or will they flee the withering community?

Politics of Love by Annette Mori

Governor Sandra Murphy is rethinking the sanity of allowing her mother to talk her into considering becoming the democratic party's choice for the presidential nominee. Sandra has enough to contend with after surviving a bomb attack, thanks to the brave border control agent working alongside the clever undercover FBI agent. Now she has to worry about a pesky reporter who seems to be everywhere scoping stories Sandra would prefer Wynter Holmes steer far away from.

Wynter admires the charismatic governor. After all, she voted for the woman. But that doesn't give Governor Murphy a free pass. A breaking story is what Wynter lives for, and she isn't about to stop digging just because the engaging governor is attractive, single, and an out lesbian. Reporting for the famously biased, right-wing media conglomerate is not exactly making Wynter a friend of the enigmatic leader.

Will repeated attempts on Governor Murphy's life where Wynter might be collateral damage bring them closer together or tear them apart from what might be a perfect match?

Out and Loud by Ali Spooner

The Bentleys have begun celebrating their success by performing live in small venues and outdoor concerts. Their music and love for one another continue to grow as their number drops to four. Stone is needed at home to run the business during his father's rehabilitation, but the Bentleys drive forward. Cedra's challenge to her bandmates to create original songs for their next album turns into brilliant love songs, rockabilly, and a Pride Festival anthem. Ride along with the Bentleys as they capture the hearts of country music lovers across the nation.

Undercover Love by Annette Mori

When the domestic terrorist cell Emma Schmidt has infiltrated summons her to an abandoned warehouse for a loyalty test, Emma immediately recognizes the battered woman. Emma must act fast to protect her cover and save the woman, Jimena Aguilar, she's never forgotten.

Emma and Jimena team up on a dangerous mission to take down the terrorist cell and save the life of the popular California governor.

Will this lead them back to the closeness they once shared or have the years in between hardened their hearts to love.

Affinity
Rainbow Publications

eBooks, Print, Free eBooks

Visit our website for more publications available online.

https://affinityebooks.com/

Published by Affinity Rainbow Publications
A Division of Affinity eBook Press NZ LTD
Canterbury, New Zealand

Registered Company 2517228